Loving Maddie
from A to Z

KELLY JAMIESON

Loving Maddie from A to Z

ISBN: 978-0-9918532-5-0

Cover by The Killion Group, Inc.
Interior Formatting by Author E.M.S.

Edited by Briana St. James

Published in the United States of America.

Praise for the Novels of Kelly Jamieson

"Kelly Jamieson delivers a blazing passionate read that tugs at the heartstrings!"
— **Carly Phillips,** *New York Times* **Bestselling Author**

"seductive and bewitching from the very start... Softly romantic and wickedly provocative"
— *RT Book Reviews* **on Rule of Three**

"Kelly Jamieson now has a permanent place on my keeper shelf and I can't wait to see what she writes next."
— **Joyfully Reviewed**

"Ms. Jamieson once again gives the reader a richly detailed story that is brimming over with sexual tension, intoxicating desires and intriguing carnal needs that is edgy and psychologically intense..."
— **The Romance Studio**

"...I love Kelly Jamieson's books and the way that she depicts her characters..."
— **Sizzling Hot Book Reviews**

DEDICATION

Special thanks to Slick Reads who suggested this title in my Sweet Heat Reader Group when I was whining about how I suck at titles! Also thank you to beta reader Michele Harvey—once again your honest and thoughtful feedback helped make this story better. And thanks as always to critique partner Nara Malone who confirmed that Aidan is a real man.

I also want to send out thoughts and prayers to the families of both journalists who are missing, and journalists who have not come home. My heart goes out to all of you. This topic was brewing in the news when I wrote this story and then during edits became tragic real life headlines. Also, thank you to those intrepid reporters who bring us such important stories from around the world.

1

Maddie eyed the black leather tails of the flogger Aidan held, imagining how they would feel slapping her skin. She fingered the soft tails, met her boyfriend's eyes and smiled, her insides quivering. "Wow. Are we getting kinky?"

He smiled back at her.

After knowing each other nine years, six of those as a couple, she still thought he was so handsome, with his short dark hair brushed back off his face and neat sideburns. His brown eyes regarded her warmly, the corners crinkled up, his full lips curved in a sexy smile. "You said you wanted to spice things up."

She nodded. "Yes. I did." She'd broached that subject a few days ago, a little diffidently, not even sure what she really wanted. She just knew that she'd been so...restless. She didn't want to say dissatisfied, because that wasn't true. She loved Aidan, and she loved having sex with him. In no way was it terrible. It was intimate, and lovely. He was generous and thoughtful, strong and physical. She worried that it was her, that there was something lacking in her, and that was why she felt something missing. So when she'd mentioned spicing things up a little, she'd been worried that he'd be hurt. His male ego bruised. But now she was relieved he was open to that.

He'd brought home a flogger. Wow.

"Maybe just a spanking would have been enough." She eyed the tool again.

Aidan chuckled and touched his lips to hers. "When do we get to try it out?"

Excitement curled in her belly. "How about now?"

"Let's go."

They left the dishes on the counter, having just finished eating dinner, and sprinted out of the kitchen and down the hall to their bedroom. Maddie jumped onto the bed and watched Aidan pull his T-shirt off over his head and toss it aside.

Her breath hitched at seeing his naked torso, another thing she still appreciated even after their years together. He exercised often and with a fierce intensity, running five miles almost every day and pumping massive weights in the gym his company thoughtfully provided their employees. His career involved crazy long hours, especially since starting his own architectural cooperative, but he managed to make working out a priority. It kept his body lean and hard, with ripped abs and heavily muscled arms and shoulders.

He stepped out of the worn jeans he'd changed into when he got home, revealing equally muscled legs, lightly dusted with dark hair. His cock was hard, surrounded by a thick patch of dark hair. Maddie's nipples tingled and her pussy squeezed.

She fell to her back and lifted her hips to push off her fleece shorts and panties, then sat up and pulled off her own thin T-shirt. She unhooked her bra and dropped it to the floor, then rolled to her stomach, wriggling into a comfortable position.

Her nerve endings tingled with anticipation, waiting for the touch of the flogger on her skin. Would he tease her with feathery strokes? Or get right into the slapping? Did he even know what he was doing with it? He wouldn't hurt her, would he? Actually…she hoped to feel a sting. A little burn.

After several seconds, nothing had happened and she lifted her head to look at Aidan.

He stood next to the bed, gazing at her. She couldn't read the expression on his face. "What? What's wrong?"

"You want me to flog you?"

She blinked. "Uh…yeah. Isn't that why you bought it?"

He gave a short nod. "Yeah. I mean, I was kinda hoping you'd use it on me too."

"Oh! I can do that. I guess." She rolled to her side and drew her bottom lip between her teeth. "I don't exactly know what to do, but I can try."

"I don't know what I'm doing either," he admitted. Then he flashed an evil grin. "But we'll figure it out." He reached for the flogger.

She loved it. She had to direct him a couple of times, gently, to not hit too many times in the same place. After that, he carefully laid the tails in different places, warming her ass and the back of her thighs. She asked him to go a little harder. But she felt he was holding back, as if he was afraid to hurt her. Her only complaint about the experience was that she wanted more—more sensation. It was a teaser.

But it was a start.

Using the flogger on Aidan wasn't as much fun. She did it, because he wanted to try it. It surprised her that he wanted it. But she held back at least as much as he had, not wanting to hurt him, not sure what she was doing. Then she tossed it aside, lay down beside him and looked at him.

They both started laughing.

"Yeah, that was weird. C'mere." Aidan pulled her closer and kissed her. He slid his tongue inside her mouth, his body hot and hard and heavy on hers. His hands pushed into her hair and held her head, tilting it to deepen the kiss. After long moments of hot making out, he eased her thighs apart with his and fit himself between them, his cock solid and pulsing against her.

"Yes," she whispered when he dragged his mouth off hers and kissed her jaw, her neck. "Fuck me."

"Did you like it?" He opened his mouth on her throat. "The flogger."

"Yeah. It made me hot." It wasn't a lie. It had been exciting. The heat that had built under her skin made her wet and achy. She wanted him inside her, fucking her hard.

And then he was, pushing into her, filling her with thick heat, her body tightening around him. His fingers tangled in her hair and tingles cascaded down her spine, coalescing at the base of her spine in a hard ache. She lifted her hips to meet his strokes. "I love you."

"Mmm. Love you too. Love your tight pussy squeezing me. So fucking hot." He slid out and thrust back in, deeper, pushing her breath out of her lungs.

Heat spiraled low inside her, growing, building. Then he pulled out and went onto his knees. She struggled to open her eyes, swiping her tongue over her bottom lip.

"Wanna fuck you from behind." He reached for her and easily flipped her. "Wanna see that pretty pink ass."

"Oh." She sighed as he arranged her into position, wriggling a hand down under her to find her clit. She closed her eyes and focused on building her orgasm again. She was buzzing, but she needed more, needed to rub herself. Her clit pulsed with need.

Aidan's big hands gripped her hips as he pushed back into her, this angle deeper, hitting more sensitive spots, intensifying her pleasure. One of his hands slid up her back, gripped her hair and tugged. "Oh I love that." She gasped, her head going back. "Yes, yes, do that." She'd told him how much she liked her hair pulled, but he rarely did it.

More. She wanted more. The words swirled through her head as she rubbed her clit and Aidan's stiff cock tunneled in and out of her with sweet friction. She didn't know what she wanted; all she could think was...more.

Aidan groaned, releasing her hair. Dammit. But he palmed her butt cheek. "Sweet little ass," he ground out. "Love your ass, Maddie." He thrust harder, smacking his lower belly against her ass, and the sensation twisting up inside her shot up sharply, rocketing her up and over the edge in a hard, shuddering orgasm.

When she dragged her hand out from under herself, Aidan pounded harder, faster, and she loved it, her orgasm stretching out in delicious, soft waves.

"Fuck yeah." He groaned, hands on her hips, holding her tight against him as he pulsed inside her. Heat flooded her pussy. "Maddie, baby, love you."

"Mmm." She couldn't form words yet, her body limp and languid.

Aidan curled over her, kissed her shoulder, her hair, the middle of her back. Then he slowly withdrew and rolled to his back beside her. She stretched out her weak legs and dropped an arm across Aidan's abdomen. He curved a palm over her butt. They lay like that for long moments, breathing gradually slowing and easing.

"Wow," Aidan finally said. "That was hot."

"Hot. Yeah." She let out a long slow exhalation, her mouth curving into a smile against the pillow.

Moments later, the bed shifted as Aidan left. She heard water running in their bathroom and then he returned with a warm wash cloth that he used to clean her up. He always took such good care of her.

Then they snuggled under the duvet and Aidan flicked on the TV mounted on the wall across the room. He started channel surfing and she wrapped her arm around him, her head on his shoulder, not paying much attention. He could find something he wanted to watch.

He'd wanted her to use the flogger on him. What did that mean? That she wasn't the only one who'd been feeling less than satisfied? The idea that Aidan found their sex life lacking made worry curl inside her. Sure, she'd been feeling that way a bit, but she still loved him. She didn't want to lose him.

But as he clicked through various channels, two words pierced her thoughts:

Zack Donovan.

Her eyes flew open and her body tensed. She lifted her head. "Did you hear that? What was that?"

"Zack. Hang on." He'd already gone past the channel. In seconds, he'd found the news channel that was talking about two journalists missing in Syria, one American, one British.

She scrambled to sit up, shoving the duvet away, staring at the TV in wide-eyed horror. "No." She covered her mouth with her hands. "It can't be."

Aidan's hand landed on her back and rubbed gently. "Maybe he's just there covering the story."

She swallowed, ears acutely tuned to the news story. Her entire body vibrated. She turned to look at Aidan, biting her lip. He lifted one shoulder and they continued to listen.

Then their worst fears were confirmed. Their best friend had been missing in Syria for over two weeks.

"Oh my god!" Her body started to shake, her stomach tightened and she pressed her hands to her cheeks. "Oh my god, Aidan, this can't be happening."

Aidan was silent, watching and listening. But they'd missed the first part of the story and the news anchor went on to another one. "Shit."

Zack. Oh no. Oh god no.

They hadn't seen him in years. He'd left Chicago seven

years ago to pursue his photojournalism career, right after he and Aidan had graduated from college. Zack hadn't been great about staying in touch over the years. In fact, he'd never even been home once, despite Maddie's emailed pleas to come home and see them. He'd emailed back, infrequently, always with some job or trip that kept him away at Christmas, or any time really. Seven long years since she and Aidan had seen their best friend.

And now...god. Her throat tightened again. Were they *ever* going to see him again?

"I'll go look on the Internet." She flung back the covers and jumped off the bed. She grabbed the robe she'd left lying over the arm of a chair and fumbled into it with shaky hands, then sprinted out to their shared home office. Her laptop sat open on the desk at her end of the room, and she dropped into the chair and tapped the keyboard.

The monitor lit up and she bit her lip as she clumsily typed out a search.

She sensed Aidan behind her and glanced over her shoulder to see him walking toward her in a pair of boxers. He rested his warm, strong hands on her shoulders.

Zack had apparently entered Syria from Lebanon on June fifth, had traveled to Damascus and then had been going on to al-Qusair. There'd been intense fighting in that area as regime forces supported by Lebanese Hezbollah fighters were trying to capture the rebel stronghold. Zack had last contacted his employer, Stockton News Agency, on April 30, and hadn't been heard from since. Over two weeks ago.

"He emailed me on April twenty-ninth." Maddie turned again to Aidan. His face had tightened into lines of stark concern. "I was asking him to try to come home this summer. For your thirtieth birthday."

"Fuck." Aidan stared at the monitor.

Zack had been all over the world, to some of the most violent places—he'd left Chicago to go to Iran, had moved on to Afghanistan, Pakistan, then Middle Eastern countries. She'd almost been relieved the time he'd traveled to Australia, such a nice, calm place, except that he'd been there covering terrible wildfires that had been almost as scary as warfare.

Why he kept risking his life covering these tragic new stories she wasn't sure she'd ever understand. In fact, it made her a little angry at him at times. And then he won awards for his photographs, including last year's Pulitzer. And she knew he was doing something important. At those moments, she was filled with pride and admiration and knew all she could do was keep in touch as best she could and support him in his career.

She stared back at the computer, scrolling down, then doing another Google search, but there wasn't much more information to be found. "I feel so helpless." Tears stung her eyes. "What can we do?"

"I don't know." Aidan's voice came out rough.

"We have to do something!" She turned anguished eyes on him. "How can we just sit here and…and…"

"I know. I know." He massaged her shoulders. "I don't know what right now, but I'll figure it out."

She nodded, pressing her trembling lips together. Aidan would fix it. Aidan could fix anything. She couldn't stop the tear that dripped from her eye and she swiped at it. The immense frustration and anger swelled up inside her, a feeling of red hot pressure.

"He has no family," she reminded Aidan. Zack had never talked a lot about his childhood but Maddie and Aidan knew it had been tough.

"I know." Aidan rubbed his chin. "Well, the first thing to do is contact the company he works for. They have to be working on this."

"Yes. Yes, good idea." She scrubbed at her stinging eyes.

Aidan crossed to his own computer on the other desk in

the den and sat. In moments he'd located a contact name and email and had sent a message.

He turned to Maddie. "There. Don't worry, sweetheart. Tomorrow I'll make some calls."

"Oh, Aidan." She slid onto his lap and his arms came around her. His strength and warmth surround her, and she pressed her face to the side of his neck. "I knew something like this was going to happen. He keeps putting himself in danger...sooner or later it was going to catch up to him."

"He's strong." Aidan rubbed her back. "He's survived a lot, his whole life. And he's smart."

She drew back to peer up at him. "Why'd you say that? That he's survived a lot?"

Aidan shrugged. "We both know he didn't have the best upbringing."

She searched his eyes. "You know more about that than I do, don't you?"

He just shrugged and looked away. He did know. He and Zack had been friends before she'd met them. Of course he knew. Maddie had her own suspicions, based on comments Zack had made, but she'd never pushed either of them to talk about it.

She sucked briefly on her bottom lip. "I know he's been in some tough situations. And he's made it out alive before. He will this time too."

"That's what we're going to believe." Aidan's arms tightened on her and she was so glad she had him there, rock solid and supportive. "He's going to be okay."

The emailed response the next day from Stockton assured them that they were reaching out to a range of contacts and doing everything they could to facilitate Zack's release. They promised to stay in close contact with any news they had. They issued a press release that praised Zack as a brave and dedicated reporter who believed the civil war in Syria was an important story for the American people to know about, and urged his captors to release him.

Aidan also contacted the State Department, and after persistently explaining that Zack had no other family and they were his closest friends and working his way up several levels, they'd agreed to talk to him. They were sympathetic and supportive but had no concrete information at that point.

As Maddie watched the news coverage over the next days, she learned how the situation inside Syria had gotten so much more complicated and dangerous for journalists since the war had begun, with multiple rebel factions on one side and diverse militias fighting for the government on the other.

A few days later, they learned that Zack and the other journalist had in fact been abducted and were being held by rebel forces, a brigade known as Al Hassaq, apparently, terrifyingly, affiliated with Al Qaeda. But little else was known.

They continued to watch the news and scour newspapers and the Internet for any mention, but after the first few days the story dropped off the media's radar as a top story. She and Aidan went to work every day, him to his architectural firm where he was overseeing a number of huge, high-profile projects, her to her public relations job at The Endicott Foundation. Aidan was under so much pressure at work with the Thorne Studio, and he was being amazing by every day trying to contact someone to find out more information. They kept in touch with Stockton News and the State Department, but Maddie couldn't let it drop. She felt helpless and felt a need to do something. So she started a Facebook page dedicated to bring Zack home.

Support quickly grew from their friends and people they'd all gone to college with, then from total strangers. She posted links to news stories, not only about Zack but about other journalists being held captive. When she read stories that ended in tragedy, her stomach twisted into knots. She agonized for the friends and families of those who didn't make it back, trying to stay hopeful for Zack. She found herself with an almost mission-like zeal to draw attention to this important and tragic issue.

She struggled some days at work, finding herself distracted and even angry. Sometimes she'd be sitting in a meeting, shaking her head at the fact that these people had no idea someone was being held hostage, possibly — likely — being tortured, halfway across the world. She marveled that they didn't know and didn't care.

They'd been such close friends, she and Zack and Aidan. She found herself reliving memories of their time in college, the way the three of them had bonded through the creative aspects of their respective majors and their mutual interest in world events. Zack and Aidan had been friends first, and had taken her under their wing the night they'd rescued her from Colton, the douchebag boyfriend she'd been trying to break up with. Colton had been drunk and aggressive, and had come close to raping her when Zack and Aidan had heard her terrified cries over the loud music of the party they'd all been at. They'd taken on Colton, kicked his ass and earned her eternal gratitude. Then when Colton wouldn't accept the breakup and wouldn't leave her alone, they made sure she never *was* alone — one of them was always with her, if not both.

She couldn't deny that she found them both attractive — god, who wouldn't? Aidan with his clean cut good looks, sexy dark eyes and hard body, Zack with a bad boy air, hair as dark as Aidan's but worn in long curls and waves over his forehead, and eyes that were so clear blue they glowed. But having just come out of a bad relationship, Maddie only wanted to be friends with them. It was a relief to just be herself around them and not worry about flirting and girl-boy stuff. And sex.

Although, they did flirt. The guys never put serious moves on her, but often joked around about how sexy she was and how no girl could ever measure up to her. It was all just teasing and fun.

⚜

As weeks went by after learning of Zack's disappearance, life went on. Maddie and Aidan had busy careers and a social life with friends in a city where there was always lots to do. She kept the Facebook page up to date. She researched other missing journalists and connections she could explore for any help. She made friends online with family members of other missing journalists. And she kept emailing Zack.

When he'd first left Chicago, she'd emailed every week, probably stupid boring emails about their jobs and daily life. He emailed back sporadically. She knew he was busy and traveled a lot. She wished he'd keep in touch better, but she knew the demands of his career.

Her emails had tapered off after a while, to maybe once a month or when something significant happened. When Aidan got promoted, or won an award for one of his designs. When she'd gotten a new job. When Zack had won awards, she'd emailed him to congratulate him. And when things had changed between her and Aidan from friends to lovers, she'd emailed Zack that they were "dating," and then moving in together, finding herself strangely hesitant to tell him that, anxious about his reaction to that. His emailed response weeks later had been a brief "Congrats. Happy for you both."

Then, on the sixty-fifth day since he'd last been heard from—Zack Donovan reappeared.

2

Zack stared out the window of the Boeing 777 as the wheels touched down at O'Hare International Airport in Chicago.

He was about to see Maddie and Aidan again.

That should have filled him with dread. He'd been avoiding them for seven years. Now...he didn't feel anything. After what he'd been through, he'd shut down. Over-the-top emotions had no place in his life. Hopes got crushed, fears got mocked. Hate made you bitter and love made you weak. He was just lucky to be alive. After the things he'd endured, seeing his two old friends, the ones he'd run from with a broken heart and never looked back, was really no big deal.

Broken heart. He almost snorted out loud. Looking back now at his youthful misery, it seemed so...over the top. Whatever.

Not that he was all eager to see them. He just...had nowhere else to go.

Sure he did. There were a lot of places he could go. There was a whole world out there. He could go visit Kate in London, hanging out in her elegant flat. He could go see Jean-Marc in Paris and have some fun in the dungeon he'd introduced Zack to.

He couldn't go there. Who was he kidding? He was a mess. He'd lost so much weight his skin was hanging on his bones. He was having nightmares and flashbacks. Neither Kate nor Jean-Marc had offered him a place to stay.

Maddie and Aidan had.

Maddie's emails pleading that he should come to them when he'd finally been released from hospital in Germany must have caught him at a weak moment. He found himself agreeing to come to Chicago and stay with them while he recovered. He couldn't imagine showing up at Kate's place in this kind of shape. She was a lovely woman, but probably not strong enough to deal with his shit. Jean-Marc...same thing.

He didn't want to do this to Aidan and Maddie either, but somehow he knew they were solid and strong enough to deal with this.

His employer had made it quite clear that he wasn't going to be working for a while. Six weeks of leave to "recuperate."

But they didn't understand—he was fine. Well mostly.

Hell.

And what was he going to do for a six weeks? Jesus. If he wasn't already whacked, he'd be really out of his mind after sitting around doing nothing for that long.

The plane took forever to taxi to the terminal, then even longer to open the door and let people deplane. By the time he was able to rise from his seat, grab his bag from the overhead compartment and file off the plane, he was antsy and itchy. Maddie had insisted they'd pick him up at the airport. Were they waiting for him just inside this building? Was he going to be able to handle seeing them together...seeing them as lovers, not just friends? Were they going to freak out seeing him like this, after all this time?

Somehow they'd kept his return under the radar. The

media had been all over the story, a happy ending story this time compared to some recent events. He'd given a ton of interviews in Germany. He knew they wanted to cover it, the homecoming, the guy who'd survived—but he couldn't handle that. He wanted to tell the stories—he didn't want to *be* the story. He knew at some point he was going to have to face the press once home, ha, even though he was one of them. He just couldn't do it right now.

So the State Department and Stockton had managed to keep all the plans on the down low, as had Aidan and Maddie.

He rubbed his face as he emerged into the terminal. He tugged a newsboy cap down over his eyes and kept his sunglasses on even in the terminal, in case someone recognized him. As if he was a fucking movie star, or something. He hated the media attention.

He followed the swarm of people toward the baggage claim, his insides tightening up. Everything turned to a blur around him as he tried not to look for familiar faces in the crowd, all the noise around him becoming a muted roar. He focused on finding the carousel displaying his flight number, shoving his hands into the pockets of his new jeans.

For some reason he didn't want to see them first.

"Zack!"

He heard her voice behind him and stopped. His shoulders tightened, but he turned.

Something inside him clamped down on his heart, squeezing it. He looked at Maddie nearly running at him, fuck, so gorgeous it made his throat ache. Her shiny brown hair was still long and straight, hanging below her shoulders. She used to wear her bangs thick and straight across her forehead, but now they were swept to one side. Her smile was as sweet as ever, her cheeks pink, her sapphire eyes shiny. Behind her was Aidan, striding fast, an intense look on his face. Aidan hadn't changed at all.

15

Maddie barreled at him, long legs bare in a pair of cut off denim shorts, flat sandals, a loose flowery top in pale grey with pink flowers flowing around her slender torso, tiny straps leaving arms and shoulders bare. Then she was nearly knocking him off balance, her arms going around his waist, her face planted in his chest.

His lungs burned and his throat closed up. His arms closed around her helplessly and he squeezed his eyes shut against the stinging he felt. Fuck. Fuck! He did not want to feel these things. He'd been dealing fine with all his crap, mostly by shutting down. But now he was suddenly terrified he was going to burst into tears. "Maddie. Baby."

Her body shuddered against his. Shit. She was crying. His hand slid up the middle of her back to press her head against him. "Don't," he mumbled. "Don't cry, baby."

"I can't believe you're here." She tried to breathe in and sobbed. "You're here." Then she reared back and stared at him, her eyebrows pinching together. "You big jerk!" And she punched him in the shoulder.

His mouth fell open and he jolted back. "Hey! What was that for?"

His mind spun. After all the care and sympathy and being treated like he was a soap bubble, about to burst if barely touched, here she was punching him, for fuck's sake! For some reason this made him smile. Christ. He wasn't sure when the last time was he'd smiled.

"You're a jerk! You haven't come home in *seven years*! You hardly ever call or email us! You're off in crazy dangerous places, putting your life at risk! We were worried sick about you! What the hell, Zack? What the fucking hell?"

He looked up at Aidan standing behind Maddie, his eyes soft on Maddie. Then Aidan lifted his eyes to meet Zack's. He gave Zack a long, measured look, his eyes narrow, his mouth grim. Emotion swelled in Zack's chest.

Fuck. They were both mad at him. "Dude," Zack said quietly. "Call your woman off. She's gonna hurt me."

The words echoed in his head, making his skin tighten.

Aidan's eyes softened at the corners and warmed, as if he couldn't stay angry. "She's too puny to hurt you." He stepped forward, nudging Maddie out of the way, grabbed Zack's hand and slapped his other arm around his shoulders. They hugged liked that for a stretched out moment, then drew back. Once again, Zack had to work at fighting down the pressure building inside him. He rubbed a hand over his mouth, sucked in air, and let it out. Jesus fuck. He'd missed this guy. So damn much.

"I'm not puny." Maddie said the words of protest, but when Zack looked at her, her eyes were brimming with tears, her mouth trembling.

"I am." Zack glanced ruefully down at himself.

Maddie's eyes tracked down and then back up. She sucked in a shaky breath. Yeah, this was more what he was used to—pity. "You've lost a little weight." She tossed back her hair and lifted her chin. "Good thing I like to cook. We'll fatten you back up in no time." Then her eyes shadowed and she moved back in. Aidan stepped aside, his lips twitching. She flattened her palms on Zack's cheeks, pulled his head down, and stared straight into his eyes. "I'm not going to ask if you're okay. Because there's no way in hell you are. But you will be."

Her forthright words made his chest tighten again.

She repeated in a fierce tone, "You will be."

And for the first time since those goddamn masked men claiming to be police officers had made him get out of the vehicle, taken him to a house somewhere in remote Syria and beat him up...he actually believed that.

At first, he'd believed that. He'd believed he'd get out of there alive. Someone would rescue them. He'd survive.

Then he'd started to have doubts. Even when weeks

later they'd escaped due to some inexplicable breakdown by their guards, as they'd run toward the border of Lebanon he'd been convinced with each step that he was going to feel a bullet in his back at any moment.

After, when he was physically safe and secure, when he knew he was going to live…that was when the real doubts had started that he'd ever be okay. But now…looking down at Maddie's beautiful face, her anger at him and yet her caring and her determination that he was going to be okay…he started to believe it.

"Thank god you're alive," she whispered.

He swallowed hard and nodded.

"Let's get your luggage." Aidan nodded at the conveyor belt where suitcases were starting to stream by.

"I don't have much." Zack gave a wry smile. "I lost pretty much everything I had. Got some new things in Germany." They moved closer and Zack searched for his big duffel bag on wheels. Eventually it showed up and he hauled it off. He traveled light so what he'd lost hadn't been much. Other than his precious camera gear. He clamped down on how much it hurt to lose that, reminding himself it was just stuff and could be replaced. At first he'd been all gung ho to head out shopping in Germany and buy a whole bunch of new equipment. Then his bosses told him he was on leave for the next month. So what was the point?

"I'll take that." Aidan reached for the bag. "You've got your carry on."

Maddie tucked her arm through his and started leading the way out of the terminal. "I can't believe you're here. Thank god you're okay. What a nightmare you've been through. You can stay as long as you want. Our guest room is all fixed up for you."

He hated that they'd gone to trouble for him. And he hated hearing "our" guest room.

Shit. After what he'd been through, this was nothing.

He could do this. It was great that Maddie and Aidan were together and happy.

Sure.

It was a warm summer Saturday in Chicago, the sun shining in a clear blue sky and a light breeze teasing their faces as they stepped out of the terminal and crossed to the parking garage where Maddie and Aidan had left their car. Soon they were in the Lexus SUV, his duffel and camera bag loaded in the back.

"Nice wheels." Zack looked around the interior of the vehicle from the back seat. "When did you buy this?"

"Last year. We had a good year."

"I emailed you about his company." Maddie shifted in the front passenger seat to look back at him. She'd slipped on a pair of aviator sunglasses against the bright sun, which forced his attention to her pretty mouth, the sweet way it curved into a smile, her lips shiny pink, her teeth all perfect and white.

Despair settled in his gut like a rock. Surely to fuck after seven years he should be over this?

He looked away from Maddie to gaze out the window as Aidan merged into traffic on Interstate 90 heading downtown. Zack knew they'd bought a condo in Streeterville about a year ago, but didn't know much about it.

"How was your flight?" Maddie asked.

"Long. I slept a little."

"What's the time difference? What time is it for you now?"

"It's about…eleven."

"Oh. That's not so bad. Can you stay awake long enough to eat dinner, or do you want to go to bed when we get home?"

Whatever. He rubbed his eyes. "I haven't been sleeping great. But I'm fine. I'll stay awake as late as I can and try to get back on track." He had some drugs they'd given him in the hospital. He hated taking drugs, but they'd been pretty clear that sleep was the foundation of recovery. Without it, everything else would only get worse.

Her mouth softened. "Whatever you want, Zack. Just name whatever you need."

"Thanks."

He watched her settle into her seat, watched Aidan stretch a hand out to grab hold of hers and squeeze.

What he needed might be some time alone, so he didn't have to watch the two of them like that.

Man, he was going to have to get over this and pretty damn quick or he wasn't going to last long staying with them. Maybe this was a bad idea.

He also had to get over this pity party.

Aidan navigated traffic easily, eventually exiting the freeway and cruising towards Lake Shore Drive. He pulled into an underground parking garage beneath a high-rise building with a rounded façade that gleamed in the summer sun.

Zack leaned forward. "Nice place."

"Thanks." When he'd parked, Aidan climbed out and rounded the car to the rear, popping the back door.

Christ. Zack had never lived in a place like this. Aidan must be pulling down some serious coin. They rode the elevator to the twelfth floor and Maddie unlocked the door to their condo, stepped in and disarmed the alarm system.

"We'll give you a key and a code." She moved farther in, letting him and Aidan follow. "So you can come and go."

"Thanks." Although Zack had no idea where he would go. Without the adrenaline rush of danger and violence, the compelling need to take pictures, capture images and tell stories, the emptiness of his life created a sudden feeling of terror. He fought that back too. "Not sure how long I'll be here." Christ. He couldn't spend six weeks here. He had no idea where else he'd go, but staying here all that time would be torture.

But then, he'd undergone true torture and lived through it. He could do this.

Sunlight streamed in big floor-to-ceiling windows that curved around a combination living and dining space. Wow. The place was huge. Hardwood floors gleamed in the bright light. A big sofa faced the windows, flanked by funky chairs, a glass table centered between them. The sweeping view through the windows encompassed the lake and harbor as well as some other downtown buildings.

Maddie's eyebrows sloped down. "You're staying for a while, right?"

He tried to smile. "I don't know, Maddie."

She advanced on him, her flat sandals a whisper on the hardwood floor, but her hands curled into fists made him worry she was going to start punching him again. He held up his hands. "Don't hit me."

She stopped and planted her hands on her hips. Her lips twitched. "I wasn't going to hit you. But don't piss me off, or I might. You're not talking about leaving when you've just walked in the door. We'll talk about that later. Now...we'll show you around. You can lie down if you want, take a shower, whatever. I've already got dinner started, just need to put it in the oven for a while and toss the salad. We can eat whenever you want."

They gave him a quick tour. They showed him the doors that led onto the balcony, where they had an arrangement of dark wicker chairs with bright yellow cushions. The galley-style kitchen was separated from the dining and living areas by a big expanse of white granite counter. Dark wood cabinets lined either side of the kitchen space, with stainless steel appliances. At the opposite end of the living area was a den, separated only by another, cozier arrangement of furniture facing a big-screen television, the two inside walls lined with built in desks. He followed them down the hall, past a closet where Maddie showed him the washer and dryer, past a powder room, then a full bathroom opposite the bedroom that was to be his. She gestured to their master bedroom at the end of the hall.

He didn't even want to look into their bedroom, giving it the briefest glance as Maddie waved at it.

His room wasn't huge, but had a queen-size bed covered with a black and white duvet, masses of matching pillows and some olive green ones tossed in among the black and white. A black dresser matched the headboard, and an olive green tub chair sat in the corner. "This is great." He parked his duffel next to the bed.

"You can use the big bathroom across the hall." Maddie pointed. "There are towels in there. Just ask if there's anything you need." She clasped her hands together and gave him a slightly anxious look. "Okay. We'll let you settle in. We'll be out in the kitchen, just come on out whenever."

Maddie brushed past Aidan leaning against the door frame, giving him a flash of a smile. Aidan didn't leave.

"What she said," he said quietly. "Anything you need?"

Zack studied Aidan, the way the T-shirt he wore stretched over his biceps and broad shoulders. Damn, he looked good. He'd sure kept in shape over the years. Beneath the hem of his knee-length shorts, his calves were muscular and tanned. A day's grown of dark beard shaded his square jaw—his weekend look, no doubt. He'd always been a confident guy but now had an air of assurance, a guy who'd experienced success. A guy who got things done. "Not that I can think of at the moment," Zack finally said.

"Okay." Aidan straightened from the doorframe where he leaned. "You've been through hell and we're here for you. It's good to see you, Zack." He gave him a searching look. "Really good. See you in a bit."

Aidan closed the door behind him, leaving Zack alone

in the elegant bedroom with the stunning view out the window, the same wall of windows that curved around the living space. Lake Michigan stretched out endlessly blue to the horizon.

He rubbed the back of his neck and took a deep breath.

He was here. He'd made it this far. He could do this.

3

Aidan paused in the hall before joining Maddie in the kitchen. He leaned against the wall and bent his head, hands shoved into his pockets. Seeing Zack again had messed up his head.

During the weeks Zack had been missing, he'd thought a lot about what Zack meant to him. He'd missed him all these years. He'd been pissed off at him all these years too, for leaving and never coming back to visit. And yeah, there'd also been an element of hurt there. Now, seeing him again, he realized just how much he cared about the guy. But everything had changed since Zack had left.

He straightened, pulling in a long breath, and walked into the kitchen.

Maddie whisked something in a bowl and looked up as he pulled out a stool at the counter and sat. He took in the droop of her mouth and the unhappy shadows in her eyes.

"He's so thin," she said quietly. "They must have starved him."

"Yeah." He'd noticed too. Zack was a couple inches shorter than him and had always been more muscular. Now he was painfully lean compared to his old self. "Damn. It's good he came here."

She nodded, dipping a spoon into the concoction in the

bowl to taste it. "Yeah. We can make sure he's okay. Shit, Aidan." She flattened her palms on the counter and leaned in.

"I know, I know. But he's here."

"He had hardly any stuff. He said he lost almost everything he had. That must include his cameras."

"I'll see if he needs any money," Aidan said slowly. "If he needs help to get back on his feet, we can definitely do that."

She bit her lip. "For sure. We'll ask him. I mean..." She sighed. "There was a time when the three of us could talk about anything. He seems so...closed off."

"He's just been through a traumatic ordeal. Give him time."

"It's not just that." Her lower lip pushed out. "He's different. He seems...harder. And even though he's lost weight, he seems...bigger. Does that make any sense?"

Aidan thought about that. She was right. Zack had lost weight but nonetheless radiated an intense energy, a puzzling mix of powerful confidence and cool remoteness. Maybe that wasn't any different than when they'd been in college. Chicks had all dug that artistic, brooding vibe he gave off.

Actually, quite a few guys had dug it too, which had irritated Aidan. Through college Zack had gradually come to open up about his bisexuality. Aidan hadn't been shocked by that, and he wasn't homophobic, but he'd been confusingly annoyed when Zack expressed even hesitant interest in another guy. Now, Zack seemed to have settled into himself, his personality bigger. Stronger.

"Yeah. I know what you mean."

"We've hardly heard from him in seven years. It felt like he deliberately distanced himself from us, even though he kept saying he was just busy. I just don't understand why."

"Maybe we'll find out."

"He doesn't seem very inclined to talk."

"He never was one to talk a lot." Zack had been a very private person.

"That's true. I remember in college, wanting to know more about his family and his childhood, but all he would say was that his parents were dead and he didn't want to talk about it."

Aidan glanced toward the bedrooms, hoping Zack wasn't going to appear while they were talking about him.

"Yeah. That's true." Zack *had* told him more than that. He'd also asked Aidan to never tell Maddie. When Zack had eventually confided in him, it had made him feel stoked that his friend had trusted him enough to share his tragic past, trusted that he wouldn't look at him any differently because of it, and trusted him that he wouldn't tell anyone else. When Zack had told him that shit, it had brought them closer together. It had also made him pissed as hell on behalf of his buddy. He liked to fix things—but how could he change Zack's past?

He couldn't. All he could do was...care. Look out for him.

When they'd met in college, and ended up as roommates, neither of them knew a single other soul on campus. Aidan had been excited to meet new people and did so easily. Zack had been more standoffish, his crappy childhood a big chip on his shoulder that gave him attitude. The bad boy attitude, shaggy hair and good looks, the artistic vibe with a camera seemingly always around his neck, had attracted tons of girls, but he'd kept people at a distance. Aidan soon had a big circle of friends, but he always made sure to include Zack, who'd gradually relaxed with people and opened up a bit. And they'd become friends.

"This dressing needs more vinegar." Maddie splashed some from a bottle into the bowl in front of her and resumed her whisking, maybe a little more vigorously than she had to, blinking rapidly.

Fuck. This was hard for all of them. After so long, to see Zack like that... Well, they had to make the best of it. They just had to be glad he was there and he was alive.

"I'm still pissed at him." She bent her head. "But it's kind of hard to stay that way when I see him and it really hits me what he's been through."

Yeah, he knew exactly what she meant.

Aidan studied Maddie. There'd been a time when he'd wondered if Maddie had been one of those girls crushing on Zack. The three of them had gotten tight, hanging out a lot. They'd all dated other people at times, but never anything serious. Aidan had been half in love with Maddie since the day they'd met, but she'd been gun shy about guys and dating after that fucktard ex of hers had tried to rough her up. And he'd seen the way she looked at Zack sometimes, which made him even more hesitant to make a move on her. She'd been devastated when Zack had left.

And so had Aidan. He just hadn't been as open about it.

He sighed. "I need a drink."

Maddie looked up at him and smiled, her eyes softening. "Great idea. Let's open that bottle of Malbec."

He rose off the stool and crossed to the wine rack in the dining room where they had an extensive collection. He selected the Malbec she'd referred to and proceeded to uncork it. Maddie slid two large-bowled wine glasses with slender stems across the marble counter toward him. When he'd poured it, he pushed one over to her. "Here, sweetheart."

She leaned against the counter and sipped her wine. Her brown hair brushed over bare shoulders. She lifted her wine glass with a toned, slender arm, lightly tanned from their weekends at the beach or cycling or relaxing out on their balcony. Christ, she was beautiful. And smart and kind and funny. He was so fucking lucky.

"Love you," he said quietly.

She met his eyes and her lips curved into a smile. "Love

you too." She took another sip of wine then set her glass down with a clink on the stone counter to check the lasagna in the oven.

"Something smells great."

They both turned to see Zack standing there. He'd showered and changed into a different T-shirt and jeans, both of them obviously new. Yeah, he was thinner, his eyes wore shadows, but his shoulders seemed broad and strong and powerful.

"Seafood lasagna." Maddie straightened from where she peered in the oven. "It'll be ready soon. How about a drink? We're having wine. Want a glass of that? Or something else?"

"Got a beer?"

"Hell, yeah. Open the fridge right beside you." Aidan gestured. "Take your pick."

Zack did so and took a moment. "Wow. Quite the selection. How about a basic Budweiser?"

Aidan snorted. "Dude. Bitching about the brand of free beer in your buddy's fridge is totally against the guy code."

For a moment, Zack looked startled. Then he smiled. It looked tight and uncomfortable, but he smiled. "Jerkoff," he muttered. "Fine. I'll drink one of your fancy microbrewery beers." He pulled one out and popped the top off.

"Want a glass?" Maddie asked.

"Nah. This is good." He tipped the beer to his lips and drank like he was dying of thirst. "What is this?" He held up the bottle to peer at the label. "Big Dick's Pale Ale?" He turned appalled eyes on Aidan. "You gotta be kidding me."

Maddie giggled and Aidan smiled. "Nope. It's one of my favorites."

"Don't know if you wanna go around telling everyone you like Big Dick's." Zack smirked.

Now Aidan laughed too, although the tops of his ears burned. "Shut the fuck up. It's good beer."

"Yeah, it is." Zack gave a gusty sigh. "Wanted a beer so fucking bad while I was held captive."

Maddie tipped her head. "Do you want to talk about it?"

Zack grimaced and hitched a shoulder. "No."

Aidan watched Maddie's throat move as she swallowed. "Well. If you do, we're here. I think it would be good for you to talk."

"Might be," he acknowledged. "Good for me, but a huge fuckin' downer for you."

Maddie laughed and Aidan had to grin too. "I think we can handle it. Now we know you're alive. Fuck, man, you had us going nuts the last few months."

Zack leveled his gaze on him, chin lowered. "Wasn't fuckin' *me*, dude. I had no choice in what happened."

Aidan closed his eyes briefly. "I know. I didn't mean that. I'm not blaming you."

"Well, I am." Maddie spoke up, lifting her little chin. "I mean, it's not your fault you got abducted. But it *is* your fault for putting yourself in that kind of dangerous situation."

The air changed, going electric around them. Zack's eyes narrowed.

Shit.

"It's my job," he said tersely.

Maddie and Zack entered into a brief stare down. Then Maddie softened. "I know it is." She sighed. "And you've done amazing things. A Pulitzer, Zack. That's incredible."

One corner of his mouth lifted. "Thanks."

"Come on." Aidan tucked his tongue into his cheek. "Anyone with a digital camera can take pictures like that." Maddie and Zack both directed their gazes at him. Then they burst out laughing and the tension eased.

"Asshole." Zack took another swig of his beer. "I believe you've won some awards yourself."

Aidan grinned. "Well, my company has."

"Tell me about your company."

"Have a seat, Zack." Maddie nodded at the stools. He moved through the galley kitchen and around the end of the counter, then pulled a stool under him as Maddie turned to the oven and removed the lasagna.

"That thing is huge," Zack said, watching Maddie.

"That's what she said," Aidan replied.

Maddie cracked up and leaned on the counter, her hands still in big oven mitts. "Riiiiight."

Zack laughed too and Aidan grinned. Making Zack laugh made him feel pretty good.

"Talking about your ego, no doubt," Zack said dryly.

"Ha ha. Anyway. I founded The Thorne Studio about five years ago. It's a collective of architects and designers. We do cross-field research, collaboration and experimentation. We test out ideas on different scales — cities and environments, material and physical properties. I've got some great people working with me and we've done some good things."

Maddie snorted and he caught the look of pride on her face as she dumped a bag of greens into a salad bowl. "Some good things. Right. Last year they called you 'a star architect in a city that loves architecture.' And one of the most influential architects in Chicago."

Aidan caught Zack looking at Maddie too and his heart gave a bump at the expression on Zack's face, which was quickly shielded as he dropped his eyes to the beer bottle in his hands resting on the counter. And expression that looked like...longing.

"We wanted to do things differently." Aidan fingered the stem of his wine glass. "Not just your typical design firm. We use a research-based discovery process. We try to actively involve clients in the design process, making choices as the project develops. Understanding our clients' project goals and strategizing methods to achieve them from the very beginning allows us to keep to the project's budget and timeline. And build a more compelling design. We're also very focused on sustainable design. We want all our team members to be LEED Accredited Professionals within a year of joining the firm, and several of our projects are targeting a LEED Platinum rating."

He knew he didn't have to explain Leadership in Energy and Environmental Design, a set of rating systems for the design, construction, operation, and maintenance of green buildings, homes and neighborhoods, to Zack—he'd talked to him about it enough back in college.

"We've had some big projects," Aidan continued. "The Griffon Tower was probably our biggest. That was the one we won the National Design Award for Architecture, last year."

Zack nodded. "Maddie told me about that in one of her emails."

"Right now we're working on a bunch of things." Aidan's shoulders tensed, thinking about the work he had to do and the problems waiting for him at the office. "Including a big new medical complex in Greektown."

"Sounds amazing, dude.

For a moment, Aidan had a sense of unreality. A week ago, Zack had been a captive somewhere in the Syrian desert, clearly physically abused, mentally abused, his life not destroyed but certainly changed. And here *he* was, talking about designing buildings. What the fuck? Who gave a crap about that?

He bowed his head. Then a firm hand landed on his shoulder. He tilted his head without lifting it to look at Zack. "I'm here," Zack said quietly. "I'm okay."

How the fuck had Zack known what he was thinking? The guy had always been eerily intuitive. Aidan nodded.

Aidan looked up at Maddie, watching them as she slowly sliced a red pepper. His eyes met hers and she gave a tiny smile.

31

Fuck, he'd missed Zack. Maddie'd been the one who'd tried to keep in touch with Zack, with all those emails she'd sent him, many of which got no reply. She was the one who'd bitched about how he'd disappeared and how she didn't believe he couldn't take time to come home for a visit. Aidan hadn't talked about it. Hadn't wanted to admit how much he missed his friend. But he had.

He couldn't say that. That would totally go against the guy code.

"I wanna hear about that stuff," Zack said. "This all feels so...normal."

"You two are such over-achievers." Maddie set down her knife. "I mean, I always knew you would be. You're both so smart and talented. I feel like a big loser compared to you."

"Fuck that," Aidan said at the same time as Zack said, "That's bullshit."

She grinned. "Okay, not a loser. But you know...I just have my little public relations job."

"Sweetheart, your job is important. The Endicott Foundation is one of the biggest philanthropy groups in the city."

"I'm sure you're great at your job," Zack added.

"Of course I am." She winked, still smiling. "But I'm not some kind of rock star like you two."

They both snorted at that. "Fuck, I don't feel like a rock star." Zack rubbed his face. "I'm the one who feels like a big loser right now. Shit. I'm homeless, don't have much more than the shirt on my back, and my employer doesn't want me back."

Maddie gasped. "What? They fired you over this?"

"No, no. I still have a job. But they're making me take six weeks off before I can work again."

"Oh." Maddie's shoulders relaxed. "Well, of course you should have time off. You need to recuperate." She lifted the cutting board and slid the slices of red pepper into the salad bowl. "Okay. I just need to toss this and we can eat. Aidan, honey, can you set the table?"

"Sure." Aidan stood.

"I'll help," Zack said.

"Nah, it's fine. Everything's right here." Aidan slid open a kitchen drawer and counted out sets of cutlery, then pulled plates out of the cupboard and carried them to the dining table. It only took a moment to arrange the place settings. Then he set the big lasagna on a hot pad on the table.

Maddie carried over the salad. "Zack, can you grab that bread?"

Zack brought the bread, Aidan refilled their wine glasses, offering one to Zack for dinner, which he accepted, and they sat down to eat.

"This is unbelievable," Zack said moments later. He'd already wolfed down two thick slices of the warm, crusty bread and was digging into a big piece of seafood lasagna.

"Thanks." Maddie picked up her glass of wine for a sip. "Eat up. You look like you could use twenty or forty pounds."

"Yeah. I did lose weight."

"Did they feed you?" she asked quietly. "At all?"

"Yeah. Our captors gave us their leftovers to eat. It wasn't much, but it was something."

Aidan watched Zack, saw his face tighten, and waited, wondering if their friend would share any more about his ordeal.

"How awful was it?" Maddie asked.

"You don't want to hear."

She pressed her lips together. "I think you need to talk about it."

"Maybe so, but I don't want to bring you guys down hearing about it."

"We can take it."

"Maddie," Aidan said quietly. "He'll talk when he feels like it."

Aidan met her eyes and she sighed. "I'm sorry. I just want to help." She reached out and gave Zack's hand a squeeze.

"You are helping." Zack gave her a tight smile. "Letting me come and stay here...feeding me this great food."

Aidan wasn't about to say it in front of Maddie, but possibly Zack would be more willing to open up about what had happened with him rather than Maddie, especially if Zack was trying to protect Maddie. Because that was what they both did, what they'd always done—protect Maddie.

"Another piece?" She reached for the serving dish as Zack finished off his first.

"Sure." As he took a second helping, he said, "When I was in the hospital in Germany I couldn't eat much. I'd totally lost my appetite. And the food in the hospital wasn't that great. But gradually they got me eating more. I can't tell you how good this tastes."

Maddie looked pleased.

After dinner they carried their wine glasses out onto the balcony. The south-east exposure had the low sun shining on them. With a light evening breeze it was comfortable. They settled into the thickly-padded chairs.

"This is nice." Zack gazed out at the view of the harbor. "Very urban and sophisticated."

"That's us." Maddie gave a soft snort. "Sophisticated, you bet."

"It's Saturday night," Zack said. "You don't have plans?"

Aidan glanced at Maddie. They'd cancelled plans to attend a fundraising dinner that evening when they'd heard back from Zack that he was coming. "Nothing important."

"You don't have to entertain me while I'm here," Zack

said. "Just go on living your lives like you always do."

"Yeah, we know that."

"It's your first night here." Maddie curled her legs under her. "Of course we're going to be here. We haven't seen you for seven years. Okay. So. You don't want to talk about what happened in Syria. Tell us some of the other things you've done since you left. I know you've been to some amazing places."

4

The next morning, while Aidan headed out for his run, Maddie mixed ingredients in a bowl to make pancakes. She was determined to feed Zack. She pulled bacon out of the fridge and separated slices so it was ready to cook once he was awake. She had real butter and maple syrup for the pancakes and she'd make sure he loaded up.

Last night they'd sat and finished off the bottle of wine, the conversation flowing easier, but mostly light and superficial. That was fine. If Zack wanted to keep it that way, they could do that. Whatever he needed. He'd been tired, so they'd all gone to bed early.

She heard noises down the hall, a door opening, another closing, then the shower running in the guest bathroom. She turned on the stove to start cooking.

By the time Zack walked into the kitchen, his dark curls damp, dressed in jeans and T-shirt again, the bacon was sizzling and she was starting the pancakes.

"Sweet Jesus, that smells good. Is that bacon?"

"Yes. Good morning."

A smile flickered on his lips. "Morning. God, I haven't had bacon in so long."

"Coffee?"

"Hell yeah."

She pulled a mug out of the cabinet and poured him a cup. "There's milk in the fridge if you use it, and sugar there." She nodded at her rooster-adorned sugar bowl on the counter.

"Black is good. Had to get used to going basic in some places."

"Did you sleep okay?" She poured a neat circle of batter onto the griddle.

"Yeah." He sounded surprised. "I actually did. First time in…well, that bed's really comfortable."

"Good."

"Can I help?"

"You can turn the bacon." She nodded at a set of tongs on the counter.

He began picking up strips and turning them while she watched the tops of the pancakes for bubbles, then flipped. "You still like your bacon crisp?"

She smiled. "Yeah. Very crisp. Take yours out if it's done enough for you. Leave me two or three."

"Plates are up here?" He reached for a cupboard, apparently remembering last night when Aidan had set the table.

"Yeah."

He pulled out two plates, also decorated with colorful roosters, and lifted some bacon onto one. She slid a stack of pancakes next to it.

"Whoa. That's a lot of pancakes."

"Fattening you up, remember?"

He laughed. "Right."

"Have a seat. I'll join you in two secs." She finished a couple more pancakes, nodded at the bacon and turned off the stove.

"Not waiting for Aidan to eat?"

She smiled. "He's out for a run. Sundays he does a really long run. He'll be back in a while. I'll make his breakfast when he gets home. There's orange juice too, if you want." She'd set the pitcher of juice on the counter with two glasses.

"Thanks. This is fantastic, Maddie. You're a great cook."

"Thank you." Pleasure warmed her inside.

Silence expanded around them as they ate, not completely uncomfortable but Maddie cast around in her head for a conversation topic. Then Zack beat her to it.

"I saw the Facebook page you started."

She blinked. "Oh. Did you?" She hesitated. "Did you get my emails?"

"Yeah."

Her mind churned. "*All* my emails?"

"Yeah."

She looked at her plate. "You didn't answer very many."

"I did, some."

Not many. But she fought back the hurt she'd felt over the years and didn't say that.

"When I got to a computer after I escaped, I read all the ones you'd sent." His voice went thick. She glanced up at him and saw his face was tight. "Saw the email you sent about the Facebook page. Checked it out." He paused, his throat working. "Can't believe you did that, Maddie."

She didn't know where to look. Looking at his face made her want to throw herself into his arms and hug him and kiss him. She blinked a few times. "I had to do something. I felt so helpless. Aidan was working hard too, staying in touch with your employer and the State Department, putting pressure on them to keep trying to find you."

He looked up and stared at her. "Jesus. Seriously?"

"Yeah." She blinked. "You're our friend, Zack. We care about you."

He just shook his head and used his knife and fork to cut a piece of pancake. "The Facebook page is amazing. I had no idea all that was going on while I was being held. Some of those other guys...I know...knew some of them. Fuck."

She nodded, her throat aching. "Zack. Don't feel guilty that you're here and they're not."

His head snapped up again, his brows pulled together. He stared at her. "How'd you know I feel guilty?"

She gave tiny shrug, sucking briefly on her bottom lip. "I think there are a lot of things you're feeling right now. You just don't want to talk about it."

After a moment of silence, he said, "I'm fine." But she could see the anguish in his eyes, thinking about some of his fellow journalists.

"I know."

He wasn't fine. But he would be. They'd make sure of it.

They talked about the Facebook page, which she still wanted to update. She'd posted that Zack was free and they were picking up him at the airport, but she hadn't updated it since seeing him. "Do you want to post something? I think people need to hear from you."

He lifted his gaze from his plate to meet her eyes and the pain she saw there made her heart clench. Then he nodded. "Sure," he said casually, returning his attention to his breakfast. "I could do that."

"We'll do it after we finish eating."

Maddie pulled Aidan's office chair over beside hers for Zack to sit on. They went to the page. First they read the comments that had been left on Maddie's post that Zack was arriving home in Chicago. It took a while to scroll through all of them and the congratulations and good wishes were overwhelming. Maddie found herself tearing up, hurting for those who were still missing family and loved ones.

She glanced at him, both of them leaning in close to see the screen. She could smell the shampoo he'd used, along with his own unique scent. Up close, could see every whisker that stubbled his jaw and cheeks, his thick eyebrows and short dark eyelashes. She let her eyes wander all over his face in profile to her while he read the comments.

"Wow." Zack rubbed his mouth.

"I'll move so you can post." She pushed her chair away a little.

He hesitated, hands hovering over the keyboard. His fingers were as beautiful as the rest of him, long, lightly dusted with dark hair, his forearms sinewy and strong.

"I don't know what to say."

"Well. Start by saying it's you. Just say…thanks." She bit her lip.

He started typing. She leaned away to give him time and space to think. A few moments later, he said, "There. Done. I think. Have a look before I post."

She leaned in again, brushing against his arm. He radiated heat and she breathed in that scent again. Her skin tingled everywhere.

She read his heartfelt words, words of thanks but also thoughts and prayers for the families of other missing and lost journalists. Her throat clogged up again. She nodded. "That's great." She cleared her throat. "Perfect. People will be so happy to hear from you. It's a miracle. Like you said, I hope it gives strength and hope to those who are still waiting."

He clicked the mouse to post.

The door of the condo opened and closed, and Aidan appeared, sweaty and flushed. He spotted them in the office. "Hey. What's up?"

Maddie spun on her chair to face him. "We're just posting on the Facebook page I created for Zack."

"Cool." Aidan swiped his brow. "Gonna jump in the shower. Be right back."

"I'll get his breakfast started." Maddie pushed away

from the desk. "If you want to use my computer for anything else, go ahead."

"I could check emails."

Maddie fled back to the kitchen. "Any time."

"I'll have to go buy a new computer."

"Well, until you do, you can use mine. Or Aidan's."

She got busy heating bacon and making more pancakes. Her heart was beating fast and she felt warm. Was that just from sitting beside Zack for a few minutes?

He'd had that effect on her back in college too, but she'd determinedly ignored it. They were friends. Although, by the time Aidan and Zack were graduating, a year before her, it was getting damn hard to ignore the fact that she was completely confused about her feelings for both Zack and Aidan.

She didn't want to think about that time, all the intense emotion and angsty internal drama, when she was trying to figure out what she was feeling and what the hell to do about it. Then Zack just leaving, and her disappointment and hurt and heartbreak. She was older now, in control of her emotions.

Then why did she alternate between wanting to hit Zack and kiss him? Why was she almost in tears one minute, then laughing the next? And why was she all goose bumps and breathless just from sitting beside him? Especially when she was in love with Aidan.

✦

Zack was undone.

He was such an asshole.

He did not deserve this. He'd left seven years ago, running away like a coward, trying to ignore Maddie's emails over all those years, rebuffing her invitations to come visit. Every once in a while he'd broken down and emailed her back, because much as he wanted to he just couldn't completely sever the connection. Clearly she'd been hurt by that. Yet when he'd been taken captive, she and Aidan had gone to all those lengths to try to find him.

This made him feel like a worthless piece of camel shit.

Reading all the comments on that post about him coming home made him want to crawl into a hole. Fuck, he so did not deserve that. Most of these people were total strangers all joining together to support him and fight for him and other journalists who'd disappeared.

During his time in captivity, he and his fellow prisoner had talked about a lot of things. Simon had a wife and kids that he talked about, more worried about how they were coping with his disappearance than he was about himself. Zack had had a lot of time to reflect on the fact that he had nobody. Nobody at home freaking out about him or his safety, nobody worried about him. He'd never imagined that Maddie and Aidan had been so impacted by his disappearance, despite Maddie's efforts to stay in touch with him over the years. It had made him question how he'd lived his life, though he'd justified it over and over again in his mind.

Now learning that there *had* been people who cared, including Aidan and Maddie, was totally fucking humbling.

He pushed away from the computer. He'd made a pretense of checking emails to give him time to get control of himself. Really he was just sitting there staring at the screen.

He stood and walked over to the kitchen just in time to see Aidan stride down the hall, move up behind Maddie and press her against the counter while he nuzzled her neck. "Smells good, sweetheart."

Maddie paused what she was doing and lifted an arm to slide her hand around the back of his neck. He gave her a squeeze, then released her. Their gestures spoke of their love and affection for each other.

Zack's gut cramped. Fuck. He had to deal with the fact that they were together now. He wasn't going to be able to stay here if he couldn't get his shit together. He forced a smile watching Aidan steal and munch on a piece of bacon as Maddie flipped pancakes.

"Any more coffee?" Zack asked.

"Yeah, help yourself," Maddie said.

"How was the run?" Zack asked Aidan as he refilled his mug.

"Excellent. Good to get out there before it gets too hot. So. What are we going to do today?"

Zack shrugged. "Whatever you usually do on a Sunday."

"Zack, what would *you* like to do?" Maddie spoke up. "We don't have plans. After months being held captive, what do *you* want to do?"

Christ, there she went again. How could she be so damn generous when he'd been such an asswipe?

His first impulse was to snap back that they didn't have to look after him. But fuck, she made him want to be a better man. To be worthy of that caring, and all that caring shown by the people on that damn Facebook page. This was an entirely new feeling for him and it fucking terrified him. But he kept his mouth shut and thought about her question.

During those interminable days and nights in the hot, dry desert, when he'd had nothing to occupy his mind but fantasies, he'd thought a lot about the ocean. He'd thought about places he'd been that were on the ocean—the Bay of Bengal, the Arabian Sea, the Tasman Sea, and especially the Mediterranean...he loved the Mediterranean. He'd thought about cool, blue water, immersing himself in it, waves buoying him.

"I wanted to go to the ocean," he mumbled.

He caught the way Maddie's eyes went soft. "Yeah?"

"And eat a hamburger and fries."

Her eyed danced now. "Okay. Excellent. We don't have

an ocean, but we have the next best thing…Lake Michigan. We'll go to the beach, and then for dinner we'll go to Big Rick's. Best burgers evah!"

He grinned reluctantly. "You two really don't have to entertain me."

Maddie have a huge, long-suffering sigh. "Oh my god. Would you stop with that? We're happy you're here. We want to spend time with you. Get it through that thick skull of yours."

He pressed his lips together to keep from laughing.

"Besides." She swiped her bangs aside. "I like going to the beach. Sundays are a day we try to take a break. Aidan works long hours, I often have fundraising events in the evenings, even Saturdays end up work days for us. I could definitely get into lying on the beach in the sun."

"Looks like it's gonna be a nice day." Aidan poured a river of maple syrup over his pancakes. "I'm not one for lying around, but maybe we can play beach volleyball."

"Beach volleyball. Jesus. Are we back in college on spring break?"

Maddie and Aidan both smiled.

"Oak Street Beach can be like that," Maddie said. "So let's pretend we are on spring break. For today."

He met her eyes and it was almost painful. She was so pretty, so sweet.

"You guys can totally go play volleyball and swim in the lake," she continued. "Also, I love Big Rick's. So again, no hardship."

"Okay." His voice emerged scratchy. "Let's do it."

"We gotta get there early." Aidan pushed away his empty plate. "That beach will be packed today."

"I don't have a swimsuit," Zack said.

Maddie's eyes saddened. She bit her lip and looked at Aidan.

"I have a few," Aidan said easily. "You can borrow one. The Speedo."

Maddie and Zack's eyes met, wide open and horrified. They both choked on laugh.

"Kidding." Aidan's lips curved. "Board shorts."

"Fuck me." Zack grinned. Goddammit. Both Maddie and Aidan made him laugh, and he hadn't laughed for a long time. "If I was in Europe I'd totally wear the Speedo. You should see the things guys wear over there."

Maddie lifted her eyebrows. "Like what?"

"One day I was on the beach in Nice and I saw this guy wearing a...I don't even know how to describe it. A bright yellow Lycra jumpsuit. Speedo-type bottom, two suspenders...Jesus."

"Oh my god." She bit her lip, laughing. "That's kind of...disturbing."

"Yeah. That's a good word for how I felt. Disturbed." He grinned. He wasn't averse to checking out hot guys on the beach, but yeah, that had *not* done it for him.

"And the women go topless." Aidan arched one eyebrow.

"Yes. Yes they do."

Maddie shook her head, smiling. "I'll get some things together."

Zack watched in surprise as Aidan started doing dishes and cleaning up the kitchen. He didn't know why he was surprised. Aidan must've caught his expression. "What?"

"You're doing dishes."

Aidan's eyebrows rose. "You didn't think I could?"

Zack grinned and rose off the stool to go help. "Wouldn't have guessed it from the state of our dorm room in college."

Aidan smiled as he dropped cutlery into the basket in the dishwasher. "Maddie made it pretty clear that she expected to share household responsibilities equally. We both work full-time, demanding jobs. She does the cooking. I clean up after. Most of the time. We try to be fair to each other."

Zack resisted the urge to make some kind of mocking comment, the words "pussy whipped" coming to mind. But again, he stopped himself. He didn't need to be more of an asshole.

And the truth was, he didn't think Aidan was pussy whipped. He was just envious of their easy, loving relationship.

Two hours later they were at Oak Street Beach. The soft pale sand warm beneath their feet, they walked across it and found a spot to spread a blanket and set up a couple of folding chairs. Already numerous blue umbrellas dotted the beach area. Maddie had packed a small cooler with drinks, and Aidan pulled out a football and a Frisbee.

Zack pulled off his shirt and stuffed it into his backpack.

"Whoa." He turned to see Maddie staring at him. Jesus, was he that emaciated? But she was looking at his tattoo. "When did you get that?"

He glanced at his left shoulder. "A few years ago. In Berlin."

She studied the swirls of dark ink that curled over his biceps and shoulder. Would she recognize the symbol in the center of it? Apparently not, though she did seem to like the tat.

"That's awesome." Then Maddie took off the loose sleeveless dress she wore over her swimsuit.

Christ.

She turned and bent to tuck the dress into her beach bag, giving him a close-up view of her sweet little ass in a tiny pink bikini. Her curves were smooth and lightly tanned. When she straightened and turned, he took in the deep V of the halter top, the gentle swells of her breasts, her flat stomach. She was gorgeous.

Trying not to stare and possibly drool, he looked away, only to see Aidan pull off his T-shirt, leaving him in a pair of black board shorts. They sat low on his lean hips. Holy fuck, he was ripped. Strong biceps bulged as he opened up one of the folding chairs and wedged it into the sand.

Zack grabbed the other chair and set it up. Maddie sat on the blanket and pulled out a big bottle of sunscreen. When she started rubbing it onto her arms and legs, he could only stare in fascination.

Apparently several months without sex was turning him back into a fifteen year old boy aroused at the sight of any kind of nakedness. Maybe the beach wasn't such a great idea.

Maybe he needed to get laid. Tie some sweet little thing up and fuck her hard.

There had to be a BDSM club in Chicago he could find.

"Gonna go look at the water," he mumbled, pushing up out of the chair.

He walked into the lake and stopped about a foot in. As he stood letting cool water wash over his feet, staring at the endless expanse of pure blue, he remembered all those time he'd imagined the ocean. Water. Coolness. After he'd escaped, a shrink had talked to him in the hospital. They were concerned he'd have PTSD or who knew what else. The shrink had talked about relaxation techniques and guided mental imagery. Zack had been using this technique as a coping mechanism during his captivity and hadn't even realized it.

Now here he was, not at the ocean, but damn, it was fucking fantastic. Hot emotion swelled inside him and he curled his hands into fists and closed his eyes. He swallowed down the burning in this throat. He was here. He was alive. God.

Deep breathing. Now, he needed that relaxation technique. Here he was where he'd wanted to be, and *now* he was having a meltdown.

A few more breaths had things under control. He again contemplated finding some kind of dungeon.

Leaving home and travelling the world had introduced

him to the kind of sex he liked. He'd explored fetish clubs and dungeons in London, Paris, Berlin, Tel Aviv. He'd met some special subs, like Kate and Jean-Marc, with whom he'd kept in touch and visited when in those cities. He'd learned a lot about himself. He'd learned about his need for control. And that world had accepted his bisexuality, something he'd only started to accept and open up about before he'd left Chicago. He'd had to open his mind and be brutally honest with himself about who he was, and it had been so freeing for him to be able to be true to himself for the first time in his life.

Maddie and Aidan in their sweet vanilla relationship would die if they knew the kinds of things he liked to do.

5

Over the next couple of weeks, life went on mostly as normal. Maddie and Aidan went to work every day. Having another man in the condo was a little weird for Maddie. Zack was trying overly hard not to be a burden, cleaning up after himself and keeping himself apart from them, but still, she was aware of him being there. After she'd wandered out of her bedroom one morning to make coffee wearing her little boy shorts and cami and had run into him in the hall, she'd been more conscious of not walking around half dressed.

One night she got up around two in the morning because she couldn't sleep. She slipped out of the bedroom and down the hall to get a glass of water, and her heart leaped up into her throat at encountering Zack in the kitchen. She slumped against the wall, hand at her throat. "Jesus. You scared the life out of me."

"Sorry." He stood in the dark room in shadows, wearing a pair of boxer shorts and nothing else. He held a book in one hand. "Couldn't sleep. Thought I'd come out here and read a bit."

She flipped on the lights beneath the cabinets. Zack's face wore tense lines and his shoulders carried tension in them. "Are you okay?"

"Yeah." He rubbed his face. "Had a nightmare."

"Oh." She reached out a hand to touch him, fingers hovering over bare skin. She drew back. "Have you been having a lot of nightmares?"

"Not that many. I had some when I first escaped. Since I've been here, they've been less. Don't know where this one came from. Fuck." He scrubbed his hand over his mouth again. "Wake up with my heart pounding, sweating, thinking I'm about to die. Hard to come back to reality."

Sympathy swelled inside her. Now she did rub his arm. "I'm sorry. That sucks."

"Yeah. I'm okay." He tried for a brief smile. "Usually if I read a bit, it sort of resets my mind."

"Want some tea? I have some herbal tea that's good for sleep."

He tipped his head. "Uh. Sure. But you don't have to lose sleep yourself looking after me. I'll do it."

"I was wide awake too. It just happens sometimes. I start thinking about problems at work, or…other stuff. I'll make us both some tea."

"They gave me some sleeping pills." He watched her plug in the kettle and find mugs and tea bags. "But I hate taking them unless I really have to."

"Yeah. Try the tea, see if it helps. What have you been doing this week?"

He'd gone out, but hadn't said much about where or what he'd done. She knew he watched a lot of television. He'd used her computer to do some stuff although she didn't know what.

They'd tried to include him in some of their social events, like a dinner out with another couple, a movie, a friend's birthday party. Sometimes he'd gone with them, sometimes he'd declined and stayed home. He'd accepted Aidan's offer to use his bike. He looked healthier, had put on weight, had gotten a little color from the sun. He still didn't talk much about what had happened.

"Gone for some bike rides. And some walks. Found a gym and bought a one month membership." He held up the book. "Borrowed some of Aidan's paperbacks."

She nodded. "You'll let us know if there's anything you need, right?"

"Sure. But I'm good."

They shared some quiet conversation as they drank their tea in the dim kitchen, then Maddie stood. "I'll let you read a bit. Hope you get some sleep."

"You too. You're the one who has to get up and go to work in the morning."

She gave him a wry smile. "Yeah. Good night."

"Night Maddie."

Yeah, having someone else living in the condo was different. But it was fine.

She couldn't blame Zack being there for the fact that sex between her and Aidan had not gotten any more satisfying, although trying to keep their sexcapades quiet didn't help. Normally they both liked to make a lot of noise, but knowing Zack was in the room next door did put a little damper on that aspect of things.

Aidan had come home one night with another toy, this time a vibrator intended for couples to use. They'd had a laugh trying to figure out how to work it, and it did create an amazing orgasm. Then he'd brought home some handcuffs. The idea of being helpless caused a little rush of warmth inside her. Yet somehow, when he'd restrained her, she hadn't felt the excitement she'd thought she would. Maybe because she didn't actually feel helpless. She felt if she'd just said to Aidan, "Take these off me" he would have. And where was the fun in that?

And as with the flogger, he also wanted to be cuffed. She did it because he wanted it, and it was no hardship exploring his body at her leisure. The muscles he worked so hard to maintain were beautiful. Her hands had explored smooth skin and rough hair, lingered over his nipples, breathed in his scent. She shifted between his legs and took her time exploring there too, making him groan and gasp as she weighed the heavy sac of his testicles, traced over the puckered seam with her tongue, then finished with a blow job that had seemed to really do it for him. Again, never a hardship—going down on Aidan was a great pleasure. She loved the taste of him, the weight of his cock on her tongue, the scent of aroused male. She was glad she'd made him feel so good, but still felt...hell, she couldn't even explain it in her own mind.

Then one night Aidan brought home a strap-on dildo.

Maddie was in bed when he showed it to her. She studied it. This time it was pretty clear who was going to be using it, because Aidan had no need to attach a fake cock to fuck her. His real cock was damn fine enough.

Unless...no. She'd never even told him about that double-penetration fantasy. That was a deep, dark secret.

She gulped.

"Um. You want me to wear that?" She looked up at him and was surprised by a hint of uncertainty in his eyes. Her stomach tightened.

"Yeah. Thought it would be fun to try."

This disturbed her for some reason, raised questions in her head that she didn't even want to acknowledge, but also made her heart go warm and soft. Clearly, he was hesitant about broaching this idea. Yet he trusted her enough to do it. They loved each other. In no way did she want to make him feel uncomfortable or embarrassed about what he wanted to try.

She'd do anything for him.

"Okay." She held out a hand to take it from him. "That's hot."

"We'll need this too." He produced a bottle of lubricant.

She swallowed. "Good thinking." She swiped her tongue over her bottom lip. "How does this thing work?"

"Wait. Wanna make out with you first." Aidan pulled

off his clothes and slid into bed with her, sliding his hand into her hair, kissing her with his delicious mouth. Such a good kisser. She drifted a little, her body heating, her pussy aching as their mouths ate at each other in long, hungry kisses.

Aidan's hard cock pressed against her hip and she shifted so it slid between her thighs, along her pussy. She wore a pair of cheeky boy shorts. He rubbed back and forth there, moaning into her mouth, caressing her cheek, her neck, her shoulder, and then her breast through the thin camisole top she wore. Her nipple, already hard, tightened even more. She arched her back and pushed her breast into his palm.

"Oh yeah," Aidan murmured. "Hot. Take this off." He reached for her cami, eased it up her torso, then tugged it off over her head.

He rubbed her breasts, brushing his fingertips over stiff nipples. Tingles rushed through her body, her abs tightening with pleasure. He bent his head and closed his lips around one nipple, tugging the bud into his mouth and sucking. Pleasure flowed through her right to her core, intensifying that ache with a sharp heat. Her pussy ached with need, his lips and tongue and hands on her body exciting her to the point she desperately wanted him inside her.

He was hard, so hard. Her fingers closed around his cock. She wanted that, needed that...but instead he rolled away to reach for the strap-on. She blinked and caught her breath. Okay. She could do this. He'd got her all wound up and needy, but she could do this, give him what he wanted.

Together they fastened it around her hips, nice and snug. When she looked down at herself, she closed her eyes. This was so not her. But she could do it.

Aidan helped her lube up the cock-shaped dildo, then handed her the bottle and rolled to his belly. Her heart thudded and she dragged her tongue over her bottom lip, staring at his ass. It was a sexy ass, muscular and round. When he shifted position and flexed, deep dimples appeared. She'd enjoyed playing with that ass other times. Now…this would be fun too.

She drizzled lube up the crack of his ass, then massaged it in with her fingers, going deep, over his anus. He groaned. "Yeah. Gonna need to use lots…go right inside with it."

They'd played this way before, a little. This was just taking it to another level. He pushed up his butt, giving her better access and, on her knees, she took hold of the dildo and rubbed it up and down the crevice. Then, sinking her teeth into her bottom lip, she pushed the tip inside him.

It was kind of hot. Watching his hands curl into fists, his hard-as-rock ass muscles clenching. The fake cock gave her a weird sensation of being apart from it all. Normally when they had sex, they both felt it—him inside her was good for him and for her. This just felt…like she was observing. But this was for him.

"Don't want to hurt you," she whispered, going deeper.

"Fuck," he groaned. "It does hurt…but Christ…it's good. Keep going."

She did so, not sure how deep exactly she should go.

"Ah yeah, there…fuck yeah." She'd hit a good spot apparently. Good to know. She began to fuck him, in and out, using her hips, steadying the base of the dildo with one hand. Her other hand held his hip. His hand went beneath him to his own cock, fisting it and jacking himself.

That was hot too.

"Not gonna take long," he moaned. "Oh yeah…Jesus. Jesus fuck. Gonna come…" And he did with a loud roar of pleasure that had Maddie's eyes widening and shifting to the wall that separated them from Zack's room.

She slowly pulled out. She wanted this thing off. She

fumbled at the fasteners and got rid of it, then stretched out on top of Aidan, who was now flat on the bed and breathing heavily. Her body clung to his damp skin as she kissed his shoulder.

"Fuck that was hot." He panted. "Maddie, sweetheart...I love you so much."

"Love you too." She paused. "When do I get *my* orgasm?"

His body shook with laughter beneath her. "Give me a minute. When I can move I'm gonna make you come so hard."

"Mmm."

He made good on that promise, rolling her to her back and going down on her with slow, luscious nibbles and licks and sucks. She bent her legs, let her knees fall open and threaded her fingers into his hair while fiery pleasure built inside her. Heat rushed through her body, sensation burning and twisting. His teeth scraped over sensitive flesh and she jerked and tightened her fingers in his hair. Then he sucked her clit into his mouth and intense pleasure tore through her. She let out an ecstatic cry, not even realizing until long, shuddering moments later that she'd been almost as noisy as Aidan.

He stretched out next to her, pulling the covers up and over both of them, snuggling her against him.

"Shit," she mumbled. "Made too much noise. Both of us."

"Ugh." Aidan kissed her neck. "Right. Damn."

"Oh well." She sighed. "Nothing to be done now."

"True that. God I love you, Maddie."

"I love you too."

The next morning she found the strap-on in their bathroom. Aidan had gotten up first to go for his run. He must have picked it up and washed it. She eyed it with doubt, then carried it out the bedroom and put it in the drawer of the bedside table where they kept their other toys.

She dressed and wandered to the kitchen. Saturday morning meant a lazy start to the day, for her anyway. She started a pot of coffee and wandered over to her computer to check email and Facebook. She stared at the monitor, tapping her fingers on the desk.

She'd had this crazy idea circling in the back of her mind for a while now. After last night and the strap-on, it was pushing its way to the forefront of her consciousness. It was crazy…

She started tapping keys, doing a Google search, sucking on her bottom lip as she studied results. *Maison de Sade – premier BDSM dungeon in Chicago, owned and operated by Dominant women. Private and discreet.*

She clicked onto the page with pictures of the women. Huh. They looked pretty normal. In fact, one of them looked a little like her hair stylist…good god, she was not risking showing up somewhere they'd run into someone they knew.

She moved on to the website for Mistress Marbella. She was…attractive, although the dark lipstick was a little scary. Maddie looked through the site, frowning.

Oh for god's sake, this was ridiculous. She could not be looking up dungeons and actually considering paying someone to dominate her boyfriend. He was a prominent businessman. That was just insane.

Why did they need someone else? They didn't. They loved each other and they'd keep experimenting until they found…something that worked for both of them.

She heard steps in the hall and quickly closed the browser, swinging around in her chair at the same time.

Zack appeared, wearing a pair of plaid boxers that sat low on his hips, and nothing else. His shaggy mop of hair hung over his forehead and curled around his ears. "Oh," he said, stopping. "Didn't realize you were up."

She smiled but as their eyes met, his skittered away and a flush climbed up his face.

The air around them went static and her skin tingled. Shit. He'd heard them last night. She immediately, intuitively knew that. And he was uncomfortable.

She considered apologizing, but acknowledging what was currently unspoken might only make things worse. So she pretended it had never happened. "Yeah, I'm up. Aidan's out for his run. Want some coffee? It should be ready now. I was going to take mine out onto the balcony. It's nice and sunny. I wonder how warm it is."

Christ, she was babbling like a fool. She rushed from the den to the kitchen. She grabbed a mug and sloshed coffee into it, scooped up the one spoon of sugar she took and picked it up.

"Coffee'd be great." Zack followed her.

She handed him a mug too, then scooted around the end of the counter to cross over to the balcony doors. She stepped outside, moved to the railing and curled her fingers around it, sucking in a long breath of already warm morning air.

"Nice day," Zack said behind her.

She nodded, closing her eyes briefly. "Lovely. We're going to go Taste of Randolph Street this afternoon. You coming with us?"

"Uh...I dunno..."

She whirled around. "Okay," she said. "Let's just get this out in the open. The sex got a little noisy last night. Sorry. Didn't mean to make you uncomfortable."

His face tightened, but he rolled his eyes. "Not like I don't know you have sex."

"Um. Yeah."

Heat rolled up into her face and she bent her head to take another sip of her coffee.

"Aidan's still into working out," Zack said.

"More than ever. He needs it. He's under so much pressure at work. They've taken on some really big projects, and he's in charge of them. He has all these people working for him, asking him questions, wanting him to solve problems. Right now they have this big project planned and they applied for a zoning variance but some historical preservation group is blocking it. Their lawyers are fighting it, but they may have to go back to the drawing board, which costs them more money and…anyway. He says working out lets him zone out, lets him shut off his brain for a while."

More babbling.

Zack nodded.

"Well. I'm going to get ready to go out." She pushed away from the railing.

"Can I use your computer?"

"Of course."

She headed to the bedroom with her mug to fix her hair and put on a little makeup.

Why was that so awkward? Their other friends all joked about their sex lives with each other, the guys alternating between bragging and insulting each other about the size of their penises, their endurance, their skills. Wives and girlfriends joined in the jokes. Once when they'd gone on a trip to Maui with their friends Ethan and Chelsea, they'd had rooms next door to each other. She and Aidan had heard the headboard banging against the wall between their rooms half the night. They hadn't let Ethan and Chelsea forget that. In fact the next night, they'd pounded on the wall and shouted "Oh yeah baby, do me harder!"and "Yes, yes, yes!", killing themselves laughing the whole time.

Jeez, if Zack knew exactly what they'd been doing, things would be even more awkward.

6

Zack sat in front of Maddie's computer to check his email. Since he'd been back, he'd found himself drawn back often to the Facebook page she'd created and some of the links she'd shared about other missing journalists. He was still blown away by the support and networks she'd helped build. Also embarrassed by the attention.

One of the people he'd found there was the widow of a foreign correspondent he'd worked with and with whom he'd become friends. Glenn Peters had been killed about a month before Zack had been taken prisoner. Glenn's wife had been pregnant with their second child when he'd gone missing, their other child only two years old. Zack had made contact with his widow, curious about how she was doing, which turned out to be not great. He also found himself using other contacts to try to do something to help locate other missing journalists.

Maybe he'd been inspired by Maddie's commitment to that cause. It pulled at him.

He needed to get his own computer. He wanted his MacBook Pro back. He hadn't replaced it or any of his camera gear. He was going to have to face that demon. Was he ever going to take pictures again?

He sighed. He missed it, with a bone-deep longing. He had a deep-seated need to capture images. He missed the creativity of it, missed the way he could observe everything from behind the lens, capturing others' emotions without involving his own.

He was already three weeks into his six weeks of leave. Of course he'd get back to it.

He clicked the mouse on the Internet browser on the toolbar at the bottom of the screen that Maddie already had open. But the site that appeared had his jaw dropping.

Mistress Marbella.

Holy fuck. Strap-on play, smoking fetish, objectification, humiliation, bondage...holy, holy fuck.

None of those were his scene at all. Well, other than the bondage. He read on. Spanking, caning, paddling, flogging...that was more like it. Pain and power...oh yeah.

Shit. What the fuck was Maddie doing looking at a site like this? He glanced over his shoulder to make sure she wasn't standing there. His head moved slowly from side to side, eyes on the monitor. Then, with depraved curiosity, he checked her browser history. And found *Maison de Sade*.

Heh. Just the kind of place he'd been considering finding. His lips twisted as he read about it. His groin tingled.

But again, what the fuck? He narrowed his eyes. Were Maddie and Aidan not as vanilla as he'd thought? Jesus.

Then the question crossed his mind...what had they been doing last night that had gotten so noisy?

Fuck, he'd been hard as stone, listening to them. He hadn't wanted to. He'd listened against his will, imagining what was happening. All kinds of pornographic images of his two best friends fucking had spooled through his mind. He'd jerked off to the sounds of each of them coming, first Aidan with rough masculine pleasure, then Maddie's softer cries. Jesus, how many times had he imagined each of them orgasming, the way they'd look, the way they'd sound, how they'd feel...

He closed his eyes and slumped back in the chair.

He'd been doing so well since he'd been staying with them. Ruthlessly pushing aside those thoughts. Pretending he didn't feel that ache of longing deep inside him. But last night had made it impossible. Now his mind was overrun with those sounds, the imaginary images. And his body was electrified, humming with arousal.

He sucked in a long breath and let it out, rubbing his eyes. Now he had to hang out with them all afternoon and pretend everything was great.

"Zack, are you..." Maddie's voice trailed off behind him. "Oh shit."

He jerked upright. Fuck! He still had the *Maison de Sade* website open. Every muscle in his body tensed. Slowly he turned to face Maddie.

She stood across the room, blue eyes wide, her lips parted. Her gaze shifted from the computer to his face and bright color rushed up into her cheeks. Their eyes met.

She sucked on her bottom lip.

Christ, he didn't even know what to say.

"How did you find that?" She twisted her fingers together.

"You left your browser open."

"Oh." She swallowed. "Shit. I thought I closed it."

"You just minimized it."

She winced.

"I saw Mistress Marbella," he said slowly. "Then I checked your history and saw this. Why were you looking at sites like this, Maddie?"

She closed her eyes, cheeks still flushed. Her fingers tightened together. "I don't know."

"Sure you do."

Her face squeezed into a grimace, then she opened her eyes. She walked over to one of the couches in the room and sank down onto it. She'd changed into a summery dress, turquoise and green swirls, with tiny straps. Her bare toes with fuchsia painted toenails curled into the rug.

She met his eyes then her gaze darted all over the room. She rubbed her throat with one hand, the other pressed over her abdomen. "This is…" She stopped.

Zack kept his gaze steady on her and waited patiently.

"I shouldn't…" She stopped again and swallowed. "I was thinking about, um…oh god, it was such a stupid idea."

"Tell me." She was so fidgety and obviously conflicted. This was more than just a little web surfing. And for some reason, he felt a surge of confidence and strength. This was something he knew and understood…what had she been looking for, exactly?

She cast her eyes down, staring at her knees. "I thought Aidan might like a, um, Dominatrix."

Silence swelled around them.

Zack kept his mouth shut while his mind went crazy. Holy, holy fuck.

His mind processed it all in lightning fast flashes. She thought Aidan might like a Dominatrix. That meant Maddie wasn't a Domme. That meant Aidan wasn't a Dom.

He, Zack, was a Dom.

What had they been up to that made her think that? What did Aidan like? And was she seriously considering introducing another woman into their relationship?

Jesus, his dick was swelling.

"I'd never have the nerve to actually do something like that," Maddie continued in a low voice. "I had the idea, but…it's crazy."

"Why do you think Aidan would like that?" He kept his tone neutral, his face composed despite his buzzing arousal and curiosity.

She sighed. "We've been trying some new things.

Trying to spice things up a bit." She flicked a glance his way. "I probably shouldn't be telling you this."

"We're friends."

"Yes, but so are you and Aidan. It's not that there's anything wrong with our sex life. It's great. It's just...we both felt like there should be more. So we tried some different things, but..."

"But what?"

"I liked what he did to me." Her cheeks got red again. "Even though it felt like he was holding back. Then he wanted me to do the same to him."

Her lack of specifics was making his imagination run wild. Of course, she *could* be talking about something as innocent as oral sex, for fuck's sake.

"It didn't work out so great. I mean, we laughed, but..." She hitched one bare shoulder. "I just wasn't...that into it."

If she was talking about something like going down on each other, he was *way* off base in what he was thinking. But he'd always had pretty good instincts. An ability to read people and know what was going on in their heads. And he was pretty sure he was figuring out what was going on here.

Holy mother of fuck.

"So you thought bringing another person into the bedroom might help."

"I know it was crazy! Don't judge me."

"Oh Maddie, baby, I am not judging you." She had no idea. "It's not that crazy. Did you talk to Aidan about it?"

She shook her head miserably. "No."

Huh. Zack rubbed his mouth.

"I get the feeling he doesn't really want to admit...what he wants. So I looked at those websites but it just seemed so...I don't know. Kinky. Sleazy. Dangerous, even. I mean, you don't know what you're getting into when you go to one of those places."

"True. You need to be careful."

She slowly lifted her gaze and met his eyes again.
"Have you…?"

"Yeah."

She blinked.

He leaned forward, elbows on his knees. "Is that all you
know about BDSM? Those websites?"

She drew her bottom lip between her teeth. "No. I know
a little about it. There've been some things I've been
curious about."

He nodded.

"God. Aidan would probably kill me for telling you
about this."

"I won't say anything. But you should talk to him about
it."

She bit her lip. "I can't. He'll think I'm crazy."

"Maybe you're right. Maybe he *would* like it."

"But even if he would, I don't have the nerve to actually
do it!"

Aidan walked into the condo at that moment. Zack
quickly turned and closed the browser window, catching
Maddie's grateful glance.

Wearing a sleeveless top and shorts, his skin gleaming
with perspiration, Aidan spotted them. "Hey. You're up."
The muscles in his legs flexed as he walked toward them.

Maddie rose with a smile. "Been up for a while. How
was your run?"

She swept over to him and threw her arms around him.
Zack totally got the message she was sending. There may
be things lacking in their sex life, but she loved Aidan.

Aidan grabbed her arms and set her away from him
with a grin. "Hey sweetheart, I'm all sweaty and stinky."

"I don't care." She went onto her toes to kiss his mouth.
"Come on. You need to shower so we can get going." She
grabbed his hand and dragged him down the hall without
a backward glance at Zack.

Zack leaned back in the chair, his mind a writhing

snake pit. He shoved both hands into his hair and held his head for a moment.

Well. This was…interesting.

Aidan studied Maddie as they walked toward Randolph Street in the summer sun. She'd seemed a little tense earlier, but now was more relaxed. But there was still some kind of weird vibe going on between her and Zack. A few times Aidan caught Zack giving both Maddie and him long, thoughtful looks that made Aidan wonder what was going on in that head of his.

Then Aidan remembered their noisy sex last night.

He closed his eyes briefly. Clearly, Zack had heard. And clearly he was wondering what they'd been doing. Aidan's gut burned at the possibility that Zack knew that Maddie had fucked him with that strap-on.

No. There was no way he could know that.

Unless Maddie'd told him?

Again, no. She wouldn't do that. She could not have been discussing their sex life with Zack. It was just awkward that he'd heard them and Aidan kept getting hot again thinking about how good that had felt.

Maddie clasped his hand and swung it back and forth as they walked.

The things he wanted…the things he fantasized about…seemed so risky. He'd never had the balls to tell Maddie all of it. All his life he'd been looking after other people, and now in his business he had the entire company on his shoulders. He loved it. He didn't want anything different. He loved taking care of Maddie, but there were times he longed for someone else to take charge. But for many people, a man wanting something like that made him weak. He didn't want to seem less in her eyes.

He loved Maddie and he'd finally gotten the guts to show her something he wanted. And she'd done it. But he could tell she wasn't as into it as he was. Which made him feel...uncomfortable.

Now, as they paused in front of shop for Maddie to peer in the window, Aidan watched Zack looking at Maddie, his eyes going hot. Almost predatory.

Seeing another man look at her like that...Christ. That made *him* hot. He was such a sick fuck.

He wasn't the jealous type, but once again he wondered about Maddie's feelings for Zack. And Zack's feelings for her.

Aidan knew Maddie loved him. He had no doubts about that at all. But he remembered how things had been just before he and Zack had graduated, how Aidan had wondered about their feelings for each other, and how much Maddie had missed Zack.

Zack seemed different. His smiles were still rare, but he did seem more at ease. He also seemed even more confident, more imposing. There was some kind of crackling energy flowing around all three of them, heating Aidan's blood. But confusing him.

They met up with their friends Ethan and Chelsea, and Nisha and Blake, and having the others with them was a welcome distraction from the tension Aidan felt. They spent the afternoon ambling along the six blocks of Randolph Street that had been taken over by local restaurants and artists and various vendors. It was a great sunny Chicago day, with lots of people out enjoying the festival.

They sampled all kinds of food and drinks. When Zack pulled his wallet out to pay for one round of beers for him and Maddie, Aidan said, "Hey, put that away. I'm buying."

"No way man, I am."

They argued about it briefly but Zack was not backing

down. When they stepped away from the cart with drinks in hand, Aidan asked in a low voice, "You okay for money, man?"

"Yeah. Hell yeah. Got paid well. Hardly ever spent money. Didn't have a home so no need to buy furniture and stuff. Just needed to get banking shit figured out, but I'm good now."

Aidan nodded. "Okay good. Just wanted you to know, if you need any help just say."

"I'm good. But thanks."

When they passed by a camera store, Zack paused to look in the windows.

"Want to go in there?" Maddie asked, her hand tucked into Aidan's, pulling him to a halt also.

"Nah. Don't need to drag you guys in there."

"I'm surprised you haven't already replaced your stuff," Aidan said.

"Insurance crap," Zack muttered. "Haven't got the check from them yet."

"But you said—"

Zack's dark frown stopped him.

Aidan narrowed his eyes at his friend. Did he have money or not? If he was waiting for his insurance claim to be paid to buy his new camera gear, maybe not. Or maybe he was just using that as an excuse...

They wandered farther up the street, pausing while the girls looked at some hand-crafted jewelry, then some unique soy candles. Then they listened to one of the musical groups that took the stage at the east end. Maddie smiled and bopped to the music in the sun, her hair shiny, her aviator sunglasses shading her eyes.

Aidan also caught all the girls giving Zack the eye as they strolled around. Once again, his shaggy dark curls, blue eyes and powerful presence attracted female attention.

Their friends left late in the afternoon, but Maddie wanted to stay and listen to one of the bands that was on stage at seven, so Maddie, Zack and Aidan ate dinner there, picking up hot dogs from one of the restaurants. They each deliberated over what kind of toppings to have, studying the many choices.

Maddie requested pepper jack cheese, caramelized onions and jalapeno peppers.

"That's gonna be hot," Zack commented.

"I like it hot and spicy."

Their eyes met and Zack's lips twitched. "Really."

Maddie's face flamed. Aidan lifted a brow at him and Zack returned his gaze blandly. More of that heat shimmered around them.

Zack ordered a Chicago-style dog with all the trimmings — mustard, onions, relish, a pickle — and Aidan ordered a bratwurst that had been soaked in beer. When the server handed his over, Maddie peered at it. "Oooh. You got a big one."

"Yes, I do," Aidan agreed. "You should know."

Zack groaned. "Here we go again. Bragging about the size of your ego."

"Not my ego she's talking about, dude." Aidan lowered his chin and gave his crotch a brief but meaningful grin. "Don't be jealous."

"Jealous?" Zack glanced at the bratwurst. "I was thinking it looks kinda small. It's all relative, I guess."

Maddie was cracking up and Aidan had to laugh too. "Dude, I've seen your dick."

"Wait, what? That's what we're talking about? And didn't I warn you about telling people you like big dicks? They could get the wrong impression of you."

Aidan met Zack's eyes and heat rushed through his veins. What the fuck. He kept his expression casual. "I said I saw your dick, never said it was big."

Zack grinned and took a bit of his hot dog. "No need to state the obvious."

"Now I'm curious," Maddie said. Then her eyes flew

open wide and she snapped her lips shut. Her cheeks went scarlet. "Um. I mean...I didn't mean that like it sounded."

Her eyes met Aidan's with a kind of pleading, don't-be-mad-at-me look. And he wasn't mad. He was...he was turned on. Fuck. "Come on. Let's go sit somewhere and eat."

Sexual tension continued to buzz among them as they listened to more of the music. Aidan found himself acutely aware of the others. Of course, Maddie—she sat next to him, moving to the music, leaning into him from time to time. But also Zack, sitting on his other side, not touching him, but...there. And occasionally leaning forward and closer to look around him and say something to Maddie.

They had more drinks, and ended up at home around ten. They'd all gotten some color from the sun. Maddie looked so pretty, and Zack looked healthier. They said good night to him and went into their room. Aidan closed the door behind them.

"That was a fun day." He pulled his T-shirt off over his head.

"Yeah." Maddie went quiet as she took out her earrings and set them on the dresser. With her back to him, her shoulders had tightened a little and the air in the room had gone thick. Aidan stepped out of his shorts and tossed them into the laundry hamper, eyeing her as she fiddled with some things on the dresser.

"I...can we talk about something?" Maddie blurted, not looking up.

"Of course." He moved toward her through their bedroom and set his hands on her shoulders. He moved them in a gentle caress, curiosity burning inside him at what she wanted to talk about.

She looked up and their eyes met in the mirror. "I don't even know how to say this."

He nodded, his insides tightening. How bad was this going to be? "Talk to me," he urged quietly. "You know I'll do anything for you."

"I know." She paused. "But what if I want to do something for you?"

"Like what?"

"Like...hire a Dominatrix for you."

He went completely still. He fought to keep his face expressionless even though his jaw had slackened. "A Dominatrix."

She swiped her tongue over her bottom lip. "Yes. I thought maybe you would like that. The things we've been trying...I want to do those things for you, but it feels weird for me."

He sighed inwardly. Yeah, he'd figured that.

"Not that I don't like it," she added hastily. "I love everything we do together. But I thought maybe it would be better if someone who knew what they were doing, um, helped us."

His mind became a jumble of thought fragments. What. The. Fuck. How did she envision this happening? Dropping him off at some sex club for the evening? Bringing someone home with them? Would Maddie be part of it too? Or would he have sex with another woman?

A bad taste rose up his throat, even though the idea...excited him. But he wasn't interested in another woman. He would never do that to Maddie.

She continued to gaze at him in the mirror, her eyes shadowed with anxiety. Christ. She was trying to do something for him. Something huge and amazing. Crazy too. But still. She knew that what they'd been trying to do hadn't been completely satisfying.

For either of them.

His chest tightened. He wasn't satisfying her either. She did those things because he wanted them, but she didn't get off on them. Fuck.

Why couldn't they find something that worked for both of them?

7

"Sweetheart." Aidan's insides felt shredded. "I am so fucking sorry."

Her eyes widened, then she blinked. "Sorry for what?"

He closed his eyes briefly, his fingers tightening on her upper arms. "I'm sorry it hasn't been good for you."

"It has been! It is! Really."

He shook his head. "No. I get it. I mean, I know you love me. I should've realized sooner that you weren't getting everything you need."

She didn't deny that. Her eyes got shiny. "I love you," she whispered. "I really do."

"I know." He turned her in his arms and hugged her. "I love you too."

"So you don't like the idea?"

He took a breath. "There are some things about it that are hot as hell. But another woman...no. I don't want to do that to you. Unless...would you be part of it? Would you want her to dominate you too?"

She tipped her head back and now her eyes were wet. "Maybe." The soft word floated between them. Her eyes tightened a bit. "I'm not sure. That would be..." She stopped. Her and another woman? She'd had a lot of fantasies, but never that. "I started looking online but I chickened out. I thought it was a crazy idea. Then I...oh, you might not like this."

"What?" He braced himself for another jolt.

"Zack found what I was looking at. I thought closed the browser but I just minimized it and he went onto my computer. Oh my god, I was so embarrassed!"

"Uh, yeah."

"He asked me questions about it."

Aidan stared at her. "What did you tell him?" The words scraped over his tight throat.

"Nothing, really. Just that I'd been curious and I was thinking about doing that for you. Um, he wasn't freaked out." She gazed at him with big eyes. "He knows about that stuff. He said I should talk to you about it. And so...I am."

"When did this happen?"

"This morning. While you were out for your run."

He nodded. Christ. Zack now knew Aidan wasn't able to satisfy his girlfriend. Fucking awesome. Just what every guy wants his buddy to know. He exhaled slowly at the stab of embarrassment. At least she hadn't told him about the strap-on, but who knew what Zack was putting together in his mind.

"I told him I knew I wasn't giving you what *you* need," Maddie clarified, watching him. "But I did say I was curious too."

No wonder Zack had kept giving him those odd looks all day. Aidan swallowed. "Okay," he choked out. "Fuck, Maddie, I don't even know what to say about this."

She nodded, dropping her eyes. "I know. I'm sorry. It was crazy. We'll just forget I ever mentioned it." She gave a small sniff. "I just wanted to make things good for you...to make you happy."

"I am happy." He crushed her up against his chest, the tightness in his chest increasing and his stomach feeling like a rock. "I am, sweetheart."

"I know you are. I am too. So like I said, just forget it."

He didn't know if that was possible, but he was willing to give it a shot. Jesus. "What kinds of things were you curious about?"

She sniffled again and one shoulder hitched. "You know. The bondage. Cuffs and ropes. I liked that. I liked it when you used the flogger on me, except…I felt like…oh I don't know." She blew out a breath. "Forget it."

He couldn't let it go. Just yet. There was something she was missing. He'd tried to give her everything she ever wanted, to look after her and protect her and take care of all her problems. He'd been doing that since the day they'd met. He'd never stop doing that. "No. Tell me. We have to talk about this."

He'd been avoiding this for so long. He had to man up and have this conversation.

"I felt like you were holding back. Even though I was handcuffed, I didn't feel like you were really…controlling me. Like, I could ask you to set me loose and you would. As if you were afraid of hurting me, but I really wanted…" She peeked at him through her lashes. "More."

His guts twisted as her words sank in.

She was right.

She was totally fucking right. He didn't want to hurt her. He *couldn't* hurt her. And restraining her…well, yeah, if she'd said, "Aidan, let me loose," he totally would have. He'd been nervous about hurting her. And what that meant became crystal clear in that moment as he thought about his own preferences. He knew what she meant, because when he'd been the one restrained, he'd felt the same. He just hadn't put his finger on what was wrong.

They'd been playing around at that stuff, trying to give each other what they wanted, when neither of them was really capable of it.

But seriously…hiring someone to dominate both of them? That was insane. Wasn't it?

"We'll be fine." He drew her back against him, his hand in her hair. "We'll be fine. We love each other." His words were as much for him as for her.

"You're right. We will be fine. Let's just forget about this."

He knew they should talk more but since he had no idea what the solution was at that point, he nodded. "Okay. Let's go to bed." He kissed her silky hair.

They moved apart, her to the bathroom to wash her face, him to the walk-in closet to take off his clothes. He climbed into bed naked, as he always slept. Maddie came out of the bathroom, slid a silky nightie over her head, then joined him without saying a word. He reached for her and pulled her to him, curling his body around hers, needing the feel of her against him, in his arms.

It took a long time for them to fall asleep. He felt her shifting against him, knew from her breathing she was awake. He couldn't shut his own mind down either.

He kept replaying their conversation in his head. Guilt rose in him, lodging at the back of his throat. He wasn't giving Maddie what she needed. He loved her so fucking much. He'd do anything for her. Even…that?

If it was what she wanted, could he give her that? He tried to imagine Maddie and some nameless Dominatrix having sex. Fuck yeah, it was hot. But…it just didn't sit right with him. It seemed so calculated. It felt wrong.

She said to forget about it. How could they just forget about it? How could you unhear something? How could you cut it out of your mind? You couldn't. It would always be there.

But then, there were a lot of things that had always been in his head that he'd kept carefully pushed way down deep.

For the next week Zack managed to keep his shit together. Maddie and Aidan had been busy, Aidan working late and Maddie attending a couple of business functions in the evenings. Zack had time on his hands and was starting to feel antsy.

He'd joined a gym, knowing that getting back in physical shape would also help him mentally, so he worked out every day. Maddie's plan to fatten him up was succeeding and he'd gained weight. He felt stronger too.

Seeing that camera store last weekend had awakened the need inside him to take pictures. He missed it. He'd totally been procrastinating on buying new gear. He couldn't explain why but he recognized that being unwilling to plan for the future was one of the possible symptoms of PTSD.

Aidan had clued in that he'd been delaying it when he'd made that bullshit excuse about waiting for the insurance money. He had more than enough to buy that new Nikon D4 he'd been wanting. Plus all the lenses and accessories. Yeah it was probably about twenty grand, but he had that easily.

So Friday, he gathered up his courage and hit a big camera store on Wabash. He weighed lenses in his hand, and the feel of them made his skin tingle all over. Pleasure flowed through him as he studied the camera. He changed the lenses out and looked through the viewfinder each time. His new Visa card took a hit, but he left there with a sweet new bag full of camera gear.

He didn't take any pictures. One step at a time.

He was sitting on the living room floor that evening with everything spread in front of him like a kid on Christmas morning when Maddie walked in, home early for once.

"Hey." She dropped her purse on a table. "What's all that?"

"New camera gear." For some reason he didn't want to

let on what a big deal this was or the complex emotions twisting inside him. The fact that this was a big step forward. "Went and picked it out today."

"Awesome." She picked up some mail and glanced at it as she walked across the room. Dressed in a fitted white suit with a silky pink blouse beneath it, she looked all professional. Her slender legs were bare beneath the knee-length skirt and she wore sleek high-heeled shoes that were sexy as hell. She sat in an armchair near him and surveyed the camera parts. "That's great. Wow."

He shrugged and began packing away the items. "No big deal."

She didn't move, didn't say anything and finally he had to look up at her. She was regarding him with steady eyes, eyebrows lifted.

"What?"

"Why are you being an asshole again?"

He frowned. But she had him. It was the only way he knew to cover up his emotions. Be a jerk. "Sorry," he muttered.

"You'd think you'd be happy now you have camera gear again."

He bent his head. "Yeah. You'd think."

"Zack. Why aren't you happy?" Her voice went soft and husky and reached deep inside him and squeezed.

"I'm happy."

"Oh. Okay. I get it. Jesus, Zack. It's not a weakness to be happy."

His head snapped up and he glared at her. "What?"

She smiled and to his utter shock reached out and patted his cheek. His body went rigid and he stared at her. "It's okay to have feelings."

His eyebrows pulled together. "I don't...what?"

"I still wish you'd talk to us."

He narrowed his eyes at her. "Babe, you don't want to hear the stuff I'd talk about. Believe me."

"Oh come on."

"I'm not the same guy I was when I left here seven years ago."

Her smile faded and she nodded. "I know that, Zack. Believe me, I know that. But still…you're someone worth knowing." She set her hands on her thighs and stood. "I'm going to change."

What the fuck? He rolled onto his back on the floor and stared at the ceiling. Why did she say shit like that? She was messing him up even more.

Because even more, he wanted her.

He closed his eyes. Pressed his fists into the sockets. He never should have come here. She thought she knew him. She thought she knew what he was feeling. She had no fucking clue.

She'd done so much for him. Cared about him. Lobbied people to try to find him. Organized support for him. And then let him come and stay there when he was wrecked, and an asshole who'd rejected her.

It was wearing on him, weakening those walls he'd put up. He was trying so hard to keep his emotional distance, from both of them, but when she was nice to him and saw stuff inside him he didn't want anyone to see…it was hard to keep those barriers up.

He sat up and looked out the window. Rain drizzled down the outside of the big glass windows, the sky a dull gray, a mist shrouding Lake Michigan. It was still hours from dusk but the heavy cloud cover created an early darkness. It emphasized the warmth and brightness in the condo, the feeling of being secure and safe.

Oh Christ. He was having another of those moments— the intense relief at being safe making him relive when he'd *not* felt safe and secure. His body trembled as memories assaulted him, memories of how he'd felt when he believed he was about to die. He tried to focus on the stuff the shrink had told him, relaxing his muscles, deep breathing. He focused on Maddie and her sweetness and generosity.

The flashbacks hadn't been happening as much. They'd told him he should see a doctor back home if he continued to have them, along with all the other symptoms they'd alerted him to. He hadn't gone to anyone because they'd been diminishing. He was sleeping better, for the most part, unless Maddie and Aidan were having sex in the next room. The nightmares had been fewer and farther between. He wasn't worried about PTSD; he was strong. Just every once in a while, he had these flashbacks when something triggered strong emotion inside him. He got...scared.

He still felt moments of helplessness. And shame. Also Maddie had called on him feeling guilty because he'd survived when others hadn't. Yeah, that was huge. That feeling of being completely different from others persisted...or maybe returned. He'd felt like that when he was younger, confused about his sexuality, messed up by the abuse his mother had dealt him, guilty about leaving her to her fucked-up life.

Meeting Aidan and then Maddie, having their friendship, having people he felt like he did fit in with had helped a lot. Then, even though he'd left Chicago unhappy, learning more about himself through BDSM had further strengthened his confidence. But it was hard not to feel a bit like a misfit when he was staying with Maddie and Aidan, and their relationship was different now. Before, they'd all been a trio. He'd loved them both and felt they'd both cared about him. Now...they were a couple. Established. In love. He stood apart from that now, despite their friendship and their efforts to include him.

He'd gotten past this hurdle—he'd bought a new camera, so he must have some anticipation of taking pictures again at some point. The frozen emotional numbness that he'd wanted to maintain was thawing, against his will. He didn't need to see a shrink. He'd be fine.

Maddie wandered back out and into the kitchen, now dressed in a pair of soft shorts that left her sexy legs bare, and a loose, thin T-shirt. "I'm going to have a beer," she called to him. "Want one?"

"Sure." He rose and joined her in the kitchen, standing beside her to peer into the fridge at the choices. They each pulled out a cold bottle. Zack took her bottle and opened it for her, then handed it back.

"Thanks." She smiled.

He opened his own and took a swallow, leaning against the counter as she closed the fridge door. Awareness prickled over his skin with her standing so close to him, smelling like exotic fruit and flowers that made him think of a pink sunset, and her soft arm brushing his. He watched her lift her own bottle to her mouth, her pretty lips closing around the rim to drink. He wanted to imagine those lips closed around something else...

"Aidan should be home soon." The glum twist of her mouth did not indicate pleasure at that. Zack frowned. "We've had such a crazy week, we're going to order in pizza and stay home tonight. Sound good?"

"Yeah. Whatever. This is your place. Maybe I should go out and give you two some time alone."

"No." Her quick response made him frown again. "I mean, that's okay." She bent her head.

He reached out and tipped her chin up. "Did you talk to him, Maddie?"

Her gaze shifted away from his. She didn't need to ask him about what. "Yeah."

"And...?"

She turned a little away from him.

"Sorry." He withdrew his hand and held it palm out. "Not my business. Never mind."

She shook her head, silky dark brown hair falling over

her face. "I shouldn't have brought it up with him. He doesn't want to do it. We're trying to pretend we never discussed it, but, of course, we both know we did. God. I'm so stupid."

"I'm sorry," he said quietly. "I guess that wasn't very good advice I gave you."

She sighed. "It's not your fault. It's all just...I don't know." Then she met his eyes. "I'm scared. If neither of us is completely satisfied, what does that mean for us? I know Aidan loves me, and I love him. We'd never cheat on each other. But I worry that over time we'll become more and more unhappy together."

Jesus Christ.

Fuck, he hated seeing her looking so worried. Was she seriously afraid this was something that was going to affect her and Aidan's relationship? He set his beer down on the counter and reached for her. He pulled her into a hug, pressing her head against his chest. "I don't know what to say, baby. I don't think that will happen." Christ, what was he, a marriage counselor? He was *so* the wrong person for this kind of talk. What the hell did he know about relationships?

Her breath hitched and her body trembled. "I don't want to lose him. Things are weird now. I'm afraid."

She felt so damn good in his arms, her soft body pressed to his, the scent of her hair filling his head. He was getting hard, and that was so wrong. He was comforting her. That was all.

She wrapped her arms around his middle and held on too, a soft little sob escaping her.

"It's okay, baby." He rubbed her back. He felt her worry and pain like it was his own, and fuck, he did not want to feel shit like that. When he felt stuff, it was always too much, too intense. He had to keep those walls up.

The sound of the condo door opening had them both jerking apart. Maddie swiped at her wet cheeks with both hands, her gaze fastened on Zack's as he took a step back and picked up his beer.

What? Why were they reacting that way? They were friends and he was comforting her.

They were reacting that way because they were guilty. She didn't want Aidan to know she was upset. Zack didn't want Aidan to know that he was hot for Aidan's girlfriend.

8

Zack lifted his beer as Aidan appeared. Aidan looked the supremely successful businessman in an expensive, well-tailored suit, like he'd spent the day in an elegant office telling people what to and solving problems and making money. And from the sound of his job, that was what he did, although Zack had also heard about visits to construction sites, tense negotiations and long stressful hours.

Zack took a big swallow of beer. Crisp bubbles burned their way down his throat.

"Hey." Aidan looked at them both. "What's up?"

"Not much. Maddie and I are just having a beer."

"Great idea. I'll have one too."

Maddie turned to open the fridge again. When she handed Aidan the beer, he leaned in and kissed her forehead. "Hi, sweetheart."

"Hi."

Zack watched them.

He hadn't seen much of them this week. Now he observed the new tension between them. Yeah. Maddie was right. Things were weird.

He kept watching them as she and Aidan talked about their day and what kind of pizza to order. They weren't mad at each other. It wasn't hostility. He sensed Maddie's worry, but Aidan...Aidan seemed off. Zack couldn't quite get a read on him. Usually he was good at that.

"What were you up to today?" Aidan asked him.

"Zack bought a new camera!" Maddie announced.

Aidan gave him an alert glance, but just nodded. "Great. You'll have to show it to me. Take any pictures yet?"

Zack appreciated his casual response. "Not yet."

Aidan went to change out of his suit while Maddie hunted up a couple of pizza menus. Zack sat on a stool at the kitchen counter and watched the rain turn the view through the windows into a silvery abstract blur. Christ. He'd thought seeing Maddie and Aidan together as a couple would be hard. Seeing them as an *unhappy* couple was worse.

He almost smiled at himself. It had hurt him to know they were together, without him, but he knew now he'd never wish for anything bad for them.

The fuck of it was, he knew exactly what they needed.

And he knew he could give it to them.

His heart kicked against his sternum. Would he really try to do something?

He could help them.

Or he could irrevocably destroy their friendship.

His mind spun with pros and cons, possible consequences both good and bad.

Aidan walked out from the bedroom wearing loose, knee-length gray athletic shorts and a T-shirt, his beer in one hand, his cell phone in the other. "Okay, what's the verdict?"

Zack gazed back at him blankly.

"Pizza?" Aidan prompted. "Where are we ordering from?"

"Guiseppe's." Maddie held up a takeout menu. "I really like their special."

Aidan nodded. "Fine by me. Extra large. I'm starving."

"Can we get a salad too?" Maddie asked. "Their house salad."

"And breadsticks," Zack added. They looked at him. "Hey, you're trying to fatten me up."

They all grinned.

"I'll buy," he added.

"Fuck no." Aidan entered the number into his phone.

"Why not? I've been eating your food and drinking your beer for weeks."

"We can afford it." Aidan lifted the phone to his ear.

"That's not the point. I can afford it too. The point is, I want to contribute."

Maddie tipped her head to one side and he caught the look she gave Aidan. Aidan frowned. "Fine," he said shortly, then into the phone, "Yeah, can I place an order for delivery?"

He ordered their food then set his phone on the counter. "So. Let's see the new camera."

Zack shrugged and they all moved the den where his new bag sat. He and Aidan spent the next half hour talking about sensor size, image processing and ISO range. Aidan was by no means a pro, but shared an interest in photography and was half-decently knowledgeable.

The evening passed eating pizza, drinking more beer, watching a movie. The three of them sat on the couch in from of the TV, Maddie in the middle of the two men. Rain continued to shimmer down outside as the city grew dark and buildings glittered. Zack's nerves prickled from the faint tension he still sensed between Maddie and Aidan but also with arousal. Merely contemplating the things he could do with them made his dick stir and his balls ache.

It had been too long.

He stopped to examine that. Was that what this was about? It had been a helluva long time since he'd had sex. When he'd escaped, that had been the last thing on his mind. But now...were his own urges giving him crazy ideas?

It was impossible to sort out all the threads of what he was feeling. Maybe the fact that he was horny was influencing his thinking, but more than anything he felt a need to *act*, to take charge and *do* something that would get Maddie and Aidan past this.

Christ. His mind flipped back and forth. Do something? Do nothing? Pretend everything was fine? Or help them if he could? But what if helping them fucked things up even more?

Jesus. They were still his friends. He didn't want to wreck that, even though he probably didn't deserve their friendship after the way he'd treated them.

The internal debate made his insides twist up into knots.

Beside him on the couch, Maddie gave a soft sigh as the movie ended.

Zack reached out and laid his hand on her bare knee. "Okay, baby?"

She flicked a glance at him and her muscles tensed beneath his hand. "Um. Yeah."

The air in the room changed as Zack sensed Aidan's awareness of his hand on Maddie's leg. Zack gave a brief, gentle squeeze and didn't rush to move his hand away. Fuck. He was gonna do this.

"Maddie," he said in a quiet but authoritative tone. "Kiss Aidan."

She turned wide eyes on him. "Wh-what?"

Zack lifted his chin. "Kiss him."

He glanced at Aidan. Aidan blinked.

"Do it," he ordered, his tone harder. He reached blindly for the remote control for the TV and turned it off.

Maddie's eyes flickered but she turned to Aidan, leaned over and touched her mouth to his. A soft, short kiss.

"Not like that." Zack kept his tone firm. "Really kiss him."

She hesitated then kissed Aidan again, tipping her head. Aidan's eyelids lowered as their mouths met and opened to each other. Zack's dick swelled and heat rushed through his body. Fuck, that was hot. And her unquestioning obedience made his blood scald his veins.

She drew back and looked at Zack, blue eyes full of questions. He nodded. "Again." He shifted his position so he could better watch. He met Aidan's eyes. "Put your arms around her."

He sensed Aidan's resistance to the order but then a jolt of electric heat hit him when Aidan too obeyed him and reached for Maddie. He pulled her closer and she set a hand on his shoulder as they kissed again, long, slow kisses. Zack watched their tongues touch, watched them tilt their heads to deepen the kiss, watched Aidan's fingers flex on Maddie's hip.

The kiss went on and on, hotter. The air in the room heated and buzzed. They pulled apart once more and both turned lust-hazed eyes on him.

"Was that hot?"

Aidan's throat worked as he swallowed hard. "Yeah," he said hoarsely. Maddie just nodded.

"Want more?" Zack asked.

"What the fuck, man?" Aidan growled in a low tone. "What're you doing?"

Electricity crackled around them.

Zack gave him a dirty grin. "Taking control. Kiss her again. This time pull her onto your lap. Put your hands under her shirt. Feel that soft skin."

Aidan gave a hard shudder and a small whimper escaped Maddie.

Aidan complied, easily lifting and turning Maddie. Now she faced Zack and her eyes met his with a burst of sparks. She held his gaze as she turned her face toward Aidan and his kiss, then let her eyelids droop.

Aidan's hands slid under Maddie's T-shirt, up her back,

over her waist. Watching Aidan caress her was hot, but it also made Zack's palms tingle with the need to feel her himself. One step at a time.

He pressed a hand to his aching cock as they made out in front of him. Maddie touched Aidan too, his shoulder, his neck, his jaw. Their kisses went on and on, their faces flushing, heat building around them.

"Take her shirt off," Zack growled to Aidan.

Aidan paused, eyes meeting his. "What is this? You have some kind of voyeurism fetish?"

Zack held his gaze with steady authority. "Nah. I'd rather participate."

Both Maddie and Aidan jolted. Their eyes met briefly then swiveled simultaneously back to Zack.

"But right now it *is* hot to watch you two." Zack let a smile play on his lips. "And I get the feeling you like being told what to do."

Aidan's features tightened and his lips thinned.

"Nothing wrong with that at all," Zack assured him quietly, leaning forward, holding the eye contact. "Some people like to give orders. Some like to act 'em out. It's all good. Whatever makes you hot is good. You hot?"

Aidan didn't answer.

"Your dick hard?" Zack deepened his voice.

Aidan's eyes closed. Then opened. "Yeah."

"Thought so. Do it. Take her shirt off."

Aidan turned his gaze to Maddie. Giving her a chance to stop him. The air thickened and pulsed as they waited for Maddie's decision. Her consent.

She bit her lip. She turned questioning eyes on Zack. He gave her a nod, letting his reassurance that she was safe show in his eyes.

She nodded.

Zack's heart exploded into a heavy rhythm that pushed the air out of his lungs as Aidan curled his fingers into the hem of Maddie's T-shirt and lifted it. Everything else in the room blurred out as Zack focused on the couple, taking in the smooth curves of Maddie's body.

He'd seen it before—that day at the beach, her bikini hadn't hid much. But her sheer pink bra hid even less. Her nipples strained at the shimmery fabric, her breasts rising as she lifted her arms for Aidan to drag the shirt off.

Christ. Beautiful. Luminous skin in the golden lamp light. Her breasts weren't large, but they were perfect. Her torso narrowed to a slender waist, her shorts with the folded-over waistband sitting low on her hips.

Aidan tossed her shirt aside and then skimmed his palms over Maddie's shoulders, down her arms, all the way to her hands and then he linked his fingers with hers as he kissed her again.

It was sweet yet erotic watching this kiss, their bodies not even touching, just holding hands. Zack's blood pumped hot through his veins, his heart thudding a primitive drumbeat, and his dick was so hard he hurt. He pressed a hand to it.

How far was he going to take this?

With a muffled groan, Aidan wrapped his arms around Maddie again and pulled her closer, going in for a deeper, open-mouthed kiss that set the air around them on fire. She wound her arms around Aidan's neck and pressed into him.

"The bra," Zack rasped out. "Take off her bra."

Aidan's fingers fumbled at the clasp on her back, then the two sides parted. He nudged the straps off her shoulders and he and Maddie separated for him to tug the flimsy garment off her. It too landed on the rug.

Zack watched Aidan cup Maddie's breasts in his big hands as Maddie gave Zack a smoldering glance. She was completely aware of him there observing. And it turned her on. Zack's dick twitched hard.

Maddie let her eyes fall closed as Aidan caressed her, then closed his fingers over both nipples. Without direction, Aidan eased her back onto the padded arm of the couch, adjusting their positions so she lay across his lap, and he was able to bend his head to suck one nipple into his mouth.

"Yeah," Zack approved in a low, rough voice. "Hell yeah."

He too leaned back into the armrest at the other end of the couch. Maddie bent one leg at the knee, stretched the other one out straight and her foot grazed his thigh. He couldn't stop himself from reaching out to curl his fingers around her foot. He lifted it onto his leg, circled her delicate ankle and brushed his fingers over soft skin and toes with nails painted fuchsia.

He sensed her reaction, looked up and met her half-closed eyes watching him fondle her foot. Then Aidan turned his head. His gaze also dropped to Zack's hand on Maddie's foot. He lifted his eyes to meet Zack's, dipped his chin and turned back to Maddie. He slid an arm behind her shoulders to bring her up to kiss him again.

Zack swallowed hard. Aidan had just given tacit approval for him to touch Maddie. While they were making out. And he was watching.

He knew how this could go. He didn't know how smart that would be. Tonight was for them, not him. Longing burned in Zack's chest but he ignored it.

"Okay," he said roughly, moments later. "Come here, Maddie."

She and Aidan blinked at him, both of them with glazed eyes and swollen lips. So fucking hot. "Why?" she whispered.

"Do you trust me?" He waited. If they didn't, this was done.

She took a moment to think about that. Fuck, he wouldn't blame her if she said no. She'd been hurt by how he'd acted and he still couldn't believe both she and Aidan still cared about him, about their friendship. And then she gave him the greatest gift she possibly could.

"Yes. I trust you."

Relief surged through his bloodstream. "Then come here." He reached out a hand to pull her up to sitting, her butt going to the couch cushion beside Aidan's legs. Zack moved closer, reaching for her. His hands craved the feel of her skin but he kept his touch to her waist, lifting her and positioning her on his lap, her back to his front. He widened his thighs so she nestled between them, and slid them both down into the couch in a sprawl. "Aidan's going to lick your pussy now," he murmured in her ear, but loud enough for Aidan to hear.

"Oh."

He kept his fingers at her waist and looked up at the other man. "Take the rest of her clothes off and eat her."

"Fuck." Aidan quickly complied, going to his knees on the rug in front of them. "Can't believe we're doing this." He easily pulled off her shorts and panties and now Maddie was naked. Lying naked up against him, her head on his shoulder, she made a soft sound in her throat. Zack's fingers twitched on her waist, her skin soft and warm.

Aidan didn't need directions to part her thighs, his gaze focused with rapt attention on her pussy. Zack wished he could see what Aidan saw, but on the other hand his view was pretty damn fine—Maddie's breasts tipped with hard, tawny nipples, her smooth stomach and the puff of dark hair where her thighs parted. And Aidan, kneeling before them, studying her.

"Take off your shirt," Zack directed.

Aidan lifted his eyes. Heat built as they eyed each other. Zack sensed Aidan's resistance. But once again, he complied, reaching behind his neck to tug the shirt off.

Zack had seen Aidan's body too, at the beach, every ripped, tanned inch of his torso, and it was just as impressive now. His mouth went dry and desire slammed into him. Fuck, he was doing this for them and torturing himself.

Maddie reached out to touch Aidan's ridged abs with her fingertips, trailing them down to the low waist band of his shorts, drawing Zack's attention to the huge erection behind the soft fabric. He gulped.

Stopping now was not an option. Whether he was going to watch everything was still up in the air, but Aidan was hugely aroused and Zack knew Maddie was too. Her skin wore an enticing flush, her nipples had puckered into tight peaks and the faint feminine scent of her arousal teased his senses, making his balls ache. So they had to finish.

Aidan leaned forward to kiss Maddie's lower belly, then nuzzle the curls, then rub his face against the crease of one thigh. "Maddie, sweetheart," he murmured. "So pretty."

Maddie squeaked and shifted against Zack.

Aidan's palms smoothed over her inner thighs, pressing outward, pushing them against Zack's own, then up. Zack released his grip on her waist to lift her legs so they were on the outside of his, spreading her even wider for Aidan. He let his hands rest on her knees, his thumbs rubbing the inside of them.

Lust pulsed in his balls as he watched Aidan lean in. The expression on his face made Zack's heart clench — so intense, so enraptured. His eyes drifted closed as he pressed kisses to Maddie's pussy. His hands slid beneath her ass, right on the edge of the couch, lifting her to his mouth. His obvious pleasure at doing this radiated through Zack in hot waves. Zack's own lips parted and his mouth watered at the thought of tasting Maddie's pussy.

God. *God*. What was he doing? His head whirled with the complex mix of emotions and arousal.

He focused again on the scene before him, sliding his hands up the outsides of Maddie's bare thighs to her hips, then wrapping around her in a tight hug as Aidan feasted on her. He licked and sucked, face pressing deeply then drawing back to circle his tongue around her clit. Her body trembled in Zack's arms, her chest rising and falling as her breathing quickened, then going still as she stopped breathing. The sexy noises falling from her lips inflamed Zack even more. She grabbed hold of his arms and held on tight, hips lifting to Aidan's mouth, and then she came. She shuddered and twisted, Aidan holding her in place as he sucked on her clit.

"Oh god!" Her head turned, face pressing into Zack's neck. "Oh my god. Oh yes."

Zack held her through her orgasm, pleasure roaring through him almost enough to make him come himself. Jesus. He was that close. That close to embarrassing himself. He sucked in a long breath and dug deep for control.

Aidan lifted his head, breathing hard, his lips shiny with Maddie's wetness. He gazed at Zack in a daze.

"Good?" Zack asked.

"Fuck yeah."

Zack tried to keep his face neutral, to not show how much he wanted to do the same. To not show how much he wanted to lean forward and lick Maddie's taste from Aidan's lips. His body pulsed in hard, weighty vibrations.

"Okay, Maddie baby?" Zack murmured. Her fingers still clamped around his forearms.

"Uh. Mmm."

He took that as a yes, the corners of his mouth twitching up.

Aidan sat back on his heels, hands still on Maddie's thighs. She sprawled there between them, limp and breathless. And beautiful.

Zack lifted his chin at Aidan. "You're next."

9

Maddie's heart raced and she panted for oxygen. Zack's arms around her held her safe and secure, although she felt like she'd just flown apart into flaming pieces.

Zack had his arms around her naked body.

Sweet baby Jesus, what was happening? Her mind spun helplessly in circles. She was naked with two men. Her boyfriend had just finished going down on her and licking her to orgasm while their best friend held her and watched them. And oh yeah, *she was naked.*

She was afraid to open her eyes and face that reality, so she lay there, eyes squeezed closed, trying to breathe. God. Oh my god.

Aidan was next.

What did that mean? What was Zack planning for them now? And why were they doing this? He'd somehow taken control and directed that whole scene, and she and Aidan had been swept up in it all, liked they'd been pulled into a powerful ocean current, unable to stop themselves.

Zack's embrace relaxed and his hands rubbed over her abdomen in a reassuring caress. "You're gonna suck Aidan's cock," he murmured to her. "Soon as you come back."

Her insides quivered. Jesus. Was she really going to do that? Give Aidan a blow job while Zack watched?

"Take your shorts off and sit down," Zack directed Aidan.

Maddie cracked her eyes open to see Aidan shoving his shorts down his legs. He often wore no underwear under loose shorts when they were relaxing at home. His cock sprang out, engorged, heavy veins pulsing. His hand immediately went to it and he gave a rough tug. Heat shimmered over Maddie's body.

Naked, Aidan moved back to where he'd been sitting earlier. She followed him with her eyes, enjoying the flex of his powerful thigh muscles and the bunch of his calf muscles as he walked. When he sat, cock still fisted, he looked at her and their eyes met.

Color stained his cheeks and his eyes glittered. Eyes locked on hers, he slouched lower into the couch cushions in invitation. He let his thighs widen and his other hand went to his balls.

Zack's body vibrated behind her. "There you go," he said softly. "He's waiting for you." His hands clasped her waist and gently lifted her off him. On legs that wobbled, she stood and moved toward Aidan, then dropped to her knees in front of him.

"Aidan." She set her hands on his big knees and gazed at him. "This is crazy."

"Yeah." His smile was gentle and he touched her face with his fingertips, first her cheek, then her lips. "You don't have to do this."

"Yes, she does." Zack's voice was firm and steady. And for some reason that calmed her and reassured her, made her more at ease with what they were doing. She needed that firmness, that direction. "She wants to suck you off. Don't you, Maddie." It wasn't really a question the way he said it, but she nodded anyway. "She wants to give you what you just gave her. Here." Zack rose off the couch and she blinked as he indicated she should move so he could set a cushion under her knees. He stayed behind her, and again surprised her as he threaded his fingers through her hair. Slowly he combed through the strands, sending tingles cascading from her scalp down her spine. "You like this?"

She nodded again. She loved having her hair played with. She loved having her hair pulled.

Zack gathered her hair into a ponytail at her nape. "There."

She turned her head to look at him over her shoulder, he gave her a nod and she turned back to Aidan. She reached for his cock, and he withdrew his own hand. Her fingers curved around him and she held him for a moment, savoring the feel of him, the hot, soft skin, the solid shape beneath pulsing in her palm. The engorged crest throbbed.

"I love how you look at me like that." Aidan's fingertips brushed her cheek again. She flicked her gaze up and met his eyes. "Like you're dying to suck me."

She swiped her tongue over her bottom lip and his eyes darkened. "I am." Her lips parted hungrily and she bent her head.

She took him into her mouth, letting her tongue slide over smooth skin, tasting his male essence. She loved the taste of him. She traced over the ridge with her tongue, closed her lips over him and sucked, then pulled off with a pop. Aidan groaned. His hands fell to the couch beside him and his head went back.

She lifted his shaft and licked from root to tip, over and over, working her way around until he was all wet and slick. Aidan's body trembled, and she became aware of Zack's breathing deepening behind her. He was watching her while he held her hair back.

Heat flared deep inside her. As it had earlier, knowing Zack was watching. His expression had been stern but watchful…almost protective. Intense. Telling them what to do seemed to come so naturally to him. She sensed that he enjoyed what he saw, that he was aroused, and it seemed like their compliance with his orders aroused him even more. She'd seen him rub the very visible erection behind the fly of his jeans.

Now that Aidan's shaft was all wet in her hand, she paused to touch the tip of her tongue to the tiny slit at the head. Aidan gave another low growl, fingers curling.

"Suck," Zack ordered her.

She did. She lowered her head, taking Aidan into her mouth as deep as she could. Now he was slippery it was easier, and she curled her fingers around the base of his cock and slid the tight ring of her lips up and down. Up and down. Her mind drifted a little, lost in the rhythm, the sounds of Aidan's moans of pleasure and Zack's slow breathing, the feel of Aidan's straining flesh in her mouth, stretching her lips and bumping the back of her throat.

"Fuck yeah." Aidan groaned. "Suck me just like that."

Her pussy squeezed and ached, despite the orgasm she'd just had.

"Lick his balls." Zack's fingers gave a tug on her hair to pull her head off Aidan and she whimpered at the tiny sting on her scalp. Zack twisted his hand, tightening his grip, spreading a burn over her scalp.

She slid her mouth off Aidan and happily complied, lifting his shaft with one hand, cupping his balls with the other and bringing them to her mouth. Her tongue wandered over the soft skin, her fingers gently massaging. His sac had tightened up against his body and her pussy heated even more at this. She kissed and licked and gently pulled one testicle into her mouth, then the other. Aidan's pleasure grunts increased.

Burning between her legs, she wished she could touch herself. She knew she was wet there, felt the liquid heat building.

"Fuck that's good," Aidan panted. "Suck me again."

"Yeah," Zack agreed. "He's gonna fuck your mouth. Put your hands behind your back."

Her eyes widened and blinked, her body tensing. Panic flickered inside her at not having control of this. As if sensing her disquiet, Zack rubbed her back. "It's okay, Maddie baby."

His calm tone once again steadied her. She took in a long breath.

"Never gonna hurt you," he continued quietly. "You trust us both, right?"

She nodded.

She did. She'd trust no one else like this. But she trusted them.

"Just let go," Zack murmured. "Enjoy. Give yourself over to it."

She let his words filter through the fog in her brain. Her pussy spasmed and flames licked over her body. Yes. Surrendering control to them excited her. She wanted them to do this, take her like this. It was what she'd always wanted.

She clasped her hands at the small of her back and obediently opened her mouth. Aidan directed the head of his cock inside. Then the men took over. Zack held her head with firm but gentle hands and Aidan slid down a little lower so he could lift his hips. He started slowly, carefully, sliding in and out of her mouth.

She focused on that, his flesh on her tongue, and Zack's hands in her hair. The pressure on her scalp intensified. Her jaw ached. All the sensations rocked through her, intensifying the experience, adding to her excitement. It was so wicked, so erotic. She sucked with wild hunger at Aidan's cock.

"Yeah." Aidan's voice thickened. "Hungry for it. You love it, don't you."

She tried to nod but Zack held her head immobile.

"Christ," Zack muttered.

She rubbed her tongue over the head and Aidan made more guttural sounds of pleasure.

"Up on your knees," Zack urged her. "You need to be a little higher…"

She rose, mindlessly obeying him even though she didn't know why. And then she did know why. Zack's hands adjusted the position of her head and the different angle let Aidan thrust deeper, the head of his cock brushing the back of her throat. It was gone quickly before she gagged and she fought to control that reflex.

"Fuck, that's deep. Fuck, Maddie."

He did it again, and again, right to her throat. Her eyes watered. She breathed through her nose, loving the way he filled her mouth.

"So good," Zack praised her. "Good girl."

Pleasure expanded through her. She was pleasing him. She was pleasing Aidan. And oh god, they were pleasing her, in ways she'd longed for and had never really found. As Zack had directed her, she turned herself over to it and floated away on the adrenaline rush of submission.

She would think more about this later, what this all meant, but at that moment she knew pleasure like she'd never experienced.

Aidan's thrusts grew faster, deeper, yet never more than she could take. Another flicker of fear came, but then disappeared as quickly as she felt herself safe and secure in Zack's hands. Aidan's body tensed. Her scalp stung where Zack pulled at her hair. Her entire world became this.

"Yeah," Aidan gasped. His fists clenched. "Close…so close." His hips fucked up into her with fast, hard strokes and then his cock swelled in her mouth. She blinked rapidly.

"You're gonna swallow," Zack murmured in her ear. "Every drop."

She couldn't nod, couldn't speak. But yes…she would.

Maybe he knew women who didn't. Some of her friends admitted they wouldn't do that. But she'd always loved doing that with Aidan. And she did it now.

The unique taste of him filled her mouth. His shout of pleasure made her skin tingle. She swallowed as he pulsed onto her tongue, savoring it. Zack's hands gentled in her hair, releasing it, then stroking through it with long, slow pulls.

Warmth slid through her, a delicious, languorous satisfaction. Aidan gripped his cock and tapped it on her bottom lip, another groan rumbling in his chest. "Holy, holy fuck. Maddie, baby. You just about fucking killed me."

Her lips trembled into a smile, her face aching. Zack's hands moved from her hair to her jaw, fingertips pressing in a gentle massage. His body heat warmed her from behind, even though he was still fully clothed.

"Amazing," he murmured. "Fucking amazing."

She swallowed and nodded her agreement, not really able to form words. Emotion swelled in her chest, and a sudden prickle stung the corners of her eyes. What had just happened here? It was the most bizarre thing she'd ever experienced. It was dirty and debauched and all kinds of wrong. Yet she felt as if something had opened up inside her. As if she'd discovered something so important and special, something she'd been looking for, for so, so long.

Zack's fingers worked in slow circles over her jaw and cheeks. He knew she was feeling it. He'd always been someone who knew what people were thinking and feeling. Sometimes she'd thought it was a curse, because he always seemed to take on others' emotions, ending up moody and quiet when one of their friends was having a rough time, or taking on the problems of the world when he read about civil wars and humanitarian crises. She tipped her head back, sinking into his ministrations, laying her hands on Aidan's muscular thighs. The crisp hair prickled her palms. He'd fallen back into the couch cushions, chest rising and falling, his half-hard cock on his belly, still thick and beautiful. *He* was beautiful, wide shoulders tapering to narrow waist and hips, ridged abdomen and dark patch of curls at the base of his cock, thighs widespread.

Wow.

Zack's fingers continued to press into her cheeks, the soft spots just below her cheekbones that were tense, then her temples. Then his fingers slid into her hair and massaged her scalp. She moaned as sweet languor spread through her.

He dragged his fingers down through her hair one last time and moved away. "I'm gonna go to bed," he said gruffly. "You two should be alone."

Her head jerked around to stare at him. He was leaving? Just like that?

"Oh no, you're not," she snapped.

He paused, turned and lifted an arrogant eyebrow. "Excuse me?"

She glared at him. He'd been giving all the orders and clearly didn't appreciate her attempt to take control. Tough shit. "You are not leaving just like that."

"Babe. You two aren't done. You don't need me here for the rest of it."

"We're done." Her eyebrows pulled together. "What about you?"

They stared at each other. The air thickened around them. She stole a glance at Aidan, who'd straightened and had his hands shoved into his hair. He was watching Zack, then looked at Maddie. "Maddie, what...?"

She didn't even know what she was saying. All she knew was, she and Aidan had both gotten off and Zack hadn't. And she knew he needed to. She knew he was aroused.

She closed her eyes, uncertainty sweeping over her. "I just...you can't just leave. We need to talk. This is going to be weird tomorrow if we don't talk."

Zack look pained. "Yeah," he finally said. "You're right."

"This is going to be weird tomorrow even if we *do* talk," Aidan muttered, pushing himself to sit straight. "And we're not talking about this naked, for fuck's sake. Hand me my shorts, sweetheart." He nodded at the crumpled clothing on the floor.

Before she could move, Zack had scooped up her T-shirt and shorts and handed them to her. She slipped them on, not worried about her underwear, while Aidan pulled on the loose shorts. She sat on the couch next to Aidan. Zack remained standing, watching them, his face inscrutable, his eyes narrow.

"I'm not sure what just happened here," Maddie said in a low voice.

Aidan muttered, "Fuck."

Zack threw himself down at the other end of the couch. "Not gonna apologize. You liked that. A lot."

Maddie bit her lip. She couldn't deny it. She looked at Aidan. He scrubbed his hands over his face. She knew he'd liked it too. What was going on in his head? "Talk to us," she said. "Please."

He still said nothing.

"Look," Zack said. "I'll admit I was testing things out at first. I had a hunch...but I wasn't a hundred percent sure you'd go for it. I told you to kiss him, to see what would happen. Yeah, you hesitated, but not much. It didn't take much for you to do it, and then to do everything I told you after that." He leaned forward. "You liked giving up control. You liked having someone take over and tell you what to do. It's what you need, isn't't?"

She stared at him. Then Aidan made a rough nose and jumped to his feet. "Yeah," he snapped at Maddie. "It's what you need. And I can't give it to you."

He strode out of the room and the sound of the bedroom door banging shut vibrated through the condo.

Maddie stared at Zack, covering her mouth with her hands. "Oh no. What have we done?"

Zack face contracted. "You better go talk to him."

She nodded, her thoughts muddled. "Yes. I will. But...Zack..." She searched his face with her eyes, but he gave nothing away. The guy who could so easily read others had sure learned to keep his own emotions hidden away.

"You two need to deal with this. Thought I was helping." He rubbed his mouth. "Didn't mean to make things worse."

"I just wish I understood." She shook her head. "I don't even understand myself."

"That's what I was trying to show you." Zack rose too, his posture stiff. "You two better talk. I'll go pack."

"What? No!"

"Don't think Aidan's going to want me around after this."

"I'll talk to him. Don't leave, Zack." She wasn't sure why she was begging him to stay. After what they'd just done, maybe it would be better if he left. But that didn't feel right. She didn't want him to go. And where *would* he go, anyway? "Please, don't leave."

He hesitated. "I'll wait till morning." He too disappeared down the hall.

Maddie closed her eyes. This was all fucked up. How had this happened? *Why* had this happened? Had they put their entire relationship at risk just to explore some crazy, erotic fantasy? Oh yeah—she needed to talk to Aidan.

10

*A*idan paced the bedroom, hands clenched into fists. A tight band constricted his chest and his stomach felt like a rock had lodged there. A storm raged in his head. He wanted to be angry at Zack. Pissed the hell off at him. Why the *fuck* would he do something like that?

But how the hell could he blame Zack when he and Maddie had just blindly done everything he'd told them to? How had they gotten sucked into that depraved game Zack had been playing? And then he was back to the why — why had Zack done that?

The other thing that wreaked havoc with his attempts to be angry was the undeniable fact that what had just happened had been hot as hell. Fuck.

He paused, squeezed his eyes shut, head going back. Fuck, fuck, fuck.

He'd resisted Maddie's timid suggestion to bring someone else into their relationship. He didn't want that. They loved each other. But guilt gnawed inside him. He knew he wasn't giving her what she needed. What if that really was a way for her to be satisfied?

What if it was a way for *him* to be satisfied?

He started pacing again.

Christ, he didn't want to go there. Having a third

person in their relationship who was another man? Unthinkable.

Except, it *had* happened. Sort of. Okay, Zack hadn't *really* participated in the sex. He'd touched Maddie, but not in a sexual way. Much. Okay, some. *Fuck!*

Aidan stumbled over to the bed and dropped to sit on the side, elbows on his knees, head in his hands.

He'd left them alone out there. With Maddie concerned that Zack hadn't been, uh, satisfied. Jesus. Was he an idiot?

Maddie wouldn't do that to him. Zack…Aidan would like to think he wouldn't either, but after what had just happened, his mind was blown.

He'd sensed something different in Zack from the minute they'd seen him again. Some kind of inner strength and confidence, a sureness of self. Aidan knew some of Zack's struggle to find himself back in college. What had transpired to bring about this change in him? It couldn't just be that he'd won a Pulitzer Prize.

Okay. Okay. He had to get his shit together here.

The bedroom door opened and Maddie slipped in. She closed the door quietly behind her and stayed there, looking at him. "You okay?"

"Fine."

"No, you're not."

He frowned, then exhaled sharply. "Whatever."

"Are you mad at me?"

He gazed at her. Her thin T-shirt was wrinkled and didn't hide her stiff nipples or the way her breasts jiggled. Her hair was a wild tangle around her head. Shadows darkened her eyes and her lips were still swollen. "No."

She swallowed and gave a short nod. "Mad at Zack then?"

"I'm trying really hard to be."

She huffed out a laugh and padded toward him. "Aidan. We need to talk."

"Yeah."

"Zack is going to leave."

His head jerked around as she sat beside him. "What?"

She nodded, her bottom lip quivering. "He thinks we want him to."

"Oh." He thought about that. "Maybe that would be best."

She tipped her head to one side, eyes tightening at the corners. "I don't want him to leave."

His chest constricted even more. "Why? You want that to happen again?"

Now her eyes flashed. "Maybe I do. But I also care about him. He's not fully recovered and he has nowhere else to go. He's our friend."

"Friend."

"He said he thought he was helping us."

"You liked it, didn't you?"

She met his eyes and slowly nodded. "I love you, Aidan. What you said...you can't give that to me...I don't want to lose you."

The rock in his gut ached. "I don't want to lose you either."

"I've been worried about us," she confessed softly, taking one of his hands. "Worried that if we aren't satisfied with each other...what will happen?"

"Nothing will happen," he said fiercely. "I love you."

She nodded, looking down at their joined hands.

He couldn't lose her either. He *couldn't*. But he got the point she was trying to make. "Maddie. If that's what you want...I want you to have it."

Her fingers squeezed his. "I'm not even sure what I want."

Neither was he. He tipped his head back once again. "I have a feeling Zack knows."

"I have that feeling too." Their eyes met. "What do we do about it?"

He'd do anything for her. Anything that was in his

power. She was his to care for and look after and if there were things he couldn't give her, he'd damn well find another way to do that. If that meant…bringing Zack into their bedroom, into their relationship…he'd do it.

He rubbed the throbbing in his chest. "I'll go talk to him."

Her eyes widened, searching his. "What are you going to say to him?"

"I'm going to tell him not to leave. Because we need him."

This terrified him. But he could do it.

Her lips trembled again. She nodded, blinking rapidly.

He rose and walked out of their bedroom and down the hall, gave a sharp rap on Zack's door. The door opened.

Zack stood there, shirtless but still in his jeans. His body had filled out the last few weeks. He'd gained some weight, but was still lean enough that the muscles he'd been working on were sharply defined. Zack just looked at him.

"We have to talk," Aidan said.

"Go ahead."

"Fuck man, I'm not going to punch you."

"Maybe you should. I was out of line, obviously."

"I wanted to punch you." Aidan leaned against the door frame. "Honestly? I can't totally blame you for what happened."

"I was the one calling the shots."

"We didn't have to do it."

Zack nodded, his mouth a grim line. "Then why did you?"

Aidan sighed. "I keep asking myself that. Obviously, we wanted to."

"You talk to Maddie?"

"Yeah. We don't want you to leave."

Zack's eyes flickered. "No?"

"No."

Silence swelled around them, hot and thick.

"I have to ask you a question." Aidan gut cramped. "Are you in love with Maddie?"

Zack was good at keeping a poker face but even he couldn't help the startled look that flashed across his features. Then it was gone and he laughed. "Christ, Aidan. What kind of question is that?"

"Answer it."

Zack's eyes narrowed. "I care about her, yeah. But I gave up on love a long time ago."

"Are you attracted to her?"

Their eyes met. Silence pulled out taut between them. "Yeah." Zack crossed his arms, biceps bulging. "Not gonna lie."

Aidan nodded. "Okay then." He lifted his chin. "She wants more of that."

Zack's jaw tensed. His chin jerked up too. "And you?"

"I want to give her what she needs," he said quietly. "If that's you, taking control, then so be it."

Zack's head tipped to one side and lifted a hand to rub his thumb over his chin. Aidan felt scrutinized, analyzed...stripped down. Zack had always had that ability to see inside people. Aidan stood his ground.

Zack nodded. "We gotta talk about some limits."

Aidan narrowed his eyes at him. "We have to talk about what you've been doing the last seven years."

To his surprise, Zack smiled. "Yeah. Maybe we should."

"Hey." Maddie's soft voice interjected. "I had to know what you guys are talking about."

Aidan turned to see her standing in the hall behind him. "C'mere." He extended an arm and he pulled her to him. They all moved into Zack's room. Music played from some small speakers on the dressers, Indian fusion music with moody vocals and exotic instruments.

"Zack wants to talk about limits." Aidan wrapped his arms around Maddie from behind so they both faced Zack.

"I need to know…what do you want, Maddie?" Zack asked.

She didn't answer right away.

"I know you want someone else to take control." Zack took one step closer. "How far do you want me to take that? What kinds of things have you been wanting?"

"I, um…we have a flogger."

Zack nodded, apparently unshocked by this.

"I like being spanked and having my hair pulled."

"Restrained?"

"Yes," she breathed. "I like that."

"How far does this go?" Zack looked at Aidan. "Tonight I touched her. Nothing more."

"Are you asking my permission to have sex with her?"

Zack's lips lifted into another smile. "Yeah."

Aidan swallowed. "It's not my permission to give. It's hers. Her decision."

She turned to look at him, eyes wide. "Aidan…?"

"You don't have to decide that right now," Zack said. "Right now you're probably thinking no way. Feelings can change when we get into a scene. But we need a safe word. So if you want to stop, I know you really mean it."

Aidan and Maddie both nodded. "But if we do have sex…" She turned again to Aidan. "You'd be okay with that?"

"If it's what you want, then yeah." He couldn't believe he was saying that. But he was never jealous. He knew Maddie loved him. He wanted her to be happy. If she wanted it, he wanted her to have it. And if it was Zack…well, who better? He was someone they both knew and trusted, not some random stranger they found on the Internet. He had no doubt that Zack would ever hurt Maddie. Even so, he said it. He met Zack's eyes. "Just take care with her, man. You ever hurt her, I will fuck you up so bad."

"I *will* hurt her," Zack said. "She wants to be flogged and spanked. You gonna be able to deal with that?"

Aidan swallowed. He got it. He knew what she wanted. What she needed. He just knew he couldn't give it to her. Their eyes met. "Yeah."

Zack nodded. "I get it." And Aidan felt their mutual understanding and connection all the way to his soul. They'd always been on the same page about Maddie— they'd rescued her the night they met her and ever since then it had been all about protecting her. Warmth expanded in his chest.

"Safe word?" Zack prompted.

Aidan's mind went blank.

"Let's keep it simple," Zack suggested. "Red if you want to stop. Yellow if you want to slow down. Okay?"

"This is insane." Maddie clutched Aidan's arms over her abdomen. Then she shivered and he recognized her excitement. "I can't believe we're doing this."

Neither could he. Yet he felt a sense of relief. A lightening of spirit, somehow, knowing that this took some pressure off him.

He lived with pressure, every damn day. At work, people counted on him to make big decisions, solve problems and make things happen. There were always problems, some big, some fucking huge, problems that potentially cost millions of dollars or problems that meant someone's pride got bruised. There were always deadlines and the crunch to make them. The pressure to make Maddie happy and the kick in the ego he'd taken knowing he could never quite do it had been weighing on him for so long, the unexpected lift of that load gave him a sense of hope and lightness. And...excitement.

And then the air in the room went electric as Zack unbuckled his belt. Aidan couldn't see Maddie, but sensed her alert attention exactly where he was looking—Zack's fingers on the belt buckle, then pulling the belt through the loops and out. He held the leather loosely in both hands. "On the bed, Maddie."

She went taut and vibrating in Aidan's arms. He squeezed her harder briefly. Okay. Here's where the rubber met the road. Or the leather met the skin. *Christ.* His insides contracted, but deep down inside he knew she wanted this, and he trusted Zack to give it to her.

"Wait," he said.

Zack looked up at him. Maddie's head turned against his shoulder.

"I want to know. I mentioned it earlier. What have you been doing for the last seven years? Why do you seem to know so much about all this?"

Maddie spoke up, her voice soft. "You said you'd been to those kinds of clubs. When you found that site for Mistress...whatever her name was."

Zack nodded, stroking the leather of his belt through with one hand. "Okay. Fair enough. Wasn't something I would've shared with you. You two seem so..."

"Vanilla?" Maddie spoke up.

Aidan couldn't help the laugh that burst out of him. Jesus.

"Yeah." Zack's lips curved into a smile. "Who knew?"

"So tell us," she said.

He nodded. "Okay. Fine. When I started traveling, a whole new world opened up to me. I'd never felt like I totally fit in. Except..." He tipped his head. "With you. You both accepted me the way I was. Fucked up and no clue."

"Zack." Maddie's fingers tightened on Aidan.

Zack shook his head. "It's true. I wasn't sure if I liked guys or girls. I wasn't sure what I liked at all. I felt restless, unsatisfied. When I got to Europe, some other journalists started taking me out with them at night. We went to some pretty wild sex clubs. The first one I remember was in Berlin. It was...a revelation. People were doing things I'd barely fantasized about. I met people..." He paused and looked at them through narrowed eyes, as if afraid they were judging him. "I met people who taught me things. I learned a lot about myself. What I wanted. What I needed." He lifted his chin. "I met women—and men—who wanted the same. They needed to be dominated and I wanted to do that. A few of them turned into semi-lasting relationships. As much as I could have, considering how much I moved around."

Maddie's body tightened again against him. Aidan sensed her displeasure at hearing about Zack with other people. That was...well, he wasn't even sure what that was. It didn't bother him. He appreciated that Zack had come home with this kind of experience and could guide them through this. And it made him happy that Zack had learned who he was and had accepted that.

"So yeah, I learned a lot." Zack fingered his leather belt. "I learned technical stuff, which is important. Even when someone is into pain, you don't want to injure anyone. But the psychological part of it is important too. Learning to read people. Know what they need. And learning to know what I need."

That still left a lot open for imagination. Or questions. Aidan wanted to know more, curiosity burning inside him. He felt a connection to what Zack was saying. He recognized it was different from Zack's preferences, but still...he got it.

Zack pulled up his shirt sleeve and revealed the tattoo on his left shoulder, a round black shape with curving spokes and three dots, surrounded by stylized black curves. "This is based on the BDSM emblem. I got it a few years ago."

Aidan studied the tattoo he'd noticed that day at the beach and nodded. He rubbed a hand over his mouth. Weird they'd all ended up here.

Maddie shivered in his arms. Was she imagining the things Zack had done? The things he could do with them?

"Now," Zack said. "Need you naked, baby. Aidan…take her clothes off again."

Aidan loosened his grip on Maddie's middle and once more reached for the hem of her T-shirt. She lifted her arms to let him pull it off, this time directly facing Zack, who studied her with open appreciation. Then Aidan gave her loose shorts a shimmy and they dropped to the floor at her feet. She toed them aside. Aidan set his hands on her waist, standing behind her. They awaited Zack's further orders.

Aidan's skin tingled everywhere and his dick began to thicken again.

"Touch her," Zack directed him. "Touch those pretty tits."

Aidan slid his hands over her ribs and cupped Maddie's soft flesh, letting their weight fill his palms. He caught her nipples between thumbs and forefingers and gently squeezed. She shuddered against him.

"She wants it harder." Zack studied Maddie's face.

Aidan pinched harder. He swallowed. Maddie moaned.

"Harder."

Christ.

"She knows the safe word," Zack reminded him. "If it's too hard, she'll use it."

Right. Right. He pinched harder, squeezing the tips between his fingers.

"Oh god," Maddie gasped. "Yes."

Aidan kept going, pinching and tugging. Maddie began to tremble in his arms.

"Is she wet?"

Aidan stroked his palm down her flat stomach and slid his fingers between her thighs. Scalding slickness met his fingers. "Yeah," he groaned. "So wet." He slid his fingers back and forth in the plump folds. She leaned back against him. Zack's eyes darkened.

"I want to taste that," he murmured. Maddie jolted and

heat flared in Aidan's balls. "But first, we're going to get her wetter. Hotter. Sit on the side of the bed, Aidan. Maddie, kneel in front of him."

Zack tossed a pillow on the floor as they followed his instructions. Aidan sat. Maddie kneeled on the pillow in front of him. He parted his thighs, but still wore his shorts, his erection throbbing beneath them.

"Hold her hands." Zack moved behind her, pulling the belt through his hands.

Maddie's shoulders tensed and she bit her lip as she peered up at him through her eyelashes. Aidan reached for her hands and gripped them tightly. Her fingers curled around his.

"Lean forward, Maddie," Zack said. "Let me see that pretty ass."

Maddie set her face on the mattress, right in the V of Aidan's thighs.

Zack was going to hit her with his belt. Aidan's gut clenched so hard he was afraid he was going to puke. Could he really do this? Jesus Christ.

His heart pounded against his sternum. He looked up at Zack and met his eyes. Zack had asked him if he'd be able to handle this and he'd said yes. He swallowed and gave a short jerky nod. He had to trust Zack. There was no one he'd trust more when it came to Maddie.

"Don't worry," Zack said. "I've done this a time or two." He lifted his arm and brought the leather down across Maddie's flesh. She jolted and her fingers spasmed on his.

"Wait for it," Zack murmured to her. "Wait for the burn."

He did it again, and again. Maddie made muffled whimpery noises. Their hands clenched together.

Aidan watched, barely breathing, every muscle in his body tight, every nerve ending on alert for any sign that Maddie was hurt. She had her safe word. She didn't use it. Zack paused and laid a palm on Maddie's ass.

Heat flooded Aidan, starting at his hairline, pouring down to pool at his groin. Zack was fondling Maddie's bare ass, rubbing it.

"Okay, baby?" Zack murmured to her.

"Yes," she mumbled. "God, yes."

"Good girl." Zack delivered several more fast blows. Aidan could sense the control, the attention Zack paid. And he seemed to know when to stop. He dropped his arm.

Aidan looked up at Zack. His eyes glittered and his cheeks wore a light flush. Aidan's gaze tracked down to the massive hard on behind the fly of Zack's jeans.

"Now," Zack said, his voice calm and controlled but with a slight rasp. "Tell me how wet her pussy is."

11

Maddie kept her face pressed to the soft cotton of the duvet on Zack's bed, eyes squeezed shut. Her breath came in short pants. Heat radiated from her buttocks through her body. Each strike had been a flash of fire, the first few distinct then melding into a sweet, dark ecstasy. She'd been climbing high to an exquisite peak and had been at the point she thought she couldn't bear another lash when he'd stopped.

She held onto Aidan to keep from flying away. Her head felt light and her pussy ached with an unbearable need. She vaguely heard Zack and Aidan talking, then Aidan released one of her hands. She whimpered as he reached down and stroked his fingers between her thighs. "Christ. Dripping."

"She needs to be fucked." Zack caressed her back, then smoothed his hand over her burning ass. "Dontcha, Maddie?"

"Yes," she whispered. "Please."

"C'mere." He lifted her by her waist. Aidan released her hands. Her heart fluttered wildly. Was Zack going to do it? Dear god...they'd talked about it, but...

But no.

"Take your shorts off and lie down on the bed," Zack

told Aidan. Once again, Zack wrapped his arms around her naked body, holding her close as Aidan shoved his shorts off and pushed himself back onto the bed. His cock rose up, stiff and flushed and beautiful. "There you go. You on top. Your ass is gonna be tender." He helped her climb on the bed. In a daze, still floating and aching, she straddled Aidan.

"Fuck yeah." Aidan groaned as she reached for his shaft. Zack's hands held her, keeping her steady in her dizzy state as she lowered herself onto Aidan.

"Oh god," she whispered. "That feels so good."

"I'm gonna be right here," Zack said from the arm chair in the corner he now sat on. "Watching. Telling you what to do. And jerking off. Because fuck, I'm so hard it's a wonder I haven't passed out from all the blood flowing south."

"Your dick's not *that* big," Aidan mumbled.

Zack laughed and a smile pulled at Aidan's lips. Maddie blinked at the unexpected humor in this most surreal of moments. She couldn't stop herself from looking at Zack and her heart lurched seeing him slouched back in the chair, his jeans opened and lowered on his hips exposing dark hair at his groin, his cock in his fist.

His cock *was* big. The air all left her lungs in a rush. That was so damn hot, watching him jack himself, his hand slow and sure, pulling his cock away from his body on the down stroke, his palm circling over the head then sliding back up, again and again. The way his wrist moved was so sexy. His other hand pressed to his groin, thumb on one side of the base of his cock, fingers on the other. His eyes met hers and his lips quirked.

Heat burned in her face and she fell over Aidan, tucking her face into the side of his neck. His arms surrounded her and his hips lifted, thrusting up into her. She contracted around him, loving the fullness, the thick heat inside her. Her clit rubbed against him and she shifted a bit to get just a little more pressure...oh yeah. *There.* Tingles rushed through her veins.

Aidan's hand went to her ass.

"Spank her," Zack directed lazily from his chair.

Aidan's hand didn't move.

"It's okay," she whispered. "I like it."

"Don't want to hurt you."

"I know." Her heart squeezed. "But I want it."

"Do it," Zack ordered in a harsher tone.

Aidan's hand landed on her ass. Already warm and tender, the small smack set nerve endings on fire again, in such a delicious way. She clenched around his cock again and he groaned.

"Yeah," Zack approved. "One day I'll flog your ass with Aidan inside you, Maddie."

They both gave another spasmodic jerk at that, her stomach doing a little flip. Aidan gave her another fiery tap. Pleasure flashed over her skin. Flames twisted inside her, tension building. Aidan fucked up into her faster, delivering spanks to both cheeks. It crashed over her so fast, so powerful, dark and edgy, she cried out. Aidan's hands gripped her butt as he went still, pulsing inside her, a long raw groan torn from his throat.

"Fuck yeah," Zack muttered. "Now me too."

Maddie turned her head and watched through a curtain of hair as Zack came too, semen spilling over his hand, his jaw tight, beautiful mouth open. His low groan in the quiet room sounded primal and carnal.

Her heart pounded. None of them moved for long moments. Then Zack finally heaved himself out of the chair and grabbed some tissues from the box on the dresser.

She watched him move, a little stunned by it all. In the space of one evening, their entire world had changed.

"Be right back." Zack ducked out of his room. She heard water running in the bathroom.

She and Aidan had done unspeakable things in front of

their friend. She'd let Zack do unspeakable things to her. Dear sweet god. She started to tremble, her chest full of emotion that threatened to swamp her.

Zack was right there, a hand on her back. "She's coming down. Here, baby." He spread a blanket over her, an extra one she'd left in the room in case the air conditioning was too cold for Zack. "Warm her up," he instructed Aidan. "Hold her tight. She needs it right now."

Aidan did so and Zack continued to rub her legs through the blanket in slow, strong motions, sitting on the side of the bed next to them. Surreal.

"Got any aloe lotion?" Zack asked.

Maddie tried to speak but words didn't come out. Aidan said, "Yeah, in our bathroom."

"Rub some of it on her ass before you go to sleep," Zack advised. "It'll help."

"Jesus," Aidan muttered.

"I'm okay, honey." Maddie stirred. Her legs were stiffening up. Wincing a little, she moved off Aidan's semi-hard cock and slid to her side. "Really. That was…" She swallowed. "Incredible."

"Went easy on her." Zack touched her hair. She felt his gaze on her. "First time."

First time. There would be a next time. He'd already talked about something else he wanted to do. Maddie pushed to sitting, keeping the blanket over her breasts. She met Zack's eyes. "You're staying?"

His eyes flickered, then he nodded. "Yeah. I'll stay. For now. But you know I'm supposed to leave in three weeks."

"Yes," she whispered.

"We can do this," Zack said. "While I'm here. If you want."

"I want to." She reached out and grabbed one of his hands.

"This is fucking weird as hell," Aidan muttered. "But…thanks, man. For giving her that."

Zack lifted his chin. "Thanks for letting me."

Maddie looked at Zack. She'd felt bad earlier because she and Aidan had both been had orgasms and he hadn't. But looking at him now, he wore a look of supreme satisfaction. More than just from masturbating. It clicked inside her that they'd also fulfilled a need for him...his need to dominate. A sense of wonder filled her.

"It's late," Aidan murmured. "Come on, sweetheart. I'll carry you to bed."

He picked her up, wrapped in the blanket, carried her to their room next door and gently laid her on their bed. "Are you really okay, sweetheart?"

"Other than freaked the hell out...yes. I am." She reached out and caught his hand. "Thank you. Are *you* okay?"

He came down next to her. "Yeah." He hugged her close. "I am."

"When you told him you'd fuck him up if he hurt me...I love you so much for that."

"I'll always look after you, Maddie. That will never change."

"Thank you." Emotion clogged her throat. After a moment, she said, "I'm a little scared."

"Of Zack?"

"No." She swallowed. "I'm afraid we're taking a big risk here. We have something so good and perfect together. What if this wrecks it all?"

"Maddie, baby." He tipped her chin up. "I love you more than anything. But we have to be honest. We're not perfect."

She gazed into his dark eyes, her lips trembling. It was true. God, it was true.

How could they love each other so much and not be enough for each other?

But maybe they'd found the way to be enough. Maybe Zack would show them the way to be enough.

12

Maddie lay on her and Aidan's bed with her wrists bound and fastened to the headboard, which Zack had been happy to see was wrought iron. Her blue eyes were huge in her small face, her hair a dark tangle on the pillow. She was so fucking beautiful it made Zack's chest hurt. Breasts high and round on her chest, tawny-brown nipples hardened into perfect points, the sensuous curves of her waist, hips, and legs were outlined against the dark green duvet cover. His gaze roamed over her flat stomach and the neat little patch of dark hair on her mound.

"Spread your legs."

Naked other than the ropes at her wrists, she obeyed him. It had been a week since that night he'd taken control and directed Aidan and Maddie to have sex in front of him. They'd played again the following night, and he'd taken things a little farther. The rest of the week had been a build-up of anticipation for all of them, heightened by a little dirty talk, a few taps on Maddie's sweet ass in the kitchen and his announcement to Maddie and Aidan that he'd gone online and ordered "a few things."

"Like what?" Maddie'd breathed, wide-eyed.

"You'll find out." And he'd tapped her cheek with firm authority.

Now he'd just finished tying her up with the rope he'd ordered, with Aidan watching. He sensed Aidan's attention to how he wrapped and tied the soft rope, firmly restraining her, but without the rope biting into her soft skin. "How does that feel?"

"Um...secure." Her eyelashes fluttered, and she bit her bottom lip. She gave a tug on the rope.

"Good."

"Are you going to be able to undo those knots?" Aidan frowned.

Zack lifted an eyebrow. "You doubt my skills?"

"Just asking." Aidan lifted his chin and met his eyes. "Safe, sane and consensual, right?"

Amused, Zack nodded. "Right. I'll be able to undo them. But if I can't..." He jerked his chin toward a pair of shears on the dresser. Aidan acknowledged them with a move of his head. "Now she's restrained." Zack turned to Aidan. "Take my clothes off."

Aidan froze. "What?"

"Take my clothes off." The command in his tone was unmistakable. He could feel the vibrations flowing off Aidan's tight body standing next to him. He held his arms out at his sides. "Do it. Now."

Aidan moved closer and took hold of the hem of Zack's T-shirt. His face was impassive, but hot color washed into his cheeks. He yanked the shirt up over Zack's chest. Zack lifted his arms to allow him to pull it off over his head. Aidan was clearly trying not to touch him, but their arms brushed together as the shirt came off. Sizzles ran down Zack's arms and converged low in his belly. Shirtless, only inches away from Aidan, he smiled a dirty smile. Aidan's mouth tightened as he balled up the shirt and tossed it aside.

Zack jerked his chin down to indicate his jeans. Aidan

unbuckled the belt, lowering his gaze to his fingers. He worked open the button and lowered the zip. His fingers grazed Zack's heavy erection behind the denim and heat flared through Zack's veins.

"Why?" Eyes still lowered, Aidan gripped the sides of the jeans and yanked down. "Why are you making me do this?"

"Because I can."

He heard sharply indrawn breaths from both Aidan and Maddie.

Yes. This was what it was about. Him controlling them.

A small fear edged his consciousness, still, a fear that what they were doing might not have the results they all wanted. For his part, he wanted to help them, to show them what they needed, to give them that while he was here. Then he'd leave, go back to traveling the world and taking pictures of how fucked up that world was, and they'd stay here in their perfect life.

"Fuck." Aidan pulled the jeans lower, along with Zack's boxers. Loose-fitting jeans and underwear pooled around his ankles. His cock thrust out aggressively, and Zack felt Aidan's attention there like a touch, everything going still and electric around them. Aidan's tongue swiped along his full bottom lip. Zack's cock twitched.

He gripped Aidan's chin and lifted it so their eyes met. "You did good." He brushed his thumb over Aidan's wet bottom lip. Aidan blinked, eyes a little dazed. "Now you go sit and watch."

Aidan stared at him.

"Now." Zack released Aidan's jaw.

Aidan moved to the chair and sat.

"Sit there and watch. You can take off your clothes, but don't touch yourself until I tell you to."

Aidan's eyes flickered and his lips thinned but he said nothing. He pulled his shirt off over his head, then stepped out of his jeans.

Zack turned to the bed to see Maddie watching them with even bigger eyes which were now bright with excitement.

He approached the dresser where he'd left the box with the items he'd purchased, and pulled out another item—a sweet little whip named "Sting." When the package had arrived at the condo and he'd unpacked it and held it in his hand, he'd gotten painfully hard. The handle fit in his palm with perfect weight and smoothness, the sleek steel tapered to a point at the bottom, topped with a globe and extending into a smooth shaft. At the end of the shaft was a strip of soft silicone that could tickle, tease or...sting.

Zack flicked it against his palm and glanced at Aidan. Aidan's eyes shifted from the whip and back up to Zack's face. Zack read the hint of anxiety. The toy definitely had an evil look with its ruby-red metallic point at one end and the silicone strip at the other.

"You gonna be able to handle this?" he asked Aidan as he had the week before. He sensed his friend's concern. Zack was about to lay this whip on his girlfriend while he watched.

There had to be trust. Aidan had to trust him to take care of Maddie. And he had to trust Maddie to know herself and her limits and safe out if she needed to.

Aidan's eyes tightened up at the corners but he nodded. "Yeah."

"Good."

Zack looked back at Maddie. Her eyes glowed. Her bottom lip parted from her top just enough to show a gleam of white teeth.

He smiled at her and she gave him a slow, uncertain smile back. He liked that she was excited but still a little nervous, because if he read her right, the hint of fear would only add to her pleasure.

"Now we play." He strolled over to the bed and stood on the side opposite of Aidan, giving him a clear view of everything he did. He touched the silicone strip to Maddie's breastbone and dragged it lightly down her abdomen, all the way to her pubic curls. He teased her there for a few minutes, then let the whip dip between her parted thighs, brushing her pussy.

Her breathing hitched and her legs shifted on the bed.

He traced over her thighs, her calves, the bottoms of her feet, making her squirm, then back up. He drew the whip in a circle around each breast, then with a flick of his wrist gave a little snap of the whip on one nipple. Maddie gasped. He did the other one.

"Nice. This baby is sweet." He liked the weight of it, the feeling of control he had with it.

He traced the silicone over the sides of her neck, across her throat and down one shoulder. He tickled the inside of one arm, stroked it up and down the arm, then moved to the other.

He watched her responses carefully, assessing every flutter of her eyelashes, every indrawn breath, every twitch of her body. She loved sensation play. This was good.

He tickled and teased her everywhere, making her sigh and whimper, finally laying a sharp tap on her pussy, the soft folds below her clit. She whimpered.

Zack withdrew the whip and turned it around. "Let's see how wet you are, baby." He slid the handle through her pussy, careful of the pointed tip, and brought it up gleaming with her arousal. He turned his head to Aidan. Then he circled the bed and moved to stand in front of the other man. "Here. Taste her."

He held the handle of the whip to Aidan's mouth. Aidan opened and Zack slipped it inside. The sight of Aidan's tongue curling around the red metal before his lips closed over it made Zack's hard dick twitch.

He let Aidan lick and suck—Christ, that was hot—before withdrawing the handle. Watching that made him ache for Aidan's mouth to close around his cock like that. Lust pulsed in his balls. "How does she taste?"

"Amazing."

"Yeah. Now my turn."

He returned to the bed and did the same thing, drawing the handle through her creamy pussy. This time he opened his own mouth and took it in. Eyes on Aidan, he slowly drew it out between his lips, hollowing his cheeks as he sucked. Aidan shifted on the chair, hands gripping the arm rests.

Zack turned his attention to Maddie, who regarded them with fascination. She touched the tip of her tongue to her bottom lip and need burned through Zack. "Your turn."

Once more he gathered up her arousal on the whip handle and now turned it toward her. Her eyes went huge and she swallowed. Her fingers curled above her bound wrists.

"Open."

Her lips tightened briefly then parted. He inserted the handle into her mouth, and watching her little tongue and lips was just as hot as watching Aidan's. He wanted both their mouths on him. Christ. Imagining her and Aidan both going down on him, sharing him...he'd store that fantasy away. He wasn't sure they'd ever get there. Aidan was being almost shockingly obedient...confirming Zack's suspicions that he wanted to be dominated as much as Maddie did. Just maybe in different ways...and maybe he didn't even realize how much.

"Taste yourself, baby. That's it."

He withdrew the handle and wiped it on his left palm before gripping it in his right again. He once again began to flick the silicone strip over her body. Excitement pounded through him. Fuck, he loved doing this. He'd pondered many times why, but had never come up with a real answer other than it was just the way he was. He supposed he was considered a sadist, since he enjoyed inflicting pain. But it wasn't that simple. He didn't enjoy giving pain when it didn't bring pleasure. After the horrible things he'd seen, he was a pacifist, opposed to war and violence. The difference between hurting someone or giving someone the kind of sensation that was pleasurable was huge — even if that pleasurable sensation was pain.

His attention returned to her breasts. He again traced around their round shape, then one again flicked her nipples. They tightened even more, darkening to a cinnamon color. He moved from one to the other, taking his time, teasing them into dark, stiff points.

"Fucking gorgeous." He climbed onto the bed, and moved between her legs, nudging them farther apart. He was hard as a post and he knew Maddie was aware of it, her gaze dropping to his erection. When she looked back up at his face her eyes were wide and hot.

"Need to taste those nipples. Are they burning?"

"Yes." Her whisper barely reached his ears. He moved over her and leaned down to lick a hard nipple. He heard Aidan's sharply indrawn breath.

"That feels good." Maddie moaned.

He licked and soothed the tender tips, then closed his lips around one and sucked. Her body twitched beneath him. She made hot little noises of arousal that he loved.

After playing with her nipples for some time, he kissed his way down her flat belly, slowly, with lingering tongue and an open mouth. When he reached her pussy, he set his palms on her inner thighs and gently pushed them wider.

"Christ." He admired the view. "That is the sweetest pussy I've ever seen."

She made a strangled noise. "Zack. Oh my god. I need…"

He knew what she needed. She needed to be touched. She needed to be fucked. That wasn't going to happen yet, but…he leaned down and set his mouth to her soft, wet skin. She choked on a breath as he kissed her there, soft, gentle, slow. He kissed all over her pussy and inner thighs, leisurely kisses and touches of his tongue. He inhaled the exotic, intimate scent of her. It made him dizzy and he had to struggle to keep his mind focused. It would be so easy to get lost in all that was Maddie and lose his mind.

He stroked her with his tongue, tasting her arousal. Pleasure assaulted his nerves — her taste, her scent, the feel of her incredibly soft flesh on his lips and tongue. The sweet sounds of excitement she made inflamed him even more. He circled her straining clit with his tongue, then brushed over it, and her body jerked.

That was enough. She was close to coming, but that wasn't going to happen yet.

He rose up onto his knees, breathing fast, his heart pounding. He moved away from her. "Roll over," he growled.

There was enough play in the rope that she could roll to her front. She bent one leg, pushed a foot into the mattress and rolled, arms above her head. Her hair fell all over her face so he carefully smoothed back the long dark strands and adjusted the pillow for her.

He traced the whip down the center of her back. He tickled her buttocks, the backs of her thighs and knees. She squirmed. A pink flush tinted her gorgeous skin everywhere. Then he snapped the whip harder on one ass cheek. She jolted and gave a whimper. He flicked again. And again.

Out of the corner of his eye, he saw Aidan grip the armrest of the chair and push forward as if he was going to rush over there. Zack gave him a direct look. "Don't move."

Aidan's eyes narrowed. His breathing was shallow, his knuckles white. "Fuck," he muttered.

"Trust her," Zack said. "To know what she needs. She has the power to stop it with one word, remember?"

Aidan gave a short nod, his lips thinned.

"More." Her voice was muffled by the pillow, but Zack and Aidan both heard her.

Zack swept his hand over the smooth curve of her bottom. "So pretty."

He used the whip more and carefully took her up, letting her experience the high of the endorphins that had to be rushing through her veins. He watched her eyes get glassy as she floated off. Then he knelt on the bed, dropped the whip, and covered her ass with his hands. He rubbed her gently, up and down her back, bent and laid his lips on one cheek. "Such a good girl," he murmured. "So hot, Maddie." He slipped his fingers between her legs and found liquid heat. Her ass lifted invitingly. He stroked deeper through her silky folds.

"Please." She lifted to his touch. "Oh, please."

"You wanna be fucked?"

"Yes. God yes."

He looked at Aidan, eyebrows lifted. Aidan swallowed. "It's her call," he said hoarsely.

"Maddie?" Zack laid his palm between her shoulder blades. "You wanna be fucked by me?"

"Yes!"

Zack picked up the condom he'd hopefully set on the bedside table earlier. Maddie was hot and wet and desperate. He wanted to take her up even higher, give her the orgasm of her life with all the feel-good hormones coursing through her, her senses all heightened. He rolled it on as fast as he could and moved over her. Her pretty ass was all rosy, as were her face cheeks.

Once more he paused to draw back her hair, smoothing it off her hot face. Then he gripped her hips and lifted. He pushed into her, deliberately not being gentle. She cried out and gasped as he filled her. She was wet, so fantastically wet, but tight.

Jesus. It had been so long for him. He'd stayed in

control through all their playing, but now, fucking a woman—fucking Maddie, for Chrissake—almost made him lose it. His head spun with incredulity and excitement. He was fucking Maddie. *Maddie.*

Maddie, who turned out to have a little masochistic bent. How had he never known this? Of course, he hadn't really explored his dominant, sadistic side until after he'd left Chicago. Before that, he'd tried to pretend that part of him didn't exist, worried about what that meant about him.

He found a quick, hard rhythm. The pull of her sweet pussy on his dick had electricity sizzling through his body, tightening every nerve ending. He laid a sharp tap on her ass, one side then the other, then reached up and gathered her hair into a tail in his fist. He tugged and her head came up and back. "Like that?"

"Yes. Please. *More.*"

He twisted her hair in his hand, loving her breathless whimpers, the sound going straight to his balls. Her begging set him on fire.

Control. He had to hang on for her. This had to be good for her, probably the first time she'd had sex while riding the high of that sweet, dark pleasure. He slid a hand around over her belly, her mound, and found her clit. She spasmed around him as he touched her there, circling wet fingers over the taut bud.

"Yes," she gasped. "Oh god, Zack. I don't think I can stand it."

He leaned over and kissed her back. "Yes, you can." He stroked his tongue over her smooth skin. "You can do it." Then he closed his teeth on the muscle of her shoulder in a primal bite of ownership.

Her body jerked and she cried out. "Aidan," she whimpered.

Aidan was immediately at her side. "What, Maddie? You okay?"

"Yes. So good. Want you…just want you here. Hold my hands."

Aidan flashed Zack a look, then reached over to grip Maddie's restrained hands.

Zack licked his lips, pinched Maddie's clit and she wailed. Her pussy rippled around him as she shuddered through a hard orgasm.

13

The violent pleasure consumed her. Heat radiated over her ass, and tingles cascaded from her scalp where Zack tugged her hair, down to the base of her spine. Her entire body shimmered with a dark, heady euphoria she'd never experienced. Zack's fingers at her clit coaxed her orgasm to the edge and then her world went black as it exploded inside her. Her body clenched hard around Zack's cock where he stroked over supersensitive nerve endings. She flew away and lost herself.

She was vaguely aware of Aidan's hands clutched in hers. She gripped him tighter as Zack continued to hammer into her, extending her pleasure almost unbearably, but she embraced it and reveled in it. So much sensation. Zack's hands gripped her hips and then he groaned and held himself balls-deep inside her. Sensitized so much, she felt his wrenching spasms inside her.

"Maddie," he gasped behind her, his voice raw. "Christ, Maddie."

She'd given that to him. She and Aidan. Her eyes stung.

Zack slid slowly out and back into her body, once…twice. His hands gentled on her, then caressed her tender buttocks. Then he dropped over her, hands planted in the mattress on either side of her. "Baby. You were amazing."

She moved her head in dissent. She'd done nothing. He was the one who'd given all that to her. Her chest squeezed with emotion and she began to tremble. As Zack eased out of her she felt a sense of loss. He knelt beside her to untie the ropes at her wrists, unwrapping her with practiced efficiency. "There," he murmured. "Okay, baby? Move your fingers. Any numbness?"

She tried to focus. Aidan's hands loosened on hers but still touched her. She flexed her fingers. "No."

"Good. Rub her hands and arms," Zack instructed Aidan. "Get into bed with her under the covers. She needs to be held and kept warm. Gotta get rid of this condom."

The bed shifted as he moved off and again as Aidan joined her, tenderly lowering her arms. He got them both under the covers, her back to his front, arms around her rubbing her hands and wrists. She trembled and tried not to cry.

Again all the emotion. It was crazy how Zack brought that out of her. And yet she also felt an incredible sense of peace and freedom.

"Okay, sweetheart?" Aidan whispered against her hair.

"Yeah. I'm good. Better than good. I don't even..."

"I know. Not sure what to say myself. I was worried at first..."

"I know."

"But I could see how much you loved it. That was so fucking hot." He stroked her forearms.

Zack returned and stood beside the bed, now wearing his boxers. "Okay?" he asked Maddie quietly.

She loved how they were both concerned about her. An overwhelming sense of gratitude rose up inside her. "I'm good." She stretched a hand out to Zack. He hesitated, then sat on the bed to take it. "Thank you, Zack."

He looked down at her hand in his. Silence expanded. "Thank *you*," he finally said in a low voice. "You have no idea what a gift you just gave me."

She swallowed. "I guess it's been a while since you..."

"Had sex?" One corner of his mouth lifted. "Yeah. That too. But it was more than just that. I needed that control. My life was so out of my control all those months. And I need that...dominance...to balance me. If I don't have that I don't feel whole. You made me feel whole for the first time in a long time."

"Oh." She let out a long breath and squeezed his hand. She thought she'd done nothing, so the idea that she'd given something to him too pleased her. "I don't...I guess I need to understand you better."

"Not much to understand," he muttered, still looking down.

"I think there is."

Zack glanced at Aidan. "You okay, man? Are *we* okay?"

Whoa. She knew why he asked that. Another man had just fucked her in front of Aidan. If she thought about that too much, she'd probably start freaking out and screaming. But it felt so...right.

"Yeah," Aidan said. "We're good."

"You liked watching," Zack stated.

"Yeah. I like watching Maddie gets what she needs. That's what I want. That's all I've ever wanted." He paused. "You like watching too."

"As long as I'm controlling the action." Like he had last weekend. There was a long pulsing moment as Zack looked at Aidan. "But I think you want more than that."

Aidan's body immediately tensed against her. Her mind raced back to when Zack had asked — no, ordered — Aidan to undress him. And he'd done it. Watching the two men together had been unbearably hot. The tension between them had crackled — Aidan's resistance yet compliance to Zack's authority along with the sexual electricity that arced as Aidan removed Zack's clothing, then Aidan's obvious study of Zack's erection.

Ideas floated around in her head, the things Aidan

wanted her to do to him, the way he obeyed Zack...and she knew that Zack was right. Aidan did want more from this. Was he willing to admit it?

Much as Aidan had been pained to know he couldn't give her what she needed, she too struggled with the fact that there were things he wanted that she couldn't do. Well, she could do them. She just didn't get off on them.

But Zack...Zack did. So far this had been all about her. But maybe it didn't have to be. Maybe they could give something to Aidan too.

"Gonna say goodnight." Zack kissed her hand then released it and pushed up to his feet. "See you tomorrow."

As he left their bedroom, Maddie watched with a heavy feeling inside her. They'd started this thing, whatever it was, but still, she and Aidan were a couple and Zack was on the outside. And she found she didn't like that.

At that moment, it all overwhelmed her, everything pushing in on her and squeezing her until she couldn't breathe. Her mind shut down. She couldn't deal with it. So many emotions swamped her—fear that she and Aidan were doing something terribly wrong, compassion for Zack, guilt and shame mixed with an incredible joy and satisfaction and longing for more.

"Going to sleep," she mumbled to Aidan.

He reached for the lamp and with a click, darkness shrouded the room. He shifted her against him, settling in, and they slept.

⚜

They all woke up late the next morning, Saturday. Maddie tried not feel weirded out by the fact that she'd had sex with Zack last night. With not only Aidan's consent, but his enjoyment.

It seemed they all had a definite kinky side that they'd

never realized about each other before. Well, why would they? They'd all just been friends back in college. She and Aidan had known that Zack thought he was bisexual. That wasn't kinky. That was just him. And as for her and Aidan…their recent attempts to fly their freak flag hadn't been all that successful. They weren't sure of what they wanted and even less sure how to give it to each other.

But wow…these nights with Zack had been incredible. Heart-stoppingly, eye-poppingly incredible.

"I'm having lunch with Chelsea and Nisha," she told the guys. "Then going shopping."

"If you bring any more shoes home, an equivalent number of pairs have to go," Aidan said. "There's no fucking room left in our closet."

She gave him a look of mock horror. "I can't get rid of any shoes."

"Sweetheart. We should call you Carrie Bradshaw."

Zack snorted, reading the newspaper.

"You like my shoes. I know you have a thing for stilettos."

Zack lowered the paper and looked over at her with a smirk. "Oh yeah."

She groaned. "You too?"

"Do you have any red ones?"

"She does," Aidan affirmed. Shockingly, the two guys looked at each other with raised brows and nodded.

"Oh yeah," Zack said. "Red stilettos tonight. And nothing else."

Her entire body tightened with a little flip low in her belly. "Um. What?"

Zack's grin was evil as he folded the paper up. "Got things planned for tonight. But you go have lunch with your girls." He looked at Aidan. "What are you doing today?"

Aidan shrugged. "I could do some work."

Maddie's mind was buzzing with the thought of what Zack had planned for tonight. Sweet Jesus.

"I'm going to the Apple Store," Zack said. "I got my camera, but I need a computer. A new Mac. And a phone. Come with me."

"Okay. Sure. I like the Apple store."

"If you come home with another computer, you have to give one of your others away." Maddie smirked.

Zack burst out laughing and a reluctant smile tugged Aidan's lips. "Oh sweetheart. That is not the same as shoes."

"Sure it is! How many computers do you need? You have a desktop, a laptop, two iPads, plus some other tablet and an e-reader."

"One's a regular iPad, the other's an iPad mini."

Zack laughed again. "Dude. Maybe you better stay away from the Apple Store."

"No. I need a new case for my phone."

Maddie grinned. "I can see you two doing some damage there."

"Not as much as you at Nordstrom."

"Oh, I don't know. Well, okay. I could do some damage there. Maybe."

"You're probably jealous now, 'cause we're going to the Apple Store."

She knew Aidan was teasing. He knew her too well. "Jealous! Ha! I get queasy walking into that store. I'm totally intimidated because I don't know anything about that stuff. I'd much rather go to Nordstrom."

"I need some new underwear," Aidan said.

She planted her hands on her hips. "Then you can go to Nordstrom after the Apple Store."

He grimaced. "Yeah, maybe I'm okay for now."

She smiled and shook her head. Feeling lighter and surprisingly merry, she walked over to kiss Aidan's cheek, then did the same to Zack. They both looked at her with their mouths hanging open as she continued through the den and down the hall to the bedroom.

Whoa. Who was this woman? Living with two men. Having sex with two men. And how did she arrive in this bizarre world?

Well, Zack wasn't *living* with them. He was staying with them temporarily. And leaving—once he was healthy and fit to return to his bad-ass dangerous job taking pictures of people killing each other on the others side of the world. Which was supposedly in...two weeks.

Her jaunty mood disappeared and she gripped the marble counter in the bathroom. He couldn't leave. He couldn't do that to them again.

She rubbed a hand over her mouth. *Get a grip.* This was all weird and wonderful, but it was only temporary.

Tonight. He had plans for tonight. She was going to be tied in knots—haha, maybe that was what he had planned!—all day thinking about what he was going to do to them.

Them. Zack wasn't just taking charge of her. He was taking charge of *them*. She and Aidan both.

How was she supposed to pretend to her friends that nothing had changed?

⌒⧼⧽⌒

Aidan and Zack walked into the Apple store, big, bright and airy.

"Fucking awesome." Zack gazed around. They were immediately approached by a young man who inquired what they were looking for. "Lots of stuff," Zack answered. "First, a laptop."

"Great. Trevor will be able to help you with that."

Aidan grinned as they followed the young man toward another guy. They were quickly linked up with another sales associate and led to the laptops. On the way, Aidan got distracted by some accessories. Yeah. He wanted that magic mouse. Then he joined Zack as he studied a couple of computers.

"MacBook Pro," Aidan said. "That's what you need?"

"Yeah." Zack squinted. "My old one was a seventeen inch. Now I have to downsize to a fifteen inch."

"Is that bad?"

Zack shrugged. "It'll work. The retina display is pretty fierce."

The sales dude rattled off a bunch of specs about the different models, gigahertz and quad-core, turbo boost, flash storage and graphics. He asked Zack some questions about what he used the computer for, which Zack answered, sounding impressively knowledgeable.

"I dunno," Zack said moments later. "Speed's the only difference between these two. Six hundred bucks."

"Technology changes so fast. In six months there'll be something faster."

"True. But I don't want to buy a computer every six months. Ah what the hell, this two point three is good."

They looked at the mouse Aidan wanted and both bought one, then they drooled over a cool pen and touch tablet, then a smart pen that wowed them both into buying one. Just before they left, Aidan remember he actually needed a phone case. He found one he liked and they paid. Neither of them winced at the credit card charges and Aiden once again wondered about Zack's financial situation. It seemed he was okay for money.

Why was he concerned about that? Zack had said he earned good money and hadn't spent much over the years he'd been traveling. Aidan guessed it was because Zack had shown up with so little, having lost a lot of his belongings. And apparently he'd never had that much to start with.

As they walked out of the store a couple of hours after they'd entered, Aidan reflected on the excesses he and

Maddie had joked about earlier. Yeah, she had a truck-load of shoes and a huge closet full of clothes. He had more tech toys than he knew what to do with. They'd been successful and they bought what they wanted. And then Zack strolled back into their lives, having lost nearly everything he had and that apparently wasn't much.

Kind of made him stop and think.

It made him also feel...something for Zack. The guy had no home base, no roots. No place that he went back to on his down time to relax, nowhere that he'd furnished or decorated or spent time cleaning and repairing. Not that Aidan had been much into decorating. Maddie'd done most of that. She'd been all into it, picking out furniture and fabrics and paint colors.

Aidan felt a pinch of...what? It wasn't that he felt sorry for Zack. He just felt a need to keep Zack with them. To show him what it was like to have a home. Family. They were sort of family.

"You know," he said as they emerged onto Michigan Avenue, "you can come back and stay with us any time you want."

Zack's head jerked around and his narrow-eyed gaze focused on him. "You want me to leave?"

Aidan's gut seized. "No! That's not what I meant. Fuck." He shook his head. "Let's go get a beer."

Zack grimaced. "Not gonna turn down a beer."

"I think there's a place across Michigan on Huron. Come on."

Michigan was busy on this summer Saturday afternoon. They waited at lights as heavy traffic passed, then crossed and found the Irish pub Aidan remembered. Inside was dim and cool, with lots of dark wood, brass accents and green leather upholstery on chairs and stools. They found a small table in the window and ordered beers. "And some chicken wings," Zack added. He grinned at Aidan. "Still catching up."

"No problem."

"I'm buying."

Aidan opened his mouth to argue, met Zack's eyes and something in them made him snap his mouth closed. "Sure. Thanks."

The server moved away and Aidan played with the paper coaster on the table. "So. I didn't mean I want you to leave, when I said that."

"Okay."

"I meant, I want you to..." Fuck he didn't know what the hell he was saying. "I want you to think of our place as home."

Zack blinked at him, his face expressionless.

"You know...a home base. Somewhere you can come back to." He paused. "You are going to go back to your job, right? Traveling?"

"Yeah. I guess. I have to go see a doctor and get a medical clearance before they'll let me start back."

"You feeling okay? Is that going to be a problem?"

"I feel great. It won't be a problem. I had a couple of broken ribs, they're still tender, but everything else is fine. They wanted me to see a shrink." He shrugged, eyes on the table. "But I didn't think I needed to."

"Why'd they want that? Were you having problems?"

"I had some symptoms of PTSD after. They gave me some pills to help me sleep, and taught me some relaxation techniques. I was having nightmares at first, but since I've been back, things have been mostly good."

"It was bad?" Aidan asked quietly.

Zack swallowed.

The server appeared with their beers, setting them on the coasters. "Your wings will be up in a few minutes," she said with perky cheer.

They both gave her absent smiles and nods.

"It was bad," Zack agreed.

"Tell me."

14

Zack's stomach clenched and he curled his fingers around the cold glass of Guinness. He hadn't talked about it all since he'd been back.

"Tell me," Aidan said again in a low voice. "I've trusted you. Now trust me, that I can handle it."

This was so true. Aidan and Maddie had both given him that amazing gift of their trust. And the words came pouring out. "We were in a convoy bringing supplies to al-Qusair. We'd driven all night through the mountains with no lights on, so as not to attract attention from the regime. But when we got there, the city was nearly destroyed. Forces had been bombing it from the air. So we decided to turn around and go back to Damascus. Just as we were leaving the city we were stopped by a truck full of masked men. They made us get out and walk to a nearby house." He paused. "They beat us up."

"Who were you with?"

"It was just me and Simon. Simon Hickham, he's the chief foreign correspondent from the BBC."

"Right." Aidan nodded. "Heard that on the news."

"They told us they were police, but it didn't take long to figure out they were rebel forces. Fervent Islamists. They prayed five times a day and talked about jihad. When we got bombed, we knew for sure they were rebels."

"Bombed." Aidan's eyes went somber.

"Yeah. Good times." Zack lifted one corner of his mouth, then took a sip of beer. "We survived, obviously. After that we had to move to another house on the outskirts of town. Then that area was bombed and we moved again."

"Christ."

"They kept us like animals, sleeping on dirty straw mattresses, locked up in this tiny room with windows that didn't open. It was so fucking hot. They gave us their leftovers to eat. That didn't bother me so much; after a while I just lost my appetite. I tried to move as much as I could, doing isometrics so I wouldn't completely lose muscle tone. Simon and I talked about everything we could think of. Our favorite movies, favorite books, favorite restaurants, favorite cities…which famous person we'd most like to meet. We talked about how war changes you and how we could be better people when we got out. Never *if* we got out. We were always positive, even though I had my doubts on the inside.

"The worst thing was the humiliation. The lack of freedom. Having to ask to go take a piss. Asking for everything. And they'd say no. They liked seeing us beg."

He swallowed, memories coming back. He'd shut them off but they were still there, dark and terrifying. But sitting here with Aidan in this cheerful pub, the sun shining outside and Aidan watching him with concerned empathy, gave him the strength to keep talking. To get it all out. "One night Simon and I tried to escape. Our guard had fallen asleep and we got out of the house. We only got about five hundred feet when we were caught. They tied our hands behind our backs and locked us in a shed. We were valuable to them as merchandise, which was all that kept us alive. They'd beat us and kick us, but they couldn't kill us."

Aidan just nodded, the corners of his mouth turned down, eyebrows pulled together, listening intently.

"Twice they made it seem like they were going to kill me. Put me up against a wall and held a loaded pistol to my head. I stood there just...terrified. Fucking terrified. Ashamed of being so afraid to die. Angry. And so fucking helpless, this asshole standing there with a gun to my head, enjoying that I was so terrified. When we cried, everyone laughed at us because we were so weak." He swallowed. His voice had gone scratchy. He took another sip of beer, finishing the glass.

The pretty blonde server appeared with their wings, two small plates and a pile of paper napkins. "Another Guinness?"

Zack nodded. "Yeah. Please."

"Sure." When she moved away, Aidan said, "I don't even know what to say, Zack."

"I know." He nodded at his friend. "You don't have to say a thing." He smiled. "They tortured us by telling us we'd be free in a few days. It didn't happen. They'd laugh at us when we got all hopeful, then they'd add '*Inshallah.*'" He paused. "That means 'God willing.'"

"Assholes."

"Oh yeah. They were lying, but it was how they made it seem like they weren't. 'God willing,'" he added bitterly. He drew in a long breath and exhaled heavily. "I thought about a lot of things during that time. About what I was doing and whether it was worth it. I don't have any family like Simon, who was going insane thinking about how worried his wife and kids and his parents and two sisters were. I didn't have anyone who gave a shit."

"Yeah," Aidan said quietly. "You did."

Zack looked down. "I know that now," he admitted. "I thought about you and Maddie, but I had no idea what you two were doing." Once again, shame scraped at him. "I thought about how Syria had become so evil, how evil was triumphing over everything else. I thought about the greed and the hatred and the fanaticism. How they showed no mercy, standing next to us who'd been beaten and tied up and starved, praying to their own god...about what?" He shook his head. "Then one night we escaped again. Every step we took, I was sure they were coming after us, or I was going to take a bullet in my back. We ran into the dark, not even sure where we were going. Luckily, we made it across the border into Lebanon. And got help."

"Christ," Aidan said again. "I can't even imagine what it was like for you." He rubbed his mouth. Zack knew Aidan was struggling for control. The fact that he gave a shit made Zack's throat thicken and his chest ache. "All I can say is, I admire your strength. Mental strength, I mean, to endure that and survive."

"Didn't feel strong." He grimaced.

"You had to be." Aidan met his eyes. "You are."

He'd survived, but he didn't attribute it to anything heroic he'd done. More, he'd been allowed to live. Sometimes he'd wondered why. "Okay. Let's eat these wings."

He was done. He'd talked about it. And fuck him if it didn't make him feel better. He knew Aidan hadn't liked hearing it, but had willingly taken on the burden of those words, reliving that with him. That was a true friend.

Emotion rose up inside Zack, not dark and scary but bright and hopeful and...just as terrifying. He'd missed Aidan all these years. He'd tried to hate him for loving Maddie, avoided seeing them all that time. But he couldn't hate him. Fuck. He blinked and looked down at the table again, a chicken wing in his fingers. He didn't want to feel this shit. He was getting involved with them, with them both, something he'd dreamed of with ridiculous improbability. He couldn't let what was happening between them now affect him.

They were a couple and he was the third, the odd man

out. He was giving their relationship some kind of kinky rejuvenation. Then he'd leave and go back to war torn countries to take pictures and they would still be together. He'd given up on being a part of that love, or any love, a long time ago. How could someone who loved two people, two people of different sexes, ever find a lasting, normal, loving relationship?

They changed the subject and talked about less intense topics like how the Cubs were playing and their next game at Wrigley Field. "Wanna go?" Aidan asked him, wiping hot sauce off his fingers with a napkin. "I think there's a game every night this week. Or Saturday afternoon."

"That'd be great." He'd never been big into watching sports, but doing something so simple and all-American as watching a baseball game appealed to him.

"Oh, next Saturday we have some big fundraiser to go to. Something Maddie's involved in. So maybe we should go to the Thursday night game."

"Fine by me."

When they were ready to leave, Aidan pulled his phone out. "Let me text Maddie and see where she's at and what we're doing for dinner." He tapped in a message and waited for the reply while Zack handed over a credit card to pay the bill.

"She's already home," Aidan reported a moment later. "Says she picked up steaks for dinner."

A short time later, they walked into the condo. Sunshine filled the big space along with the loud beat of a Bruno Mars song. Maddie was in the kitchen bopping to the tune as she whisked something in a bowl.

"Hey, you're home." She eyed them and lifted her eyebrow. "Those are some big packages."

Zack and Aidan exchanged a glance and opened their mouths at the same time. "Thank you," Aidan said modestly with a glance down at his crotch. Zack had been about to say, "That's what she said" their minds working along the same dirty line. Pleasure and amusement swelled in Zack's chest.

Maddie laughed and shook her head. "What'd you buy?"

They took turns showing off purchases. Maddie had not bought any shoes. In fact, the only thing she'd bought was underwear for Aidan, despite her protest that he could buy it himself. "Just one of those days I didn't see anything I had to have." She smiled and shrugged.

"Thanks, sweetheart." Aidan kissed her forehead.

"I've got some work to do now," Zack said. "Getting this computer set up. Unless...need help with dinner?"

"No, no. Go on."

He headed to his room. He sat looking at his new computer for a few moments, thinking about what Aidan had said. Aidan wanted their home to be his home. Not permanently. A home base to come back to after he left. Because he was leaving.

His insides knotted up. Fuck he was a mess. He was starting to have feelings he didn't want to have. He didn't even want to think about how much he longed for this to be his real home. He knew he couldn't have that. He also recognized that the idea of leaving did not fill him with excitement or anticipation. More like...dread. But he could not get crazy ideas in his head about what was happening between him and Aidan and Maddie. He couldn't.

He went online to Adobe to download Photoshop, then the FTP software needed for transferring images to the agency, and got his email program installed.

He'd gone out last week and taken photos, just wandering around downtown snapping anything that captured his interest—architecture, flowers, a homeless vet sitting on the sidewalk, a little girl in a pink sundress eating a dripping ice cream cone. It felt random and pointless, and completely freeing. Now he looked at the images on his computer and smiled.

When he got his email program up and running on the new computer, he clicked through his inbox, pausing on one email. It was from one of his journalism profs at Northwestern, one he'd gotten close to. Brian Bridges had mentored him and encouraged him, and Zack had stayed in touch with him sporadically over the years. He'd heard from him after winning the Pulitzer and other awards. Now Professor Bridges was emailing to say he'd heard Zack was back in Chicago, expressing his great relief that he was okay, and saying he'd love to talk to him, inviting him to have lunch.

Zack made a face as he replied saying he'd love to have lunch. Professor Bridges had done a lot for him. It would be cool to see him again.

He had a number of other emails. He'd found himself more and more involved with Reporters Without Borders. He felt a need to do more, to try to have some kind of positive impact so he wasn't just sitting around on his ass waiting until he could go back to work. He'd also started putting together some of the things he'd written, almost like journal entries, over the years. He'd saved them to cloud storage luckily, and had been going through them, finding some common themes. He'd started thinking that maybe he could put them into a book along with some of his images. Would anyone be interested in that stuff? Who knew? Maybe he'd send some queries to literary agents and see if there was any interest.

The scent of grilled steak drifted to the bedroom and his stomach reminded him that he was hungry again. Those wings had been hours ago. He used the bathroom then headed out to the kitchen. Aidan stood out on their balcony in front of a stainless steel barbecue, a pair of big tongs in one hand and a beer in the other.

Maddie was in the kitchen, now dancing to One Republic, cutting up a head of Romaine lettuce and humming.

"You seem in a good mood today."

She looked up and smiled at him. She had such an amazing smile, wide and luminous and sweet. It reached inside him and warmed him. "I guess I am." She shrugged. "I just feel good." Her smile dimmed faintly. "How about you?"

Surprisingly, he did feel good. Having something to do helped. Having talked to Aidan helped. Being here with Maddie smiling and bopping to music helped. But feeling good made him nervous. Usually in his life that meant something shit was about to go down. "Yeah. I'm good. You look good too. Nice outfit."

She looked down at her loose T-shirt and black shorts.

"It'll look great with the red stilettos later."

Her eyes shot back up to his, her pretty lips parting and color washing into her cheeks. He gave her an evil grin.

She licked her lips. "Um. I think I need a glass of wine."

His smile widened. "Good idea. I'll have a beer." He moved to the fridge.

"Aidan's cooking the steaks. You should go tell him how you like yours done."

"Okay." He poured Maddie a glass of wine, grabbed a cold one and headed toward the balcony. He inspected the meat on the grill, requested medium, which was what Aidan and Maddie were both having. Maddie's steak was half the size of the other two, which made him smile.

He leaned on the railing, the sun low in the sky softening the view of city and lake. Maddie joined them and they shot the shit, talking about this and that until the steaks were done. Maddie'd brought out some veggies— mushrooms, peppers, zucchini—that Aidan also cooked on the grill. They carried the food inside. Maddie had set the table and there was a big Caesar salad and baked potatoes.

Zack dug in appreciatively. Putting weight on wasn't a problem the way Maddie cooked. "Damn, this is good," he said moments later. "What's on the steak?"

"It's a rub I made," Maddie said. "Mustard seed, peppercorns, coriander seed, garlic...and some other things."

"It's fantastic."

"Thank you."

They told Maddie they were going to a baseball game Thursday night, and she just nodded. "You can come if you want," Zack offered, since Aidan hadn't.

She shook her head. "No thanks. Baseball's not my thing. You guys go and have a good time."

"We were going to go to the Saturday game but I remembered we have that fundraiser Saturday night," Aidan said.

"Right." She tipped her head. "You should come to that with us, Zack."

"Uh..."

"It'll be fun. It's being held at Buckingham Fountain. It's the Starry Nights gala to raise money for Alzheimer's research."

"A good cause," he murmured, though he wasn't anxious to go to some big party. "I don't have anything formal to wear."

"Rent a tux," Aidan said. "You can do that next week."

It seemed rude to argue, so Zack nodded. "I guess I could do that."

After dinner, Zack and Aidan did the dishes and cleaned up the kitchen. When they walked into the den where Maddie had the TV on, Zack's eyes widened and he stopped short at seeing her lounging back on the couch, one red-stiletto-shod foot on the coffee table, the other leg crossed over top with a sexy red shoe dangling from her toes.

"Holy fuck," he croaked

Maddie gave them both a slow, sexy smile.

15

Maddie's heart hammered in her throat. She flattened her damp palms against the upholstery of the couch as Aidan and Zack stopped and stared at her.

She never wore high heels around home; that would be silly. So given their earlier conversation, both guys knew what this meant. She was ready for whatever Zack had planned for them for tonight. She was more than ready — she was eager.

She'd slipped into the bedroom while they were cleaning up, retrieved the shoes then waited for them. The shoes did make her feel sexy. It wasn't a bad look, even with the casual shorts — she'd seen lots of girls in clubs wearing shorts and heels.

Excitement had built inside her as she imagined what was going to happen. The not knowing was a big part of the thrill. Imagining Zack planning what he was going to do, how he was going to take charge and direct things…god, that made her pulse spike and her tummy flutter.

"Wow," Aidan said. "Those look good on you."

They both managed to move their feet again, moving toward her with hot eyes and intent expressions. Maddie's insides warmed with the feminine power flowing through her. It seemed they liked what they saw.

Aidan sat on her right, Zack on her left. Zack ran his hand down her bare calf, easing her heel back into the shoe. "Sexy shoes."

Aidan set his hand on her other thigh and kissed her cheek. "Oh yeah." He smelled so good, the aroma of his zesty shower gel and shampoo teasing her senses. On the other side, Zack's body heat warmed her as he caressed her leg. When his fingers lingered on her ankle, she shivered. Who knew her ankles were an erogenous zone?

They both started petting her, their hands everywhere—her shoulders, her arms, her breasts. Heat flowed through her veins and her limbs became heavy. Aidan twined his fingers through hers and kissed her mouth, a soft lingering kiss. When he moved back she turned to Zack. Their eyes met.

He'd fucked her but they hadn't kissed. Kissing was...intimate. Okay, that didn't make sense. How much more intimate could you get than having a man inside you? But, there was a difference. You could fuck someone without emotion. But kissing...kissing was an expression of emotion.

Not that their sex that night had been emotionless. Far from it. She'd been thrown into a tumult of emotion that night.

Now...she wanted to kiss him. Feelings for him swelled up inside her, right to the back of her throat. She liked him. A lot. She cared about him. A lot. She always had. Maybe more than she should have, considering how he'd left and how much that had hurt. And maybe she shouldn't care now, because he was going to leave again. But how could she *not* care? Maybe some people could shut it off. Like Zack seemed to do. Or maybe they just pretended. Maybe they even pretended to themselves they didn't care.

Heat built between her and Zack as they looked at each other. Her gaze drifted down to his mouth, then back up to his eyes, which went heavy-lidded in response. His fingers tightened on her bare thigh. Her breath trembled in her throat.

He leaned in closer and touched his lips to hers. "Maddie." Her name was a sigh against her lips. Her insides quivered and heated. She kissed him back, a soft joining of their lips. A groan rumbled in his throat and he tilted his head and kissed her again, this time deeper, harder…longer. She opened to him, touched her tongue to his. He tasted good. He felt good. His lips were fuller than Aidan's, his scruff of beard longer and silkier. His tongue stroked against hers then slid deeper into her mouth. She moaned and sank into the kiss.

When he drew back he looked at Aidan. "Your turn."

Aidan's eyes blazed with arousal. He turned Maddie's face to him with his fingers on her chin and kissed her again. Hard. Hot. His unique taste and feel was more familiar to her and she loved it, she loved him. She loved…oh god. She was going crazy.

She abandoned thought and turned herself over to sensation, which the two men delivered admirably, with hands and mouths and tongues. Hands slipped between her thighs to cup her throbbing pussy. Hands slid under her T-shirt. Fingertips lingered along the lace edge of her bra on the swell of her breasts. Mouths kissed her everywhere, lips and jaw and throat.

She was burning up, a crazy reckless hunger growing, a need so consuming and driving she couldn't resist it. She needed more. God, so much more.

"Bedroom." Zack growled out the order. "Now."

She blinked, dazed, but wanting to obey. She just wasn't sure if her legs were strong enough to stand. But no need to worry—Zack and Aidan both rose and tugged her hands, pulling her to standing. Still in the sexy heels, closer to their eye level, she smiled at them, feeling almost drunk. "Thanks."

They turned her and Zack gave her butt a tap as she walked. She focused on breathing, on putting one foot in front of the other, down the hall, into the bedroom.

She moved to the side of the bed and turned on the lamp, then faced them. The two men seemed to fill the space with their presence. Both tall, strong and muscled. Zack had gained weight and muscle. Aidan was as ripped as always, his manic workouts giving him a lean shredded look that she loved. And even though Zack was the one who always took control, Aidan's strength and presence was not diminished by Zack's air of command.

In the space of seconds, she reflected on that. She'd always admired Aidan's confidence and authority, the easy way he had of dealing with people, getting them to agree with him and do what he wanted. She knew he directed so many people in his work. His talent and hard work had led to a successful career and it didn't surprise her at all. He was a force. He made things happen and got things done. So when he let Zack tell him what to do—when it came to sex with her—it surprised her. It didn't diminish him in her eyes, though, because she suspected this was something he needed. She'd suspected it for a while. Something he needed that she couldn't give him. And she wanted him to have that.

"What do you want us to do?" she asked Zack, confirming him as the leader of this scene.

"Take off your clothes. Everything but the shoes."

She dipped her chin, then pulled her shirt over her head.

"You too." Zack nodded at Aidan.

She met Aidan's eyes. His lips twitched and they shared a look of amused excitement. He loved this as much as she did. Oh god. That was so incredible. Aidan yanked his shirt off forward over his head and dropped it.

Aidan moved to her as she lowered her shorts, hands at his own button and zipper. He kicked shorts and underwear off, and set his hands on her hips. Big and warm, his hands comforted her. His naked body right next to her had her bones turning to liquid. "Maddie," he murmured. "I love you so much."

"I love you too."

He reached behind her and unhooked her bra, then drew it down her arms and off. She was just shimmying out of her panties when Zack spoke. "You said you have a flogger."

Her eyes flicked to him, every nerve ending going alert. "Yes."

"Where is it?"

Aidan moved to the bedside table and pulled open the bottom drawer. "Here."

Rolling his lips in, Aidan glanced at Maddie, then handed the flogger to Zack.

Maddie swallowed.

"Have you used this?" Zack slapped the tails against his palm.

"Yes." She whispered the word and looked at Aidan. "We both tried it on each other."

"Did you like it?" He paused. "Wait. Let me clarify. Did you like using it? Or did you like having it used on you?"

She met Aidan's eyes. No point in anything but honesty. "I liked it used on me."

"Yeah." Aidan's voice came out rough. "Me too."

She didn't elaborate that she'd liked it even though she'd felt Aidan had been holding back.

"Perfect." The sadistic gleam in Zack's eyes made her pussy squeeze. Aidan's erection twitched. "Okay, here's what's gonna happen. Aidan, on the bed on your back. Maddie, you on top. Gonna flog you while Aidan's fucking you."

She drew in a long breath and went very still, other than a faint quivering. Holy shitballs. Getting fucked *and* flogged? It was...she gave her head a quick shake and her pussy squeezed. It was too much. Too hot. Too good to be true.

She followed Aidan onto the bed, wearing nothing but the red heels. She straddled his hips on her knees and looked down at him. He set his hands on her waist and their eyes met. Once again, humor sparked as the corners of his mouth lifted. Yeah, it was crazy, that they let Zack boss them around, making them do these dirty things. But obviously they both liked it. She sank her teeth briefly into her bottom lip to stop a big smile from breaking free, but she knew Aidan saw it. "You want this," he murmured.

"Yes." She both feared it and wanted it, anticipating the pain but also the pleasure it would bring. Only this time she'd be sharing it with Aidan. A shudder worked over her body.

Aidan was hard, his cock lying on his belly. She dropped her gaze there and curled her fingers around it. She stroked him, letting her thumb brush over the head. He groaned and thickened even more in her hand.

"That's it." Zack encouraged her. "Stroke his dick and get him really hard."

"He *is* really hard. And hot."

"Mmm." Zack's appreciative noise had her gaze turning to him. He watched her touch Aidan with a hungry look on his face. She'd sensed this before. He liked touching Aidan. Aidan had studied Zack's naked body too. There was a sexual tension between them she'd noticed and it made her go all hot and shivery inside.

"How about you?" Zack moved closer to the bed. "You wet, Maddie?"

She swallowed. She was wet. She'd been turned on when they started kissing and touching her on the couch. Now she was aching and her breasts were heavy and full. Zack's fingers slipped into her pussy from behind and stroked her. "Oh yeah. So wet. That's nice, baby." And her eyes went huge as Zack moved and offered his slick fingers to Aidan.

Their eyes met. Thick heat surrounded them. Aidan's cock twitched against her palm. "Open," Zack said softly. "Taste her."

Aidan opened his mouth, eyes fastened on Zack's face. Zack slid his fingers inside and Aidan's lips closed around them. His eyes fell shut too as he sucked Maddie's taste off Zack.

Zack's thumb lingered on Aidan's bottom lip when he withdrew. "Good?"

"Yeah." Aidan's throat worked.

"If I wasn't wet before, I am now." Both guys choked out surprised huffs of laughter. She cupped one breast with her free hand, gently squeezing it with the pressure she craved there. Her hips moved. "Need you inside me."

Aidan groaned as she rose up and moved above him so she could center the head of his cock at her opening. "Fuck yeah," he moaned. "Wet. So hot. Do it."

She bit her lip and eased herself lower onto him. His girth stretched her, filling her with delicious force. She planted her hands on his chest and watched his face as her body closed around him.

Zack moved from the side of the bed to the foot, behind her. She felt his presence like a vibrating energy field. "You have no idea how hot that looks. Watching his cock slide inside you like that. Watching your pretty pussy take him."

His velvet voice stroked over her like a touch. She shivered and her toes curled in her shoes. She looked over her shoulder at Zack. His eyes smoldered and he tapped the handle of the flogger against his other palm like he was dying to use it. Their eyes met with a jolt of electricity.

He stepped closer again, wrapped his fist in her hair and turned her face to his to kiss her. Their mouths met in a hard kiss that seared her senses. Aidan inside her. Zack's mouth on hers. A sharp forbidden thrill ran through her.

Zack released her hair, but kept his hand on her back.

With gentle force he pushed her down so she lay on top of Aidan. Her feet pressed against Aidan's thighs. Aidan curled one hand around the back of her neck and pulled her down to his mouth. She kissed him too, then buried her face in the side of his neck. Anticipation curled through her, dark and edgy.

Zack started teasing them, dragging the tails of the flogger over her back and her ass, down over Aidan's legs, making him shudder. She felt Zack linger on Aidan's inner thighs, then stroke down over her butt cheeks and lower. He had to be stroking Aidan's balls. His cock jerked in her pussy. *Oh yeah.*

The flogger traveled up her back then down. And then he pulled it away and she felt the air move as Zack twisted it. She squeezed her eyes closed, longing for a sharper touch spiking inside her. The first slap made her start, from the feel of it and the sound. It wasn't that hard, but she felt it, a flash of fire. He set a slow rhythm.

Each slap of the tails on her ass intensified. At first her body stiffened, but as the fire turned into a glow that spread through her body, she relaxed into it. Near her ear, Aidan murmured, "Holy shit. He really knows what he's doing."

Distantly she recognized Aidan must be watching Zack wield the flogger. It would be something to see. But at that moment, all she wanted was more of that sensation.

The pressure intensified, vibrating to her core. She sank into it, letting herself go.

"Fuck her," Zack ordered Aidan. Aidan bent his legs and planted his feet into the mattress, lifting his hips to fuck her.

"Christ, Maddie, you're like liquid around me. Never felt you so wet. This really does it for you, doesn't it?"

He didn't know that she couldn't speak, couldn't form words, barely registered his question. All she could do was whimper. Sensations flowed together, the heat on her skin, the pressure of Aidan inside her. It was drugging her, making her high.

She wanted to come. So bad. She ached for it, burned for it. It wasn't quite there...and Zack was slowing the slaps of the flogger on her. She whimpered another protest.

"Yeah." Zack paused and laid a palm on her ass. "Sweet. Okay, Maddie?"

She whimpered a protest. "Don't stop," she managed to say.

Zack chuckled, his hand caressing her. "You want to come, baby?"

"Mmhmm. Please." Her voice had gone high. "Oh please." She craved it, shook with need for it.

"You need to be patient, little girl." He stroked down the backs of her thighs, then the sensitive undercurve of her buttocks, and a shiver worked over her body.

He was torturing her. She ached with enormous need, pulsing around Aidan's thick shaft inside her. Aidan whispered words of encouragement to her.

"Please," she begged.

"Okay." And he resumed his strikes, slow at first then picking up speed and force. It was amazing. She floated, weightless and glowing, letting her mind drift. Sensation curled inside her, a delicate twist that built. And built. Higher. God. Oh *god*, it kept going up and up and...and then she got scared. The intensity of it all scared her. She was so high, panic rushed over her.

Her head reared back and she pushed up on her arms. "Stop," she tried to say. It came out a mumble. "Stop, please. I mean...*red.*"

The flogger immediately stopped and Aidan went still. Then she was flipped onto her back on the bed and Aidan lunged at Zack.

Aidan grabbed the flogger. "Stop it," he snarled.

"I did stop," Zack said calmly, relinquishing the tool. "What the fuck?"

"She used the safe word. You were hurting her." Aidan shoved at Zack's chest. Zack stumbled back a step, frowning. "Jesus Christ."

Maddie blinked, dazed, knowing she needed to stop what was happening but physically unable to move and barely able to form coherent thoughts.

16

Aidan went to go after Zack again, ready to punch him in the face, but Zack stepped aside, closer to the bed. "For fuck's sake, she needs to be looked after. You can't just stop and leave her there."

Guilt slammed into Aidan and he squeezed his eyes shut briefly. Yeah. Maddie. She was the one hurting. He'd punch Zack's lights out later.

He climbed back into bed and pulled Maddie into his arms. He stroked her hair. "Okay, sweetheart?"

Zack watched with eyes full of concern, crouching on the bed on the other side of her, hands on his thighs.

She nodded against Aidan's chest, small and soft and trembling a little in his arms. Christ. Christ, what were they doing? Playing at this crazy kinky shit, and now she was hurt.

"I'm okay."

"Take a deep breath," Zack said quietly. "You're okay, baby. We're here for you." He reached out and set his hand on her bare leg. His calm presence subdued Aidan's jittery nerves as much as Maddie's. Aidan sucked in a breath.

"Talk to us," Zack continued. "Tell us what was going on for you. I thought it was all good."

"It was. It was good. So good." Then she laughed. *What the fuck?* "I got scared. I was so high."

Aidan squeezed her, relief coursing through him. She was okay. She was giggling.

"I'm sorry," she continued. "I just…got scared."

"It's okay." Zack smoothed a hand down her leg. "I get it. It *is* scary. You were doing great, babe. So great."

"I was." She flashed a little smile at both of them. Aidan's heart squeezed. Fuck, he didn't know what to think. "I can do it. I know I can do more."

"We'll try some other time," Zack said.

"No. I want more. I want it now."

"We'll wait a bit. Maybe I went too far, too fast. You got hypersensitive. It can be stressful for you, mentally and physically."

She nodded.

"I thought you were hurt," Aidan said.

"Well, yeah. But…I liked it." She tipped her head and met his eyes. "I'm okay, Aidan. Really. Please don't blame Zack."

"Maybe I need to flog Aidan," Zack said. "So he knows what you were feeling."

The air in the room went static. Aidan looked at Zack and saw the teasing glint in his eyes. He shook his head slowly, reluctant to admit his own curiosity about how that flogger would feel in the hands of someone experienced and knowledgeable. Someone with that edge of sadism that Maddie sure as hell didn't have.

"Erotic pain is different than just regular pain," Zack said to him. "It's a rush. The endorphins made her feel like she was high. It adds another layer to the pleasure she was getting from you fucking her. It's different than just hitting her."

"I get that."

"It might have looked like I was hitting her hard, but it wasn't that hard."

"You said he knew what he was doing," Maddie reminded Aidan.

Aidan looked down at her and nodded. When he'd seen Zack start to flip the flogger around he'd been amazed. The way his wrist flexed, the way he swung in that smooth figure-eight shape, bringing the tails down on Maddie's ass with perfect control, had impressed him. It was nothing like his own feeble attempts. It was powerful and graceful and erotic.

He wasn't jealous. He admired that. Did he want Zack to use the flogger on him? His breath stuck in his throat. When Maddie'd done it, it somehow hadn't been as exciting as he'd hoped. Maybe… "He does," he affirmed in a low voice. He sucked in a breath and let it out. "I could see he knew what he was doing. It was…amazing, actually. I just…lost it when I thought you were hurt."

"I'm sorry." Her big blue eyes stared at him, then she turned to Zack. "I'm sorry I ruined it."

"You didn't ruin it," Zack soothed, his hand caressing her leg. "It happens. I should have known it was too much, too soon. You don't know yourself yet. It takes time." He lifted one shoulder. "It takes a lifetime. There's always more to learn."

Zack's experience and composure continued to reassure Aidan. He said, voice gruff, "Sorry, man. I overreacted."

Zack met his eyes steadily. "We're all learning. Right?"

Aidan nodded.

"I'll get you some water." Zack moved off the bed. Aidan cuddled Maddie closer, feeling protective of her.

"I really am okay, honey." She touched his face. "It was amazing. So good."

Zack came back and handed her a glass. She drank some and handed it to Aidan, who shook his head. Zack took the glass and also drank.

"Okay, I'm ready," she announced.

Zack chuckled. "Babe. Maybe we really should stop for tonight."

She bit her lip. "But…"

"What?" Aidan smoothed hair back from her face.

"I thought we were going to…I've always wanted…"

Her cheeks flushed a pretty pink and Aidan lifted his eyebrows.

Her gaze darted all around the room, then dropped to her hands. "Double penetration," she whispered.

Whoa. Aidan's eyes snapped up to meet Zack's. One corner of his mouth lifted. "Maddie," he said softly. "You kinky girl, you."

She lifted her head, smiling too. "It's a fantasy."

Aidan's lungs seized. She'd fantasized about that? Jesus. "You never told me that."

"I know. I think there are a lot of things we never told each other." Again, their eyes met.

Yeah. This time with Zack was stripping them bare, revealing all the things they'd kept hidden…from each other and maybe even from themselves. There were things he wanted too that he'd never been completely honest about. He nodded slowly. "Yeah. So. Thanks for being brave enough to share that."

Her pretty smile deepened. "I'm getting very brave these days."

Fuck, she was, and it was beautiful.

"And so are you." She laid her palm on his cheek.

Yeah. Letting Zack take control and order him around made him feel more naked and vulnerable than he ever had in his life. The fact that Maddie recognized that and saw inside him and still loved him anyway…Christ. His heart rose into his throat and he crushed her to him in a brief, powerful hug.

"How was it for you?" she asked him softly. "Inside me while Zack flogged me."

"It was…" He choked on the words and swallowed. "It

was fucking amazing. Feeling how you reacted. Your pussy squeezing me more and more, every time... Giving that to you. Both of us. Fuck, Maddie."

"Thank you. So. Can we go on?"

She looked at Zack. Looking to him to take control.

"Yeah," he said. "Good girl for using the safe word if you were scared. Always do that if you need to, yeah? If you want to slow down, yellow."

"I got it." She gave a nod.

"Let's give our girl what she wants," Zack said to Aidan

The idea of both of them fucking her turned him on painfully, but more than that, he wanted to fulfill her fantasy. Once more, he wanted to give her everything he could. "Yeah."

Relief filtered through Zack. Okay. He hadn't fucked it up. Maddie was fine, and Aidan got it. It was all good.

For a few minutes there he'd been terrified. Had he misread Maddie's signals? Was Aidan ready to call this whole crazy thing off? And was he about to get beaten to a bloody pulp by his best friend?

He wasn't so worried about that. He could defend himself, even if he probably wasn't as fit as Aidan. The guy's muscles had muscles. Zack had been working out since he'd been back, but Aidan put some serious effort into his body. Which Zack appreciated. Looking at him. Touching him. *Not* getting the shit beat out of him.

Anyway. Looked like they were all good. He'd have to watch Maddie closely and definitely take things slower. Like he'd said, she was learning about herself. So was Aidan. And so was he.

Yeah, he was learning things about himself too. He swallowed hard. The fact that he'd been so terrified about fucking things up told him he was starting to care way too much. If he ever really hurt Maddie...Christ, he'd rather have his balls cut off. And if he lost Aidan's friendship because of this...fuck, he was afraid to go there, because how in the *hell* did he think this was ever going to end well? Maybe he hadn't screwed up everything up today, but that day was going to come, as sure as shit.

"Let's lose the shoes." He slipped them off Maddie's feet. They were sexy, but those spiky heels might be dangerous considering what they were about to do. He dropped them on the rug and slid down onto the bed next to Maddie. "Lie down." She and Aidan followed him. With Maddie between them, he and Aidan picked up where they'd left off out on the couch, making Maddie feel good with kisses and caresses. "Gonna go slow," he murmured against the inside of her elbow. "Take you up real slow, baby."

Her sigh burned through him to his soul. Hunger rose in him, the hunger to dominate and the hunger to fuck her. He and Aidan having her at the same time...Jesus. When she'd confessed that juicy tidbit, his dick had nearly exploded. He'd done some crazy shit, including a couple of threesomes, but that had been two women. So this was going to be new for him too.

He liked that. He was the one showing these two the way, and loving every minute of it, but he liked that they were going to give him a unique experience.

He kissed his way down her arm, opened his mouth on the inside of her wrist and gently sucked, then kissed her palm. Aidan was sucking one nipple and Zack shifted to join him, taking the other nipple into his mouth. Maddie's hands came up to their heads, holding them there as she blissed out. She tasted sweet and her nipple hardened against his tongue, perfect and delicious. He sucked and used his teeth, then licked over it.

Aidan's face was right there, so close to him. Zack saw

every dark whisker, the chiseled shape of Aidan's nose, the small white scar near his eyebrow he still had from the night they'd rescued Maddie from that asshole.

Aidan's eyes opened slowly and met his. So close. If Aidan couldn't read the longing in his eyes, he was blind. But maybe he wasn't ready for that yet.

Zack let his eyelids drift shut and suckled more at Maddie's sweet breast. Her little gasps and mews of pleasure urged him on. But...slow.

He slipped a hand between her thighs. Wet. Still. Or again. She moved her legs restlessly, opening to him. He stroked through soft lips and silky heat. Need whipped through him, hot and urgent. His dick was on fire and his balls ached.

"You're really wet, baby," he murmured. "But we're gonna need lube. You got any?" He pushed away from them.

"Bottom drawer." Aidan waved a hand.

"How about a condom?"

Aidan snorted. "Fuck no. Haven't used them in years."

"Must be nice," Zack muttered. He shook his head. He moved to the bedside table and opened the drawer where Aidan had found the flogger. His eyes searched and found the bottle of personal lubricant. But his gaze also fell on something else—a strap-on dildo.

Holy fuck.

He shut the drawer without saying anything. He pushed thoughts of Maddie and Aidan using that out of his head. He needed to focus. He tossed the bottle onto the bed near him. "Be right back. Got condoms in my room."

He strode out, grabbed two condoms, and sprinted back. The condoms landed on the bed beside the bottle of lube. "Okay. Gonna get that flogger now."

"Mmm." Maddie smiled and rolled onto Aidan, stretching out over him. She kissed his mouth and he adjusted their positions, pushing his cock deep into her pussy, hands parting her thighs, then sliding up her back and into her hair.

Zack fought for control, his blood running hot through his veins. He tested the flogger then flicked it toward Maddie's sweet cheeks. Her small yelp pleased him.

He continued, watching her carefully, observing her reactions to each slap as she relaxed into it. Just like last time. He had to trust his instincts, and his experience. Aidan watched him, as he had last time as well, eyes burning hot. Aidan's compliment to his skill had surprised him and warmed him, especially after what had happened.

He took in the gorgeous sight of Aidan's thick cock, shiny with Maddie's arousal, powering up into her pussy. He studied Aidan's balls, full and round and succulent. Scorching need burned across his skin.

He dropped the flogger to the floor and knelt on the bed behind Maddie. "Baby. How are you doing?"

"So good."

He palmed her ass, the skin nice and hot and pink, then bent to press his lips there. He opened his mouth in a hungry kiss, groping around blindly for the condoms he'd tossed there earlier. His hand closed around a small packet. He ripped it open, rolled it on, then grabbed the lube. "Okay, baby. You've done this before?"

"A long time ago."

Zack blinked, and glanced at Aidan's frowning face. "Okay, we'll go slow and easy. Like everything." He kissed the hollow just above her ass, then strung kisses up her spine. On his knees, he squeezed lube into his hand. Using slow, sure strokes, he massaged it over her skin, dipping between her ass cheeks, lingering on the tight pucker. He swallowed.

No worries about whether he was hard enough. More lube had his dick slicked up. Aidan's cock and balls right there tempted him to let his hands wander. Not tonight. But they *were* going there.

He played as long as he could without driving all three of them insane, breaching her with his thumb, petting her pussy, brushing against Aidan's cock. He saw the set of Aidan's jaw and knew he was trying not to come. Maddie was panting and squirming and whispering, "Please, oh please."

Finally he planted one foot into the mattress with a bent leg, edged up close to Maddie's pretty ass and found that tight entrance. Christ. Oh unholy mother of fuck. He gritted his teeth as he pushed into her.

"Relax, babe," he panted. Then he gave her a swat. And another. That worked. She opened around him. He pushed in deeper. She cried out, her head lifting, fingers curling into the sheets, but she didn't use the word that would stop him. So he didn't stop.

Aidan's hands gripped her ass, pulling it toward him, moving her on his cock. Maddie pushed up onto straight arms to look at him over her shoulder, small cries falling from her lips. Her hair fell all around her face, and holy fuck she was sexy. Then she fell back down onto Aidan.

Fuck, wasn't going to take long. Fiery, tortuous ecstasy rolled through him. Pleasure licked over every nerve ending like flames, and his heart pounded. Every muscle in his body tightened. He knew Aidan was on the edge too. Just had to make sure Maddie...Maddie had to come first, she had to be coming out of her skin.

Aidan's feet pushed into the bed and his hips powered up, fucking her in short, fast strokes and Zack did the same, using care not to be too rough, matching Aidan's rhythm. Her ass shook with every impact. Damn that was hot.

He bent over her back. Sweat dripped from his forehead. "Baby. What do you need?"

She gave her head a violent shake. "Just...just...this...oh *god!*" Her words became a long wail, and she contracted around him in a series of pulses that yanked him over with her. Fire raced up his spine and shorted out his brain. His cock jerked inside Maddie, wrenching pulses that seemed to come from so deep inside him. He was making animal noises that he could barely hear over the mad beating of his heart and his harsh panting breaths.

When every last drop had been wrung out of him, he dropped his head down. "Holy shit. Holy fucking shit."

He stroked a hand down Maddie's back, a bit taken aback to see his fingers trembling. Then hands gripped the backs of his thighs. Big, strong, male hands. Aidan, reaching around Maddie to touch him. Pressure burned in Zack's chest as he savored that touch. Aidan's hands squeezed him, then released. That meant something. Zack wasn't sure what, but it definitely made what had just happened about the three of them coming together—not just two guys fucking Maddie. It had meant something to Aidan too.

"Okay," Zack mumbled. He had to take care of her. He pulled out, careful to hold the condom in place with the tight grip of her body. He stumbled across to their bathroom, ditched the rubber and washed up as fast as he could. He wanted to get back to her and make sure she was okay.

She and Aidan had rolled to their sides, eyes closed, holding each other, their chests still rising and falling quickly. He admired them for a moment, all that warm glowing skin, Maddie's pale gold, Aidan's darker. Then he joined them, sliding onto the bed behind Maddie. He stroked her hair, her shoulder, her arm. "Okay, baby?"

She nodded but he felt the fine trembling of her body. "Under the covers," he said abruptly. "Sorry, but we gotta move."

He let Aidan roll her away from him while he yanked the duvet and top sheet down, and together they lifted her beneath it. Without question, he and Aidan joined her there, using the heat from their bodies to warm her, their hands to soothe her. "We're here. You're okay."

"Y-yes. I'm okay. I'm really okay. I just get all shaky and shivery and…kinda feel like crying. But I'm not sad."

"That's normal." Zack pressed his lips to her shoulder. "Totally normal. When you go up you have to come back down."

"I learned that in science class," she mumbled. "The law of gravity."

Aidan chuckled and Zack smiled. "Yeah, sort of like that." He kissed her again, then swallowed a sigh. "Guess I'll head to my room."

"No." She turned to him, eyes wide. "Don't go."

His heart slammed against his ribs and he stared at her.

"Stay here. Sleep here. I need you both."

An ache of intense longing swelled inside him, pushing at his skin, so fierce it stole his breath. That alone was enough reason not to do it, never mind the other hundred reasons it was a bad idea. But he nodded at Maddie and relaxed into the bed. "Okay."

17

"Jesus." Zack tugged at the collar of his shirt just behind his tie. "I've never worn a tux in my life."

"Seriously?" Maddie admired him, brushing a hand over one shoulder. "You look amazing."

He grimaced. "Thanks."

He did look amazing. His bad-boy messy dark curls hanging in his eyes and his heavy dark beard stubble juxtaposed the traditional, formal tuxedo. The fine black wool with a white shirt beneath gave a layer of polish to his rough, raw sexiness.

"It fits you perfectly."

"Yeah, the guy at the tux place said I have perfect proportions so it was easy."

She could see that. His shoulders were just the right width, his waist and hips narrow. Perfect.

"Don't know what the hell I'm doing, going to a shindig like this," he muttered. "This is so far away from where I was six months ago. Or ever."

She tipped her head. "I know. Are you getting anxious to get back to that?" Only one more week and he was supposed to be returning to work.

He shrugged, avoiding her eyes. Her body tightened. Did he want to leave?

"I've been keeping busy."

Aidan appeared then, fastening a cufflink on his own white dress shirt. He too looked gorgeous. His short dark hair and freshly-shaved face gave him a more clean-cut appearance than Zack. His powerful body radiated strength and confidence.

"You look hot too." Maddie moved to help with the cufflink. "I'm a lucky girl tonight."

Not just tonight. These two guys had been rocking her world for the last couple of weeks. She'd never felt so at peace with herself and her life, a blissful feeling of being desired, protected and cherished.

Yeah, she still had problems at work to deal with, from an annoying coworker to a full blown PR crisis when one of their high-profile spokespersons had been arrested for DUI last week. But she felt more competent to deal with things, stronger and calmer. She couldn't explain it, but there it was.

Now she was going to an elegant party with two stunning men, both dressed equally stylishly but one with a wicked smile and sadistic glint in his eye that made her want to do whatever he bade her, the other a polished professional who wielded power in a different way.

"You look gorgeous too, sweetheart." Aidan's gaze swept over her. "Let's see the shoes."

She'd worn this dress before—a strapless black dress, the skirt layers of chiffon that wrapped around her bare legs—but she really liked it. She posed with one foot extended, showing off the sexy, strappy heels and laughed when both guys groaned. "Glad you approve." She fluttered her eyelashes. "Will I be wearing these in bed tonight?"

God, where did this bold flirting come from? She supposed the confidence came from knowing she had two men lusting for her.

"Hmm." Zack rubbed his chin. "Yeah." That dirty smile

curled his lips and his eyes went back and forth between her and Aidan, studying them up and down. "Yeah, definitely."

Heat curled low inside Maddie and her breath quickened. "Can't wait."

"Gonna be thinking about that all night now," Aidan muttered.

Zack grinned. "Me too. It'll add some spice to the party."

Aidan had arranged a car service to pick them up and take them to the event. Luckily the weather cooperated, since it was being held outdoors. Buckingham Fountain was illuminated, the city skyline creating a spectacular backdrop behind it. The dark rectangles of office buildings were silhouetted against the sky, glittering with gold lights. Above them the sky was a deepening blue with wisps of clouds tinted deeper blue. White lights glittered in shrubbery around the pavilion. The music of a jazz quartet at one end of the pavilion drifted on the evening air—saxophone, trumpet, bass and drums overlaid with the hum of conversation.

"Wow," Zack muttered. "Uh...how much was the ticket for this hoedown?"

Maddie choked on a laugh. "A lot. But don't worry about it."

"Jesus. I have money. It's for a good cause. Holy crap...is that Vince Vaughn?"

Maddie followed his gaze. "Yes! He came! I'm so glad."

"You know him?"

"No! But I knew he was a maybe, and we kept telling people he was probably going to be here to get them to buy tickets. Awesome!"

People gathered in groups talking, drinking champagne and eating hors d'oeuvres being served by servers in white shirts and black pants. Maddie moved easily from group to group, greeting people, making introductions and small talk. Aidan knew some of the people but Zack knew none, so she introduced him. "This is our friend, Zack Donovan. Zack's a Pulitzer-prize-winning photojournalist."

He scowled at her.

She bugged her eyes out at him and tipped her head. What? What was the frown about? That was who he was.

That was a conversation starter for sure. People were interested to know what he'd won the Pulitzer for, where he'd been, segueing into a discussion of American foreign policy. When Zack mentioned that he'd been in Syria, someone clued in that he was the journalist who'd been missing for months. Zack deflected most questions about his ordeal, preferring to talk about the humanitarian crisis there and the difficulty in providing aid to the people. He talked about the suffering, the growing evidence of war crimes and human rights violations. When someone asked his opinion of military pressure, Maddie listened with pride and admiration as he explained why a political solution had to be the answer rather than more violence. But then he shifted the conversation to something uplifting and positive.

She watched as people listened with fascination to what he had to say, hoping that he was okay with talking about these things. He still hadn't said a lot about his experiences there. Aidan had told her that Zack had talked to him about his time in captivity and she'd been glad that Zack had finally opened up about it.

But he had good things to talk about too, even making people laugh at some of his stories.

As the conversation moved on to other topics she and Aidan and Zack came together. "I hope you don't mind talking about your experiences." She lifted her champagne glass to her lips, eyes fixed on Zack.

"I actually enjoyed it." He hitched one shoulder. "It was okay."

The next people they ran into were a prominent

property developer and his wife whom Aidan knew. They paused to make some small talk with them, conversation naturally turning to Aidan's biggest project. And once again Maddie found herself watching and listening with pride.

She had to disappear for a while to take care of some logistical issues. Fortunately they had a great team of volunteers in place to keep the event running smoothly, but she liked to check in. She stopped to talk to the chairman of the board of the Chicago Chapter of the Alzheimer's Foundation and his wife. Dennis Sahak was also the CEO of Illinois Financial. She'd met him and his wife a few times at various fundraising events. He greeted her warmly and introduced her to others there, the Vice Chair of the board who was an attorney, along with her husband, and a director who was a partner of a major accounting firm. She chatted with them, then as she tried to find her way back to Aidan and Zack she got waylaid by some other acquaintances. She spent a few minutes there, laughingly encouraging everyone to spend lots of money on the silent auction. "There are some fabulous prizes," she finished. "So nice to see you all here!"

She found Aidan and Zack talking to their friends Ethan and Chelsea who'd just arrived. She greeted them both with hugs and smiles. They spent a while talking to them.

"How are your feet holding up in those sexy shoes?" Zack asked Maddie at one point. "They're hot, but those heels are high."

She extended a foot to look at it. "Yeah, my feet'll be killing me by the time we're done here."

"Damn." He winked at her.

She smiled back at him then became aware of Chelsea looking at them with curiosity. Oops. Maddie bit her lip, realizing how flirtatious that had sounded.

This raised a whole other potential problem – keeping

what was going on between them private. Which meant they had to act differently around other people.

Chelsea and Ethan were their best friends—well, other than Zack. But they would never in a million years understand what was going on. Would they? No.

But this was a temporary thing because Zack was leaving in a week. Maddie pushed away the wave of sadness that thought brought on and pasted on a party smile.

Hours passed in a whirl of glittery lights and sparkling champagne, speeches and prize drawings, chit chat and laughter. Much later, when she and Aidan and Zack finally connected again, they moved away from the crowd, into the shadows of the neatly carved hedges. Maddie said, "You two are giving me an inferiority complex."

They both lifted eyebrows at her and exchanged baffled masculine glances. "Huh?" Zack said.

"What do you mean, sweetheart?"

She smiled. "You're both so frickin' accomplished. You with your big project and mega deals. Zack with his Pulitzer, sounding so smart about things happening on the other side of the world. Important things."

"Babe," Zack said. "You sounded pretty knowledgeable too, when you started talking about how complicated and dangerous things have become for journalists in Syria."

She shrugged. "I learned a lot when you were missing."

"Yeah. I guess you did." His voice softened into a sexy rasp. "Also, been watching you flit around all night. You're amazing. The way you talk to people...make them laugh...plus you're gorgeous and sexy."

She smiled. "Aw. Thank you. I'm having fun. And it actually seems like you might be too, even though you didn't want to come."

He gave a crooked grin. "I guess I'm having an okay time. Black tie and champagne's not my usual comfort zone. More like boots and cargo pants and beer."

"It's not like we do this every weekend. Maybe that's why you guys look so especially sexy in those tuxes. Because it doesn't happen very often."

"Good thing," Aidan said.

"She's right." Zack gave Aidan a wolfish look. "You look fucking hot in that tux."

Maddie's eyes popped open and her blood sizzled. Immediately the air around them went electric. To her surprise, Aidan gave Zack a wry smile. "Asshole."

"I gave you a compliment!"

"You're pulling my chain."

"Ha. Pull this." Zack dipped his chin.

Maddie watched this with heated fascination.

Zack tipped his head with the arrogant air of a man who knew he had both of them at his command. "Can't wait to see you two together," he continued in that low tone. "Fucking in those oh-so-classy clothes."

Her tummy flip flopped. She blinked at him. "Oh," she breathed.

"Maybe we should start now." Zack bent his head closer to her. "No one's around. Aidan could unzip his pants, pull out his cock and pull up that pretty skirt."

Her heart exploded into a rapid percussion. Her eyes did a sweep of the area to see who was close enough to hear them. Luckily no one, but her pulse raced. She remembered Chelsea noticing the sexual tension between them earlier. If she saw this...

"What are you wearing under that sexy dress?" he asked.

She rolled her lips in and then burst out laughing. He lifted an eyebrow and one corner of his mouth quirked. She glanced at Aidan, whose mouth was still open and his eyes dark. "No way in hell are you seeing what's under this dress." She tried to stifle more giggles. "I'm wearing Spanx."

"Ah. Dude." Aidan shook his head. "She won't let me

see her wearing them. Probably for the best. I've seen them in the laundry."

"They are the unsexiest undergarments in the world." She gave another snort of laughter.

Zack grinned. "I'll take your word for it. You can get rid them before we commence."

Her skin went hot again. "Um. Okay." Holy hell. Commence what? Now she shivered. "But as for what else I'm wearing under the dress…nothing."

Zack smiled and brushed his hand over her breast in a casual gesture. "Nice."

"Maybe it's time to go," she breathed.

"You know what I like about you?" Zack leaned in so his mouth was right at her ear. "How much you love sex."

Her pussy squeezed. She captured her bottom lip in her teeth and looked up at him through her eyelashes, then over at Aidan. His smile went wicked. "She does." Aidan also moved closer. Now she was sandwiched between the two men. A warm slide of lust pooled low in her belly.

"I love sex with *you*," she clarified. "Both of you." She met Aidan's eyes and the understanding there. But then despair trickled through her like ice water. What would happen when Zack left?

Not that things had been bad between her and Aidan. They loved each other. They'd been trying. Only now they knew what had been missing, it was hard to imagine going back.

She took a deep breath. She didn't want to ruin this magical evening with worry. Tonight adrenaline bubbled through her veins like champagne and now her insides were twisting and heating with excitement.

"If you're done here, let's go," Zack ordered.

"Okay."

Aidan called the car service to pull up on Columbus. She excused herself to use the ladies' room before they left. In the small stall, she hesitated, then wriggled out of her

Spanx. She rolled them up as small as she could and stuffed them in her purse. Couldn't get it closed. Oh well. She held it in both hands as they made their way across the pavilion and past the glowing, splashing fountain. The two guys held her arms to help her so her spiky heels wouldn't catch in the bricks. Then she was in the backseat of the town car, once again a hot guy on either side of her.

A big, warm hand landed on each of her knees. She swallowed, looking down at them. Her world narrowed to the interior of the car, lights and shadows sliding by beyond the windows. There in the warm dark interior, her skin tingled and she felt breathless and edgy. Aware.

They both caressed her bare thighs, sliding up under her dress. How far would they go? They couldn't do much with the driver right there in front of them. Heat flared in her along with an aching hunger.

"Sweetheart," Aidan whispered. "Where's your underwear?"

She smiled. "What underwear?"

Both guys jolted and hissed in a breath. Exploring fingers moved higher. And higher. Aidan's brushed over her pubic curls. "Damn," he muttered. "Were you bullshitting us earlier about what you were wearing?"

"No."

"Maddie, you dirty girl you," Zack murmured.

She jerked her head toward the driver. They'd kept their voices hushed but still... Although it was a little exciting that someone *could* overhear them...know what they were doing... Dear god, she *was* a dirty girl. Her smile deepened.

They feathered kisses over her neck, her throat, her shoulders, bare in her strapless dress. Zack ran his tongue up the side of her neck to her ear and caught her lobe in his lips. She let her head fall back against the leather upholstery as they touched her legs, parting them so they could dip into her wet folds. If the driver could see them in the mirror, two guys making out with her...her veins heated at the thought, her pulse beating in a mad frenzy.

"Can't wait to get you home," Zack whispered.

Home. The word registered then floated away.

"Both of you," Zack added.

The air inside the car swelled with vibrating heat.

She got braver and reached for their laps. Hey. Two — no, make that three — could play this game. Her fingers brushed over hardness beneath the fine wool of their tuxedo trousers. She curled her fingers over the thick rods and gave a gentle squeeze that had both men sucking wind. "Mmm. Nice. I can't wait either."

18

Aidan was throbbing everywhere as they entered the condo. His body had been humming with sexual tension pretty much the entire evening, aware of the sexy couple he was with. Maddie looked so hot in that strapless black dress and strappy heels, and Zack was all broody bad boy in a tux that showed off his broad shoulders and lean build. And Zack was flirting with him.

It made him so fucking hot.

All night in the back of his mind he'd been wondering what Zack had planned for them. What kinds of things was he going to make them do tonight? Excitement shimmered close to the surface at the thought of giving up control to Zack, and then the way Zack had looked at him with hot eyes, the way he'd casually brushed his hand over Aidan's ass as they mingled in a crowd, the things he'd said...made Aidan even hotter, contemplating even more wicked things Zack could do.

"Your bedroom," Zack growled once they were in, again taking charge immediately. "Turn the lamp on. I'll be right there."

That made it easy. No awkward wondering what to do. Aidan and Maddie exchanged glances. He took her hand and led her down the hall and into their bedroom. Inside, he released her hand and crossed to the lamp beside the bed to flick it on. A warm glow spread around the bed, the corners of the room remaining shadowed.

Zack appeared in the door. He'd lost the tie and undone the top buttons of his shirt. He carried a coil of rope in his hands, and a wicked smile curled his lips.

Aidan's dick twitched.

Zack moved toward them. He stroked a hand over Aidan's shoulder through the suit jacket, then Maddie's bare skin. "Stand back to back," he ordered them in a low tone. "Arms at your sides."

With a sideways glance at Maddie, questions burning on his tongue, Aidan complied. Maddie moved too and their backs pressed together. To his shock, Zack began to circle them both with the rope, starting at their hips and wrists, binding them together, their arms trapped at their sides. Holy fuck.

Aidan closed his eyes at the sensation of the rope embracing him, snug and firm. The helplessness. He swallowed. He wasn't completely helpless…his legs were free…but how could he move with Maddie tied to him?

When they were securely bound, Zack moved them, turning them and adjusting their position, his hands strong and sure on them.

"Look." He gestured to the mirror across the room.

Aidan looked. His eyes met Maddie's in the mirror, hers huge in her small face, her lips parted. His own mouth was tight, his jaw clenched. He studied the image—both of them fully dressed, the elegant black suit now striped with pale rope, Maddie's smaller body the same, ropes crossing her bare chest and shoulders. His fingers curled into his palms at the erotic sight.

"Beautiful." Zack ran his fingers over Aidan's tight jaw, then Maddie's cheek.

What was he going to do to them like this?

Nerves fluttered. Excitement curled inside him.

Aidan was in control, all the time, at work—directing people, making decisions, solving problems. Now, at this moment, control having been taken away from him, he could only let go of it. And the relief of that spread through him in a melting heat. He felt his muscles relax, his jaw slacken. He closed his eyes and let the voluptuous pleasure of giving up control flow through him.

He opened his eyes and met Zack's. There he saw lust and excitement and…hope.

Zack had needs too. And the idea that Aidan could fill those needs added depth to his pleasure. He wanted to do this not only for himself, but for Zack.

"Okay?" Zack asked quietly.

Aidan still didn't know what was going to happen. He had to trust Zack. Was he strong enough to release all his doubts and worries and leave everything to him? *Everything*?

He nodded.

He looked back at the mirror to see Maddie watching with fascination. Again their eyes met and they shared a moment of connection, the feeling of being in Zack's control…together…owned by him.

His head went quiet and his heart felt free.

"I only have control because you give it to me," Zack said, as if reading his mind.

Aidan nodded, one corner of his mouth kicking up. "I know." It was true. Zack wasn't taking control away from him…he was relieving him of it. He was setting him free.

Zack moved around them. He kissed Maddie's mouth and her bare shoulder. He stroked her breasts through the chiffon dress. He circled again and Aidan sucked in a sharp breath when Zack's hand cupped his erection through his suit trousers. He gave a rough squeeze that had fire ripping through Aidan's balls.

That wicked smile played on Zack's lips as he fondled Aidan, then moved again to stand in front of Maddie. Zack held her face and kissed her, long and slow, with tongue that Aidan could clearly see in the mirror. Fuck, that was hot.

When Zack drew back Maddie gazed up at him, beautifully entranced. Aidan's dick pulsed.

Zack's hands wandered down over Maddie's body, over the ropes, and he lowered himself to the floor to kneel in front of her. Aidan watched the show in the mirror, feeling the vibrations of Maddie's body pressed to his, her inhalations and trembling. He heard her sighs and gasps as Zack ran his hands up her legs, beneath her dress. He caressed her thighs for long, heated moments, then pushed the dress up to expose her to him. Standing sideways to the mirror, Aidan couldn't see the same view Zack could, but knowing she was bare beneath the dress made his blood sizzle.

The soft sounds escaping her mouth intensified. Aidan groped and found her fingers and squeezed her hands.

"Tell him." Zack's warm breath brushed over her, his mouth at the juncture of her thighs. "Tell him what I'm doing to you."

"Oh god." Maddie whimpered. "He's…he's licking me. Kissing me."

"Spread your thighs, Maddie. Good girl."

They both had to shift to balance as she widened her stance. The leg visible to Aidan looked so sexy, long and smooth, muscle flexing in calf and thigh as she planted high heels into the rug. Bare all the way to her hip, the dress crumpled at her waist. Zack held it there as he leaned in, mouth on her pussy.

Aidan watched Zack's dark hair as he pressed into Maddie's softness. Her trembles increased and he tightened his own muscles to keep them from topping over.

"His tongue's inside me. Oh god. Now he's licking me again."

"You taste so sweet. Amazing. Love licking you, tasting you on my tongue." He slipped the fingers of one hand between her thighs and Aidan's dick lurched again.

"Now...now his fingers are inside me," Maddie said. "Oh yeah...that feels so good."

"Wanna make you come, baby." Zack kissed her thighs, then went back in.

Aidan could only feel the tension increasing in Maddie's body, her fingers tightening around his. He planted his feet, still in shiny black dress shoes, more firmly into the floor, holding her up as she came, soft cries surrounding them, her legs shaking.

Fuck. Sensation sizzled up his spine to his brain. His heart thudded wildly, and his balls grew tighter at the base of his throbbing cock.

Zack massaged her legs, up and down, up and down, sitting back on his heels. Aidan watched him lick his lips, studying Maddie's pussy. Aidan was struck by the gentleness of Zack's touch even as he emanated power and command.

"So beautiful," Zack murmured. "Good girl."

Maddie made a sound almost like a sob. Aidan's gaze shot to her face. Was she okay? She knew how to stop things. *Don't stop things.* Selfishly, he wanted to know what came next in this scene they were acting out in front of the mirror. She met his eyes, hers heavy, her smile slow. She was okay.

Zack stood in a graceful push to his feet. Aidan's heart skipped a beat as Zack moved again to face him. "Want to taste Maddie?" Zack whispered. He gripped Aidan's chin. For a moment their eyes met and clashed. Forbidden heat ripped through Aidan as he waited, helpless. Then Zack leaned in and brushed his mouth over his.

Fuck. Aidan's eyes closed. He sank into the brief sensation. Zack pulled back, eyes blazing and knowing. Aidan licked his tongue over his bottom lip, tasting Maddie...and Zack.

"Very good," Zack praised him softly.

Maddie moaned behind him.

Then Zack caressed him too, his shoulders through the suit jacket, his chest, his abs beneath the thin dress shirt. Zack's hands bumped over the ropes and then lower to the bulge of his dick. He rubbed him with firm strokes, over his cock, sliding lower to squeeze his balls. Aidan gasped, lust punching through his stomach. Zack looked up from where his hand cupped him to hold his gaze.

Thoughts bounced around in Aidan's head. A dark hunger grew in him, heat rushing through his body so hot he felt he could set his clothes on fire. He glanced at the mirror and saw Maddie watching with an equally hot and hungry look on her face, but also a hint of concern.

Was she worried Zack was making him do things he didn't want? She had to know he could put a stop to it at any time with one word.

He didn't.

He met her eyes and gave a small nod. She smiled.

Fuck, he might as well be stripped naked for how much he was revealing to both Maddie and Zack. His fingers tightened on Maddie's.

Zack lowered the fly and opened Aidan's pants, not slowly now, but with a sure, confident touch. With the fastener still closed, he reached into the opening, dug around and found bare flesh. Aidan hissed out a breath as Zack's fingers closed around his cock and gently pulled it out through the opening. Maddie whimpered.

Christ. Oh Christ. Fiery burning ecstasy twisted through Aidan. Zack's hand on him was big and strong and fucking hot as hell. Zack stroked him with firm assuredness, watching his own hand on Aidan's dick. Aidan's chest burned with every shallow breath he took. The tension in his spine became painfully acute.

He turned his head to look in the mirror. The scene was erotic...obscene. He and Maddie bound together, fully dressed in their formal clothing, her dress tucked up in the ropes around her waist, revealing her lower body, his cock protruding from his pants with Zack's hand on it. It was the hottest fucking thing he'd ever seen.

Zack's touch was making his blood simmer, making his head swim. And then Zack once again went to his knees. Aidan's eyes stung at how fucking much he loved this. He swallowed past his heart lodged in his throat and tried to pull air into his burning lungs. His balls were excruciatingly tight.

He turned his head and dropped his gaze to Zack in front of him, holding his shaft and studying it like it was the Holy Grail. Then he rubbed the glans over his cheek. Aidan's legs trembled. He expelled pent-up air from his lungs.

Zack looked up at him. Those neon-blue eyes glowed, surround by thick dark lashes. Drawn in, helpless to resist, Aidan stared back at him, watching in expectant fascination as Zack opened his mouth and closed it over the head of his cock.

Zack's eyes drifted closed, his pleasure evident, and gratification slammed into Aidan. He wanted this, wanted his cock sucked like you wouldn't believe, but the notion that Zack wanted this too, that he was giving Zack something that apparently pleased him so much, made Aidan's heart expand hard against his breastbone.

Zack's mouth moved on him, lips and agile tongue, his hand firmly gripping the base.

"That's so hot," Maddie moaned. Aidan leaned his head back against hers and rolled it from side to side, communicating with her. He was giving *her* something too.

His body was crazed for more—more pressure, more wetness, more sensation. Zack obliged, letting his saliva lubricate Aidan's flesh, his lips sliding, his mouth drawing on him in long, clinging pulls.

Aidan closed his eyes, burning up with it. He almost wanted to cry. His skin prickled all over and pressure gathered fast and dark in his balls. The pleasure shut down his mind—like the workouts he punished his body with, he could let everything else go and exist in sensation. The rest of the world disappeared and he went quiet in his head with the freedom to feel without having to think.

Zack pulled off with a sucking pop and looked up at him with wet lips. Aidan breathed hard. "Do you have any idea how long I've wanted to do that?" Zack breathed. "Do you know how incredible it makes me feel to have you surrender like this to me?"

Aidan again swallowed hard. He didn't know what to say. He hadn't known that, but he could see how much it pleased Zack. All he could think was... *I've wanted this too.*

Finally, from some long submerged place he could let that desire out into the open and admit it to himself. And to Aidan. And to Maddie.

Maddie. God what was she thinking of him? He was allowing both Zack and Maddie to see him at his most vulnerable—not just helpless because he was bound, but because they could see his most secret desires.

"Stop thinking about it," Zack ordered, recognizing something in his face. "Just let it all go."

Yes. Yes. He'd been doing that. He'd surrendered to the sensation. He closed his eyes again and surrendered.

Zack's teeth caught the tender rim of his cock and erotic pain streaked through him. He groaned. He longed to reach for Zack's head and sink his fingers into those shaggy curls, holding him there where he wanted him. But Zack was in charge here. And Aidan loved it.

Heat coiled and his thighs quaked with tension. Zack sucked him with a quick hard rhythm. So what if a man was sucking his dick? It felt good. Better than good. It felt dark and edgy and sublime. Zack was fucking amazing at this.

Zack set a tempo fast and hard, using his fist and his mouth and tongue. He took Aidan deeper, holy fuck, so deep he released his shaft with his hand. "Christ," Aidan croaked as his cock squeezed into Zack's throat. Zack's nose pressed briefly to his pubes. "Jesus fucking Christ!" Still helpless, his fingers gripped Maddie's.

Zack slid his mouth off him and paused to lick him, breathing hard himself, then dragging his tongue over the sensitive head, tracing around the rim. He fingered his balls, looked up at him with glistening swollen lips. If he could have, Aidan would have reached out to touch his face. He held Zack's gaze.

"Yeah," Zack rasped. "Fuck yeah."

Emotion swelled in Aidan, hot and huge. Once more Zack greedily licked and sucked him, bringing every sensation rocketing to a peak. Aidan gulped for air, throat aching. The base of his spine tingled, his thighs flexed, his head went back, bumping against Maddie's. Together they turned their heads to watch in the mirror, eyes meeting in a flash of heat, then dropping to Zack on his knees sucking Aidan's cock.

Then Aidan couldn't keep his eyes open any more. A groan rumbled in his chest and fiery sensation raced up his spine, pure ecstasy exploding in his balls. His orgasm crashed over him, his cock jerking in Zack's mouth. Searing heat streaked though him, out his dick and into Zack's mouth.

Holy fuck. His legs were giving out. He couldn't collapse with Maddie tied to him like this, they'd both go down in a heap and she'd get hurt. *Be strong. Be strong.* Quivering and quaking, he used every particle of strength and will he could find to stay upright, teeth gritted together, muscles locked.

Zack finished him off, licking, sucking, smiling. Then he surged to his feet and reached for the ropes that bound Aidan and Maddie. In seconds they were free. Aidan went down. He couldn't help it. He sat heavily on the floor, head bowed, reaching for Maddie's hand. He tugged her down onto his lap and buried his face in her hair. His entire body wracked with shivers, he held her tight and sucked in air.

Her hands were all over him, touching his face, his neck, his shoulders. She kissed his hand, twined her arms around his neck and snuggled into him.

Zack. Where was Zack? Aidan cracked his eyes open. Zack stood apart from them, holding the rope in his hands, coiling it up. Watching them.

A swirl of emotions choked Aidan. He wasn't even sure what they all were. Should he feel guilty? Ashamed? Honestly, that wasn't what he felt. He felt…good. Fuck. He felt relieved, he felt free. Definitely vulnerable. Yet not as vulnerable as the look on Zack's face at that moment as he watched him and Maddie hug.

Instinctively, without thinking about it, Aidan held out a hand to his friend. Zack was the one in charge, but it was Aidan who said hoarsely, "C'mere."

Zack hesitated, then dropped the rope. He stepped closer, lowered himself to the floor, folding his legs, and put his arms around Aidan's shoulders, with Maddie between them. Zack set his head against Aidan's and for long moments they sat like that together.

19

On Monday, Zack met with Brian Bridges at a coffee shop near Northwestern. Seven years hadn't really changed him much. At twenty-three, Zack had been a little older than some of the other students, having worked a couple years between high school and college, but Professor Bridges had seemed a lot older and wiser than him. Now, Zack wondered how old the guy actually was, because with Zack being thirty, Professor Bridges didn't seem much older.

Professor Bridges rose from the table he'd already been seated at to greet him. They shook hands and clapped each other on the shoulders with big smile. "Wow, great to see you, Zack. You look good."

"Thanks. Feeling a lot better. And good to see you too."

"Have a seat."

They settled in, ordered coffee and sandwiches. Then Professor Bridges grinned. "Pulitzer Prize, huh. I have to say it wasn't a surprise to me."

Zack smiled. "Thanks. Learned it all from you."

His old prof snorted. "Right."

"Seriously, Professor Bridges. I really did learn a lot from you."

"Call me Brian." The prof waved a hand. "I'm not your professor anymore."

"Okay." Zack grinned.

"Tell me about that story. How you got it."

They talked and Zack slipped into technical talk with ease, moving from one subject to another, things he'd seen, things he'd learned, even touching on his captivity. Zack mentioned Reporters Without Borders, and Brian told him he knew one of the founding board members, who now worked as contributing editor for the Washington Post. "They've got a really solid reputation in Washington. Defending freedom of information. So important."

"Yeah." Zack sighed. "I feel myself becoming cynical. We all want to think we can make a difference. That maybe some torture will stop because it's highlighted in the media, or corrupt politicians will stop illegal activities because journalists dig into what they're doing and make it public. But..." He shook his head. "I don't know. Do I feel like I made one damn bit of difference? Not really. There's still so much evil out there." He'd sure experienced that first hand.

"It's hard for one person to feel you're making a difference." Brian nodded. "You have to look at the big picture."

They continued talking, and when Zack glanced at his cell phone to check the time, he was shocked to see they'd been sitting there for nearly two hours. "Wow. You have classes to get back to?"

"Nah. Summer session is not as intense. I should get back to the office, though. Got a student coming to see me at three."

"Let me buy." Zack pulled out his wallet.

"No, no, I'm buying. I invited you. Listen, I wanted to ask you something. How long are you going to be in town?"

Zack shoved his wallet back in his pocket. "I'm supposed to leave next week."

"Oh. Damn. I was going to ask if you'd come talk to one of my classes. Or more than one. It would be a thrill for them to have a chance to hear from a Pulitzer-Prize-winning photojournalist. An alumnus, no less."

Zack blinked at that. It sounded cool. But he was leaving. "Yeah," he said slowly. "Sorry."

"Fall session starts in a few weeks, it would've been great. Ah well. I was actually wondering if you might even stay permanently, after what happened. We're looking for an adjunct professor. It might be something you could do along with other work."

Zack laughed. "Professor? Me?"

"Sure, why not?" Brian studied him. "You'd be great at it, especially with your experience."

Zack shook his head, smiling. "Well. Never thought of that. But the agency is expecting me back in the field."

"Yeah, no doubt."

They walked out of the restaurant. Clouds had moved in, obscuring the sun, and the low gray ceiling above them looked like rain was imminent.

Brian shook his hand again.

"Thanks for lunch," Zack said. "Enjoyed it."

"Yeah, great talking to you. Could talk for hours more. Stay in touch, okay? And if you happen to be back, let me know and we'll get you up in front of one of my classes."

Zack smilingly agreed, though he knew he wouldn't be back.

Dammit.

As he rode the train back toward Aidan and Maddie's condo, he reflected on the offer and mention of a teaching position. The idea surprisingly intrigued him. It wasn't something he'd ever contemplated as he'd pursued his own education. He'd been eager to travel and see the world and tell important stories. A classroom didn't have the same adrenaline rush or have the same import.

Well, that wasn't true. When he thought about the

impact Brian's teaching and mentorship had had on him, he had to admit teaching could have a big value. The idea of sharing his knowledge and mentoring kids was actually kinda cool.

But he was leaving. Next week. He had a doctor appointment on Thursday and if the doctor gave the okay and cleared him to return to work, he'd be booking flights to...well, he wasn't sure where yet. He'd go where they sent him.

His heart felt as leaden as the skies above him as he contemplated that.

Leaving Maddie and Aidan. Leaving their home that had come to feel like *his* home. Leaving Chicago, which he'd fallen in love with. Why hadn't he appreciated the city when he'd been in college?

He'd been a busy student, immersed in his studies. He'd also been focused on his future, on the rest of the world, and getting away. He'd always been focused on getting away, had never really taken the time to get to know the city. The here and now. There was a lot to like.

No, it wasn't a Damascus or Beirut or Mumbai or Cape Town. But when he thought of cities like that, he got a weird tight feeling in his gut. Even talking to Brian about it, he'd had that vague anxious feeling, much as he'd enjoyed their discussion.

He pushed away those feelings and thought about Aidan and Maddie. About what had happened on the weekend. How he'd sucked off his best friend. And how Aidan had loved it.

He'd had a niggle of worry, a nudge of doubt as he'd carried out the plan—the fantasy—that night. Aidan's reaction had surprised him. But then again, it hadn't. If he'd truly thought Aidan would freak out and yell red, he wouldn't have gone there. Deep down inside, he'd known...or had a feeling. One of his "hunches" or intuition.

But what did it all mean, in the grand scheme of things? He was showing Aidan that he was kinkier than he'd known, showing him and Maddie how to give each other what they needed. Then he'd leave. They didn't need *him*. This was all kinky fun, but not something that would last forever. They all knew that.

But heat spread through his body, remembering...the feel of Aidan in his mouth, the taste of his come, the absolute bliss on his face. Zack had wanted that for so long. Now he was wondering if Aidan had wanted that too.

He couldn't start thinking things like that. Getting ridiculous hopes up. Letting those old feelings for both Aidan and Maddie develop again.

He'd cared about them back then, because they'd let him in. They'd accepted him. Aidan was always rescuing people and fixing things. He'd befriended Zack when he was lost and clueless and confused, earning his undying loyalty and gratitude. They'd saved Maddie from her fuckface boyfriend.

Now, there were more reasons to care. They were both so fucking brave. Zack knew how scary it was to make yourself vulnerable, to reveal your deepest, darkest secrets. They'd done that. With him. They'd trusted him. Christ. A giant fist squeezed his insides.

They had great lives — successful careers, loads of talent and smarts, friends and family. And the hugest thing of all...they cared about him, enough to do all the things they had. When he still felt he didn't fucking deserve it.

He'd always known that someone like him, who wanted such perverted weird things, weird things like wanting two people, one of each sex — who did that? Nobody. He would never have a normal kind of relationship. Normal people fell in love with one person, sometimes the opposite sex, sometimes the same sex. The world was coming to accept that. But someone who loved *two* people was just fucked up. Plus, he liked to do kinky things to people, like tie them up and flog them. He'd accepted that part of himself and wasn't going to deny it anymore, but there were also people in the world who thought *that* was fucked up.

Which was why, long ago, he'd given up hope that he'd ever have any kind of relationship. Who would want him? Maddie and Aidan had turned to each other, two nice normal heterosexual people, maybe not as vanilla as they'd thought, but still…they were for each other.

The next day, Zack picked up the prints he'd had made of some of his photographs and went to a framing shop. He had no idea why he was doing this, but for some reason he had some kind of urge to display his work. Only, he had no actual home with walls on which to display it. Whatever. He was doing it. He picked out frames and left the prints at the shop to be picked up Friday.

Then he met Maddie for lunch, since he'd mentioned he was going to be downtown near her office and she'd immediately suggested lunch. Aidan's office wasn't that far, but when they'd invited him to join them, he'd had to decline because he was meeting with a couple of city administrators.

"Big shot." Zack had ragged on him.

"And don't you forget it." Aidan had grinned.

So Zack and Maddie met at a diner just off Michigan Avenue. She ordered a salad and he went for a big burger.

"Still craving burgers?" she teased him.

"I'll always crave burgers. And hot dogs."

They talked and flirted a little while they ate. They talked about Aidan, who was probably a favorite topic of conversation for both of them.

"He still tries to look after his brother and sisters." Maddie stabbed an olive in her salad and set it aside. He smiled at her dislike of olives. "Even though Liam just graduated from college."

As the oldest of four, Aidan had taken responsibility for his younger siblings from the time he was very young. In college, he'd always been stressed out about what was happening with them since he'd left home and he was always on the phone or texting them about their school work and activities and safe sex, for god's sake.

"I could never understand why two such self-absorbed, career-oriented people had four children," Maddie said about Aidan's parents, shaking her head. "Then they paid no attention to them."

"Could be worse. Could've had my family."

She looked at him with her head tilted and eyes soft. "Tell me about your family. Your mom."

"Eh." He poked a French fry into a puddle of ketchup on his plate. "Not much to tell. Never knew my dad. Mom was a drug addict and ended up basically a prostitute to get her fix."

"Oh my god." She blinked.

Zack wasn't sure why he was telling her this now. He'd told Aidan back in college, but had never wanted Maddie to know. For some reason, he'd had this worry that if she knew what had happened to him, it would poison her feelings for him. And he'd needed all the friends he could get. But now...well, maybe she *should* know the truth about the guy she was screwing around with. Because that look on her face the other night that had looked like she cared about him...she needed to get over that.

"Yeah. It sucked. I was a teenager and I had to listen to my own mother banging guys in the bedroom next door. Then she got the brilliant idea that she was going to pimp me out."

"What!" Her hand flew to her mouth, her eyes going wide.

He gave her a grim smile. "I had a friend. Rory. I didn't bring him home much, because...well, Mom. I didn't bring anyone home. One time she saw us together though and she somehow figured out that I was attracted to him. She started bugging me about being gay. Then one night she was drunk and high and this new dealer was gay so she couldn't trade sex for drugs with him. So she offered up me." He kept his voice as light and nonchalant as he could and it wasn't that hard since that had all happened thirteen years ago. It did still make his stomach heave though, remembering her saying, "Hey, Zack likes boys. C'mere, Zack."

He'd tried to back away, tried to ignore the assessing look the dealer gave him while his own mother tried to sell him, his heart working in painful beats, adrenaline and fear making his limbs shake.

"Oh my god." To his shock her eyes went liquid. "How could she do that? To her own son."

"Hey, don't cry. It was a long time ago. I survived. After that I ran away." He kept his tone matter-of-fact. "I was almost eighteen, about to graduate from high school. I left with nothing. Had to leave my cameras behind." Even then, his cameras had been precious, hard-earned through a bunch of crap part-time jobs. It had shattered his already damaged heart to leave his cameras behind. "I lived on the streets for the next few weeks."

"What about your friend? Rory?"

Zack's lips twisted. "He wasn't my friend for long after I tried to kiss him one day."

"Oh. Oh no."

He shrugged, pushing away that painful memory. "I had a little money, was able to buy some food, but I sure couldn't afford somewhere to live. But I was determined to finish high school. I knew education was the only thing that was going to save me."

"I know you worked for a couple of years before you started college."

"Yeah."

"You never saw your mother again, after that, did you?"

"Nope." His chest constricted with guilt. "Left her to that life and eventually it killed her." He bent his head. "Always wondered if I could have done something different. If I'd stayed. If I could have helped her, once I'd finished school and gotten a job."

"Zack." She reached out and gripped his hand on the table. "If she was addicted to drugs, you getting a job would only have helped pay for those drugs. Unless she was willing to go into rehab or something."

"Yeah. That's what I'd had the crazy idea of doing. Getting a job and paying for her to go to rehab. Even after I left, I thought I might still be able to do that, if I saved up enough money. At one point I had three jobs, lived in a crappy rooming house." He couldn't make himself go home after what had happened, fear and crushing disappointment and betrayal keeping him away. But even so, he'd felt guilty for just leaving her there. "She died before that could happen. Overdose. No idea if it was accidental or maybe she wanted to die." He wasn't sure he could bear knowing, because if she'd wanted to die he'd feel even shittier about leaving her, selfishly running away to save himself, but in the process abandoning her.

"Oh, Zack." Tears dripped down her face.

"But in the end, the money I'd saved helped pay for college." He smiled, though his lips felt tight. "So that was good."

"Do *not* feel guilty." Her voice came out choked. "Do. Not. You were a kid. You were not responsible for her. She was your mother, an adult. *She* should have been looking after *you*. And rehab would only have worked if she'd been willing to do it."

"True. Christ, Maddie, don't cry. I'm fine. I didn't tell you that to make you cry."

"I can't help it." She sniffled. "I'm sorry. Oh Zack." She squeezed his hand.

Shit. This was backfiring. He'd told her that sad story

expecting her to withdraw. Instead she was crying her eyes out. Over him. Fuck.

"Hey, I have some news. Good news." He told her about his book idea and the email he'd gotten from one of the agents he'd queried. "He thinks he can definitely sell it to a publisher. He had a few editors in mind already."

"Oh wow." She tipped her head, and swiped some last tears away. "That's awesome. What a great idea."

"Thanks. So now I have some work to do to put together a formal proposal."

"You've been doing a lot of work with the Facebook group."

"Yeah." He bent his head. "I enjoy it. Actually, I had an idea of something I want to do. Just not sure how to do it."

"What?"

"Glenn Peters. A reporter who's still missing. His wife was pregnant when he disappeared. She's had the baby now, and they also have a two year old. She's having a tough time supporting them, since she just had a baby and can't work. I thought about trying to do some kind of fundraiser to help her out."

"Oh." She stared at him with soft eyes. "That's an awesome idea. Where does she live?"

"Boston."

Maddie's forehead wrinkled. "Hmm. How about something online? I know! An auction! We could get people and businesses to donate things to auction off. I have lots of contacts."

Emotion filled Zack's chest. "Would you do that?"

"Of course! It's what I do. I think it's an amazing idea." She smiled at him, and he was glad he'd distracted her from her earlier tears. "We'll get to work on that."

When they were done lunch, he walked her back to her office building. They paused on the sidewalk. Her hair was all shiny in the sun and he couldn't resist touching, stroking some strands away from her face. Her eyes were still a little pink, her smile still half-hearted. Fuck, he didn't like seeing her sad. "Maddie, baby." He let his fingers linger on her soft cheek, and they smiled at each other, eyes locked together.

"Hey, Maddie."

They both turned to see Maddie's friend Chelsea.

"Chels! Hi!" Maddie moved away to hug her friend. "What are you doing here?"

"I have a dentist appointment. In the building next door."

Zack caught Chelsea's searching looks, the way her gaze flicked back and forth between them, her forehead furrowed. He could only imagine how intimate their posture had been at that moment, standing close together staring into each other's eyes, his hand on Maddie's face. Yeah, he'd wanted to hold her and kiss her, and that had no doubt been blatantly obvious.

"Zack and I just had lunch." Zack picked up the tightness at the corners of Maddie's mouth. She'd also seen Chelsea's curious looks. "He was downtown this morning doing some errands."

As if she had to explain anything. Zack sighed inwardly. "Yeah. I'll let you get back to work." He smiled at Chelsea. "Nice to see you again, Chelsea. Bye, Maddie."

He left the two women there, insides churning as he imagined Chelsea interrogating Maddie. What would Maddie say? She probably didn't want to tell their friends what was going on between them. Christ. Zack rubbed his eyes.

He shouldn't have put her in that kind of position. Guilt ate at him for the rest of the day until she got home that evening. She walked into the condo, dressed in the bright turquoise sleeveless dress that hugged her body and tan strappy heels he'd admired earlier. She dropped her purse, shoved her hands into her hair and met his eyes. Her eyebrows lifted.

Shit.

"I'm sorry," he said immediately. "I know how that must have looked to Chelsea. Did she ask you what was going on?"

"Yeah." She blew out a breath and crossed the living room. "She actually seemed annoyed at me."

"She thinks you're cheating on Aidan."

"Yup." She lowered herself into an arm chair. "That pisses me off. How could she think that of me?"

He didn't want to remind her of how incriminating they probably had appeared. "What did you tell her?"

"I told her that we're friends. And that's it." She grimaced. "I don't know if she believed me or not."

Things only got worse. When Aidan arrived home he shared more of the soap opera with them. "So." He strode into the kitchen where Maddie was slicing chicken breasts and Zack was chopping vegetables for a stir fry. "Chelsea saw you two having lunch together."

Zack's shoulder and neck muscles tensed and he glanced at Maddie. Her hands went still and she looked up at Aidan. "Oh no."

"Not exactly." Zack corrected him. "It was after lunch. I walked Maddie back to her office and we were saying goodbye on the sidewalk out front."

Aidan lifted a brow. Zack studied him. Was Aidan pissed? Didn't really seem like it, unless he was keeping it well controlled.

"It probably looked bad," Zack admitted. "Already apologized to Maddie. I'll apologize to you too. It's not fair to you to be put in that position."

"How'd you know?" Maddie demanded.

"Ethan called me this afternoon. Chelsea called him, told him what she'd seen, said you denied there was anything going on. But she said you seemed guilty. And she was worried about me."

"Fuck," Maddie muttered, and Zack lifted his

eyebrows. "She's worried about you, and doesn't trust me. I thought she was my friend." Her bottom lip pushed out.

Zack's heart sank to his toes.

"And I wasn't guilty." Maddie lifted her little chin. "I'm *not* guilty. I was…nervous, though."

"Because you were lying," Aidan said softly. "There *is* something going on."

"Was I supposed to tell her the truth?" Maddie flared. "Jesus, can you imagine?"

"No, sweetheart." Aidan shook his head. "I wouldn't expect that."

"Fuck, I'm sorry," Zack repeated, his gut clenching.

"It's okay," Aidan said. "I told Ethan I knew you two were having lunch and I trust you both. That's all he needs to know."

Zack stared at Aidan. Just another fucking reason he cared about this guy. Rock solid. Christ.

"It's the truth," Aidan added.

Zack looked at Maddie, whose eyes were reddened and her bottom lip trembling. She met his eyes and gave him a shaky smile, then looked back at Aidan. "I love you so much," she whispered.

Yeah. Fuck yeah. Zack looked down at the broccoli florets on the cutting board in front of him. Shit. He should never have put them in that position. What the fuck were they doing?

"Zack." Maddie edged closer. "This is not your fault."

"It's not our friends' business what we're doing," Aidan added.

"Fuck them!" Maddie said fiercely. "I'll tell them! They think I'm cheating on Aidan!"

Zack's head snapped up and he gaped at Aidan. Aidan laughed. He fucking *laughed*. "Not every last detail, maybe." His eyes gleamed with humor.

And yeah, there it was…another reason to love them both. That Aidan was laughing about this, and that

Maddie would tell her friends the truth about them, to set them straight. That she'd rather they know she was fucking two men than cheating—what the fuck could he even say about that.

She gave Aidan a narrow-eyed look. "Okay. Maybe not every last detail. But they need to know this is all consensual. It's not cheating when it's a…a threesome."

"You're not telling them anything," Zack snapped. Jesus. For once he had to be the one who saved them. "I'll be gone in a few days and there won't be an issue."

Thick silence descended over the room. Maddie blinked rapidly, and the light in Aidan's eyes dimmed.

"Right." Maddie bent her head and attacked a chicken breast with her sharp knife. "Right. No issue."

After a short pause, Aidan said, "I'm going to change. Back in a few."

Zack and Maddie continued preparing dinner. He hacked sightlessly at the broccoli, nearly taking off a finger. Yeah. The sooner he got out of here, the better for everyone.

The next day, Zack bullshitted the doctor when he asked about lingering symptoms of PTSD, ignoring those knots of anxiety in his gut, and got his medical clearance. And he called his boss in New York to talk about getting back to work. He'd talked to Dave a few times while he'd been in Chicago, when he'd checked in on how Zack was doing. To his shock, his boss offered him assignments in Chicago. In September, the G7 Summit was being held in Chicago and they wanted him to cover it. That was huge. And…interesting. Yeah, it was different than documenting war and humanitarian crises. But it was still a professional challenge.

"That wasn't what I had in mind," he said carefully.

"How about Great Britain? There's another royal baby due soon."

Jesus fuck! They wanted him to go hang around outside

a palace in London waiting for a baby to arrive? "I was thinking more like the Ukraine or Sudan—"

"You know, you've done your time in the trenches," Dave said. "You got your Pulitzer. You can take your pick of whatever assignments you want. You sure you want to go back to that?"

Hell no. The words popped into his head. But he didn't say them out loud. Because how could he stay here? He couldn't get any more involved with Aidan and Maddie. He had to get out before things got way too messy. He wanted to help their relationship, not destroy it, and he sure as hell didn't want to hurt their relationships with their friends.

He told his boss he'd give it some thought. He'd been ready to hang up and go online to start booking flights. Now he ended the call and sat in the chair in his bedroom, staring into space.

The longer he stayed the more dangerous it was. The more chance there was that he'd let on how he felt about them. How he'd felt about them seven years ago when he'd left. That couldn't happen. He in no way wanted their pity, which he knew they would feel if they found out the pathetic hopes and dreams he'd had. And which were starting to form again inside him.

He'd thought he could do this. He could give them this, and get something in return, something he needed. But he could not let his feelings grow for them again.

Only he had this sick feeling in his gut that it was too late for that.

20

Maddie called Chelsea at work the next morning. Her stomach was in knots but she was also pissed. She recognized the irony in her anger. She was mad at her friend for thinking she would cheat on Aidan; meanwhile, she was in fact having sex with another man. Only, she was doing it with Aidan right there.

"Chelsea Dalhart."

"Hi, Chels. It's me, Maddie."

"Maddie. Hi."

Maddie normally would have made some small talk but today had no patience for that. "We need to talk."

"Uh. Okay."

"Can we meet for lunch?"

After a short pause, Chelsea agreed and they settled on a restaurant and time. Maddie tried to focus on work for the rest of the morning, but was distracted by planning what exactly she was going to say to her friend.

She and Chelsea both worked downtown but not that close, so she took a cab to the restaurant they'd agree on. She arrived first and let the hostess seat her at a small table. She was sipping coffee when Chelsea showed up.

Once seated, Chelsea grabbed her menu and her gaze flicked over it rapidly. They both ordered the Santa Fe salad and the server departed with the menus tucked beneath her arm.

"So." Chelsea gave a bright smile, her fingers moving to the necklace she wore, rubbing the beads and twisting them. "What's up?"

"You know what's up. You called Ethan yesterday and told him about seeing Zack and me."

"Shit. Ethan called Aidan, didn't he?"

"Yeah. He did. Because he was worried about Aidan. Apparently you both think I'm cheating on Aidan."

"Was Aidan...mad?" Chelsea's eyes widened. "I didn't mean to cause trouble. I just thought...he should know."

"That really hurts, Chelsea."

Chelsea bit her lip. She twisted the strand of beads again.

"And no, Aidan wasn't mad. He knew we were having lunch together."

"So nothing is really going on between you and Zack?"

"I told you that yesterday," she said quietly. "Apparently you didn't believe me."

Um." Chelsea swallowed and her eyes shifted away and then back.

"If I just said, I promise you I'm really not cheating on Aidan, would that be enough to convince you?"

"I guess so."

"You don't sound convinced."

"You two looked pretty...intimate." She played with her necklace. "He looked like he was about to kiss you."

Maddie knew Chelsea was not wrong. She'd seen the look on Zack's face, his concern because she'd been upset at hearing about his bitch skank addict mother. He *had* wanted to kiss her. And she'd wanted that too.

"Okay." She sighed. Here it was. Critical juncture. She'd debated with herself all last night and all morning what to say at this moment. "I'm going to be completely honest with you." Her heart beat quicker. "There *is* something going on with me and Zack."

Chelsea's eyes flew wide.

"But not what you think. It's all three of us...we're kind of..." Words deserted her.

"Like a ménage à trois?" Chelsea whispered, leaning forward.

"Yeah." Maddie picked up her cup and swallowed a mouthful of coffee. "Like that."

"Oh my god! Seriously?"

"Yeah."

"With two guys?" Her voice got louder.

"Hush." Maddie glanced around.

"Eep. Sorry."

"Yeah, two guys."

Chelsea slumped back in her seat and slapped a hand to her chest. "Holy shit."

The server appeared with their salads and refilled their coffee mugs. Conversation halted during this service.

Once they were alone again, Maddie said, "Look, it's not that big a deal." She wasn't going to share all the details with Chelsea, like how Aidan liked to be told what to do and even let Zack blow him. That was too much info. "Zack's staying with us for a while. He's supposed to leave next week. We're just..." Her throat closed up. "Ahem." She took another sip of coffee. "We're just fooling around."

And then, to her horror, tears welled up in her eyes.

Jesus Christ, she wasn't going to cry again, was she? She'd gone back to work yesterday with a red nose and eyes, if she showed up like that again today they'd wonder what the hell she was doing on her lunch breaks.

She fought back the emotion. Chelsea's eyebrows pulled together above her nose and she straightened and leaned forward again. "Are you okay, Maddie?"

No. No, she was not okay. "I don't want him to leave." Oh Christ, why did she blurt that out?

"You...care about him?"

Maddie blinked rapidly at the sting of tears. "Of course

I do. We've been friends since college." To her horror, a sob escaped her.

"Well, you're more than friends now," Chelsea pointed out. "Um. Wow. I'm kind of lost for words here. I hate seeing you like this. You obviously have feelings for him." The corners of her eyes pinched up. "Have you fallen in love with him?"

"I know what you're thinking." Maddie fished around in her purse for a tissue. "You're thinking I've fallen in love with Zack and *out* of love with Aidan. But that's not the case. I love Aidan. I just...might...maybe...love Zack too."

Chelsea's eyes went big again. "How can you love two men?"

"I don't know! Oh Jesus." She blew her nose. "Even back in college, I think I loved them both. There. I said it." She swiped her nose again. "I was so confused back then. Wasn't sure what I was feeling. I knew I couldn't love two guys. I mean, how does that work? Then Zack left. Just up and left. Aidan was still there. I loved him and I was so happy when he wanted to be more than friends. But I tried to keep in touch with Zack. Even though he hardly ever answered my emails."

"Wow," Chelsea breathed. "I never knew that. This is better than any reality show."

Maddie frowned briefly. "I love Aidan. I really do. But I'm going to be so sad when Zack leaves. Again. In fact, I don't know if I can bear it."

Chelsea touched her fingers to her lips, eyes full of concern. "Oh, Maddie."

"I haven't admitted that to anyone else." Maddie dropped her gaze to her uneaten salad. "Definitely not to Zack."

"Would you tell Aidan? He might not understand." Chelsea's forehead furrowed. "Isn't he jealous, seeing you with...another man?"

"No." Maddie shook her head decisively. "Not at all. He likes it." Just as she'd liked watching the two guys together. Her belly did a little flip, remembering. She bit her lip.

"That's really..."

"Fucked up?"

"No! It's just hard to believe. I can't imagine Ethan ever wanting to watch me with another man. With another girl...oh yeah." They exchanged wry smiles. "His biggest fantasy. Not gonna happen. But okay, you say Aidan's down with it. But he might be hurt if you're actually in love with another man."

Maddie blinked, considering that. Chelsea had a point. Maybe Aidan was okay with all this because it was temporary. Because he knew Zack was leaving. Maybe it was okay because it was just...sex. And a little pain. And a little domination and submission. "It's complicated," she finally said. "But maybe I do need to talk to Aidan about it."

Chelsea sucked in a sharp breath. "I don't know, Maddie..."

"We love each other," Maddie said firmly. "And lately we've gotten even closer. We're honest with each other." This was true. Now. In the past, maybe they hadn't opened up to each other as much as they should, but now they were sharing everything. She was convincing herself as much as Chelsea. They *had* gotten closer. They'd both revealed parts of themselves they hadn't before, thanks to Zack. Their love was deeper now they'd shared such intimate secrets and desires.

But she had to admit she too wondered what Aidan would think if she told him she loved Zack. She was pretty sure that wasn't what he'd had in mind when they started this crazy three-way relationship.

"I'm sorry, Maddie." Chelsea's bottom lip pushed out. "You probably didn't want to tell me all that. I'm sorry I jumped to the wrong conclusion."

"I guess I probably would have done the same," Maddie admitted. "Although, I don't know if I'd ever believe you would cheat on Ethan."

Chelsea dropped her eyes and her cheeks flushed. "I'm sorry. Really."

"Are you disgusted by what we're doing?" Maddie took a deep breath, waiting for her friend's answer.

Chelsea quickly shook her head. "No. Not at all, Maddie. I'm concerned, because you're upset. I've never had a threesome, but I've heard there's big potential for things to go wrong. Jealousy. One person feeling left out."

Maddie nodded. Chelsea was totally right. But she didn't understand what was happening between the three of them.

Oh fuck, neither did Maddie, when it came right down to it.

"Well, thanks for not judging us." She picked up her water glass. "I was prepared for that, but I didn't want you to think I was a cheater." Chelsea met her eyes and her lips quirked. And Maddie laughed. "A skanky slut, maybe. But not a cheater."

Chelsea laughed too. "Maddie, I really didn't think you were cheating. It just looked…funny. I didn't know Ethan was going to blow it all up and call Aidan. I called him because I wanted him to reassure me that you two were fine and I was crazy."

"So it's Ethan who thought I was a cheater." Maddie's smile went crooked.

"You can smack him for it next time you see him. And I don't think you're a skanky slut. If you three are having fun, that's awesome. I just don't want you to get hurt. You're such a sweetheart. And you and Aidan are, like, the perfect couple. We all envy you."

Maddie cast her eyes downward. People didn't always know what was going on beneath the surface. And like Aidan had said… "We're not perfect. But we do love each other. We're going to be fine."

"Good." Chelsea gave a firm nod.

But Maddie didn't talk to Aidan about it. Nerves kept her edgy and silent. What was the point of stirring up shit if Zack was going to leave?

But she didn't want him to leave.

God, *god*, things were so messed up.

CRRRRO

Things got even more messed up that weekend, when Zack once more took control and had them doing everything he ordered in their bedroom.

Not that she was complaining.

They all had a shower together, which was new and exciting. The bathroom attached to their bedroom had a huge shower stall which she and Aidan had showered in together, but wow, there was even room for three. Zack directed the intimate washing of her pussy, shocking her when the soapy wash cloth slid up between her butt cheeks. He took his time cleaning her there, then did the same to Aidan, pushing him up against the wall, hands flat on the tiles while Zack washed his cock and balls and anus.

What did he have planned? Maddie watched, enthralled. She was already wet and achy by the time they dried each other off and padded naked into the bedroom. It was like a dance and Zack the choreographer, occasionally stepping into the sequence for a kiss, a stroke, a tap on the butt. He brought out ropes and tied both their hands together, Aidan's behind his back, Maddie's in front. Curiosity zoomed inside her along with arousal.

Then she was on her back on the bed, Aidan kneeling between her legs with his mouth on her pussy. At Zack's direction he teased her until she was even more aching and wet and quivering, licking her inner thighs, her pussy lips...and then Zack was there, hands on her thighs, pushing her legs up and back, and he said, "Lick her asshole."

Sharp excitement zigzagged through her, a hot thrill at the dirty words.

"Christ," Aidan muttered.

They'd never done this. But oh...it was hot. He nipped at her butt cheeks, licked her there, then circled her back entrance. She closed her eyes, her insides squeezing hard. Hot, wicked sensation spread in shimmering waves.

"You'd never do this." Zack held her legs, watching, as naked as they were. "Would you?"

Aidan made a noise in his throat. Maddie wasn't sure what it meant, and deep thought was beyond her as Aidan teased her sensitive flesh. Yeah, they'd never done this. She'd never even thought of doing it. She didn't know if Aidan had. But wow...she was melting into a puddle of lust.

"You told me to," Aidan's husky voice responded.

"Yeah." Zack reached out and grabbed Aidan's hair, pulling his head up. "I did. And you obeyed me. That makes me so fucking hot." And he leaned in and laid a hard kiss on Aidan's wet mouth.

Sparks zapped straight to Maddie's pussy. She gazed at them wide-eyed. Sweet Jesus, that was hot. Aidan stared back at Zack, his chest rising and falling. Maddie panted in shallow breaths, her bound hands going to her chest, forearms pressing against her swollen breasts. Wanton. Wicked. She loved it.

"Lick her more," Zack ordered.

Aidan lowered his face and did as he was told, and Maddie's eyes fell closed as his mouth closed over her flesh. Tingles ran circles where his tongue touched her, licking over sensitive, forbidden territory. When his teeth grazed her flesh, she jolted with electric shock. His tongue blazed a slow path up to her clit and circled it. She quivered with agonized wanting.

"Like that?" Zack whispered.

"Yes."

He leaned over and kissed her and she turned to him, needy and desperate. Their mouths fused as Aidan continued to torment her, tonguing her clit. Her orgasm built and she moaned into Zack's mouth.

He pulled back and the bed moved as he stood. She cracked her eyes open to see where he was going. He pulled out the bottom drawer of the nightstand and grabbed the bottle of lube along with a condom. Then he walked around the bed and then the mattress shifted again as he knelt behind Aidan.

Oh god.

Aidan was in a crouch, bound hands behind his back, mouth on her pussy, his own ass exposed. And Zack started touching him there. Aidan's mouth went still on her, and she sensed his entire body pulsing.

God, god, she wished she could see what Zack was doing. His hands played behind Aidan. Was he touching his ass? His cock? His balls? Oh sweet Jesus, that made fire burn inside her.

Zack's face wore a look of intent arousal and needful yearning. On his knees, his gaze went to where he touched Aidan. Aidan's mouth moved on her, but she sensed his distraction, the tension humming in his body as Zack played with him.

"Don't stop licking her," Zack ordered gruffly. "You're gonna make her come."

She was buzzing with it but not there yet. She swiped her tongue over her bottom lip, enthralled with what was happening between Zack and Aidan. The lube. The condom. God.

Anxiety flickered through her. She caught Zack's eye. *Please, please, be gentle with him. Please, make it good for him.* She tried to express what she didn't want to say aloud. Zack's taut face softened minutely and his eyes warmed.

He nodded. And she knew. He cared about Aidan.

This wasn't just about giving Aidan what he wanted. It was about Zack getting what he wanted too. He wanted Aidan. And now she understood that he always had.

All these years, she and Aidan had both been missing something. Now she knew. They needed Zack.

Thoughts swirled in her head. Had Zack left because he was in love with Aidan? And Aidan hadn't felt the same way? But her thoughts flew away as Zack leaned in and put his mouth on Aidan. Aidan's head jerked back and he made a rough noise of pleasure that she loved. She waited patiently as Aidan got control and moved back to her. Then Zack rolled on the condom, slicked up his cock with lube and rubbed Aidan's ass. She would think about this later.

"Fuck." Aidan's breath puffed hot against her flesh. "Zack..."

Zack bent over Aidan's back. "I saw the strap-on," he murmured near Aidan's ear. "You want to be fucked up the ass, don't you?"

Aidan went very still. His eyes closed. He vibrated.

Maddie waited for his answer, her body quivering. Would he admit that to Zack?

Then Aidan groaned again. "Yes."

"Gonna fuck you." Zack rubbed Aidan's shoulder, then dragged his hand down Aidan's back as he straightened. "Gonna fuck you so good. Christ, Aidan."

Maddie watched in a daze, her body on fire. Aidan's tongue moved on her, kissing and suckling, licking over her clit. Sparks shimmered through her veins, and a tingle radiated from her center, spreading through her body in hot waves.

Then his mouth stopped again and he sucked in a sharp breath. His body tensed. He lifted his head to look at her, eyes hot and desperate, full of the same yearning she'd seen on Zack's face. She reached out to him, cupped his face in her bound hands, holding his gaze. "I love you. You want this. You need it. I want you to have it."

"Christ, love you too, Mad." His head jerked back and she knew Zack was entering his body. "Fuck yeah. Fuck me."

She shivered with delight, her pussy clenching hard.

Zack's hand slid around Aidan's body to his cock and pulled. Aidan groaned again, pressing his hot cheek to her inner thigh. His face tightened into a look of pain that she recognized—that dark erotic pleasure pain she loved so much.

For him. This was for him. She floated, breathless, flames burning beneath her skin.

"Lick her," Zack reminded Aidan. His hands gripped Aidan's hips, lifting him to his groin. *Oh my god. Oh my god.* His face had tightened into fierce lines, his eyes burning with sexual hunger and excitement.

Aidan's tongue found her clit and flattened on it. Sensation jolted her, and those tingles intensified. Her womb contracted and pleasure spread. She couldn't stop the helpless noises that escaped her lips, whimpers and near sobs. Then Aidan closed his lips over her straining clit and sucked. Wave after wave of heat rippled through her, surrounding her in a hot throbbing glow of pleasure. She came hard, knowing that Zack's cock was buried inside Aidan, her pelvis lifting to Aidan's mouth. He held her clit so gently until she relaxed, limp and breathless.

"Good man," Zack said. "Beautiful orgasm, Maddie."

She nodded, dazed, blinking up at them. Zack's body moved behind Aidan's. Hands bound behind him, Zack's arm supporting him, Aidan looked at her again, a soft look of pleading she'd never seen before. She gave him a shaky smile. "I love you."

His jaw tightened and his eyes went cloudy and drifted closed.

"He feels good, Maddie," Zack told her. "Tight on my dick. Hot. D'you like knowing I'm fucking him?"

"Yes."

"Good." Zack worked Aidan's cock as he thrust into him, again and again. Maddie's gaze went back and forth between their faces, loving how they looked, the tortured bliss, the dark pleasure.

"Aidan. Gonna come," Zack gritted out. "But not until you do." His hand moved faster on Aidan's cock.

"Yes." Aidan groaned and then shouted as he came. Zack gave him one last long squeezing pull, then released him and gripped his hips, pounding against his body, flesh slapping against flesh, Aidan gasping for air. Then went Zack still and taut. His eyes closed and his mouth opened into a silent grimace of ecstasy.

Maddie's heart slammed against her breastbone. It was so beautiful it hurt—an erotic, agonizing pain of pure joy.

21

O nce Zack had untied their wrists, Aidan turned his hands in circles.

"Okay man?" Zack reached for Aidan's arms and massaged his wrists.

"Yeah. I'm good." He swallowed, letting Zack caress his arms, watching his face. He knew Zack wasn't just asking about his arms. They'd done something there was no going back from.

He'd wanted it. He'd been curious for so long, probably since the day Zack had confessed he thought he was bisexual. Aidan had never been interested in men, but found himself not liking the idea of Zack fucking other guys. Not because of his sexuality. Now he knew he'd wanted Zack himself.

After Zack had left, he'd turned off that part of himself. He had Maddie. Then when she'd wanted to start trying new things, that curiosity had come rushing back and he'd brought home the strap-on.

Zack's face held hints of uncertainty at odds with the way he'd taken charge. Aidan didn't want that for him. "I'm good." He leaned over and brushed his mouth over Zack's. Then he reached for the condom Zack still wore and dealt with it for him, his instinct to look after Zack. He got rid of it while Zack rubbed Maddie's wrists. She curled into Zack who then tugged the covers over them. Aidan turned off the lamp, slid in behind her and wrapped an arm around her...and Zack.

"You two were so hot," Maddie mumbled.

One corner of Aidan's mouth lifted. "Yeah?"

"Oh yeah."

Talking ceased. Aidan sensed their breathing change and deepen as they both fell asleep. But his mind was active. Thinking about what had just happened.

It meant something.

He just wasn't sure what.

Being fucked by a dildo was nothing like being fucked by Zack. He swallowed, remembering the edge of pain, then the fiery pleasure, the violent orgasm. So what did this mean about his sexuality? He wasn't gay. He loved Maddie and had always loved women.

He loved Zack. He always had. He'd thought it was a brotherly love, a friendship. Had he been in denial all this time that there'd been more to it than that? Or had things somehow changed for him? Spending this time with Zack, being with him, had gradually made him open to his true self. Parts of him he'd never even known existed.

It wasn't just about the fucking, although that was fantastic. It was about Zack taking control. Setting him free. Letting him give up all the problems he carried around that people expected him to solve, letting him shut off his brain and just have peace. To just do what he was told. The feeling was addictive.

He recognized now that he'd wanted that all along. That feeling of submission. And he recognized that Maddie would never be able to give that to him. Because she needed it too. And he also recognized that he'd probably never do it with anyone but Zack.

For a man to submit to someone else made him weak in many people's eyes. But Aidan trusted Zack. Zack understood. He understood because he knew what it was to submit, except for him it hadn't been by choice. Zack would never mock him or lose respect for him—instead, he'd praised him. Admired him. Zack understood the strength it took to give up control.

And Aidan trusted Maddie, that she too would still respect him and admire him and love him. There were no other people in the world he could imagine doing that with.

But Zack was leaving.

Aidan carefully rolled to his back in the dark and sucked in a long breath. They'd known all along Zack was leaving. It was partly why Aidan had allowed this to develop. While Zack was there, he'd learn from him how to give Maddie the things she needed.

But who would give him the things *he* needed?

Sadness and longing washed down through him. They'd learned so much about themselves, he and Maddie, these last few weeks. He loved her more than ever. But dammit. He loved Zack too. He wanted to make sure Zack was safe. He wanted to offer him a home, with them. He wanted to take care of him, the way he took care of Maddie.

Zack got something from this too. As a Dominant, he had needs as well. And for Aidan and Maddie, filling those needs had been amazing and special. Although they'd known there were things they wanted, and had been amazed and gratified to get those things from Aidan, they'd also learned that they were giving him something in return…the feeling of meeting a Dominant's needs.

Aidan was the one who solved problems and fixed things. But he didn't know how to solve this problem. He weighed options in his mind. Telling Zack the truth about how he felt. Begging him to not to leave.

But Zack was a talented, award winning photojournalist with an important goal in life. He wanted to leave, to get back to his passion, telling the stories the world needed to know. How could Aidan ask him to give up that?

And what about Maddie? Would she even understand his feelings for Zack? She was amazing, encouraging him to take what Zack was offering, wanting him to have it. She was loving and generous and beautiful. But would she welcome that kind of relationship?

They knew of open marriages. One of their friends was open about the fact that he had a wife and a girlfriend. The two women knew each other, liked each other, and accepted each other. He and Maddie had talked about it. They didn't judge their friends for their choice, because hey, it seemed to work—but they had a hard time understanding it.

Now here he was contemplating a similar arrangement. Except instead of another woman, he loved a man. But the other difference was that Zack and Maddie were involved too. They'd had sex. Aidan knew Zack was attracted to Maddie, he'd admitted that, and they were friends who cared about each other.

Fuck, it just made his head hurt.

He rolled out of bed and padded naked into the bathroom to find some ibuprofen. He washed down a couple of tablets with some water. Maybe that would help him sleep.

When he woke up the next morning, Zack was gone from their bed. Maddie slept on. Aidan's head hurt again and his neck and shoulders were stiff and tight. He dragged himself into the shower, hoping the heat would loosen things up. The shower reminded him of last night, Zack and Maddie in there with him, all steamy and soap-slippery, Zack's hands on his cock and balls and ass. Aidan had been hard and aching with anticipation, wondering what Zack was going to do with them, and holy hell, he'd blown his mind.

Once showered, he dressed in a pair of loose sweatpants and an old T-shirt. He paused outside Zack's bedroom door and saw his duffel bag on the neatly made bed with some piles of clothes.

Shit.

With a sinking heart he continued to the kitchen. There Zack sat at the counter with a mug of coffee and the newspaper.

"Hey."

Zack looked up at him. Their eyes met with a jolt of heat. "Morning." Zack paused. "I made coffee."

"Great. Need some." He poured a cup, added a big splash of milk, then picked it up. He leaned against the counter. "Saw your duffel on the bed. You're packing up?"

"Yeah." Zack too sipped his coffee. "Gonna fly to Washington for a few days while I figure out where I'm off to next. Been in touch with Reporters Without Borders there. Might do some lobbying work."

"Huh. Sounds interesting." Sounded like shit.

"Got a flight out tonight, actually."

"Jesus!" Aidan couldn't stop the word that exploded from his lips. "Tonight? Seriously?"

"Yeah." Zack's eyes narrowed and his mouth tightened.

"Okay. Well." Aidan looked down into the creamy coffee. He rubbed the back of his tight, aching neck. His chest hurt too. "I know you're eager to get back to work. So. Last day here."

"What?" Maddie stood in the entrance to the kitchen. "Whose last day here?"

Shit. Aidan shot Zack a narrow-eyed look. "Zack's. Apparently he's flying to Washington tonight."

She tipped her head and padded into the kitchen on bare feet. She wore a silky yellow nightie edged with white lace, her hard little nipples poking at the fabric. She'd stopped worrying about modesty around Zack a while back. She stopped in front of Zack. "But you're coming back?"

"Nah." He shook his head. "Just figuring out with head office where I'm off to next."

Her mouth moved and her eyes shifted from Zack to Aidan and then back. Tension hummed in the room. "I see." Her shoulders drooped and she nodded. "Well, then it is your last day here. We should do something fun."

Her voice had gone flat and monotone as she turned away and also reached for a mug in the cabinet. Fuck, she was as disappointed as he was. Aidan shot Zack a glare. He could fuck him over all he wanted, but hurting Maddie's feelings was unacceptable.

When she had her coffee, he pulled her against him, his arm around her waist. She smelled so good, her usual sweet pea fragrance mixed with Zack's unique scent and the smell of sex. Fuck, he loved her. He pressed a cheek to her silky hair, comforting her as much as himself.

He caught Zack watching them, his face etched into tight lines. Then Zack dropped his gaze.

"Yeah." Aidan rubbed his hand over Maddie's hip through the thin silk, warm from her skin. "Sure. Something fun."

"We don't have to do anything special." Zack folded the newspaper. "I'll need to leave for the airport around five. I'll take a taxi. And I need to do a load of laundry before I leave, if that's okay."

"Of course it's okay," Maddie said, a little snappish.

"Great." Zack ignored her tone and rose off the stool.

"And we'll take you to the airport," Aidan added.

Zack opened his mouth, then closed it. "Thanks. I'll get my laundry started."

When he'd gone, Maddie and Aidan stood there. She trembled against him. "Are you sad that he's leaving?"

She sighed. "Sure." She swallowed. "I'm going to miss him. And I'm going to worry about him."

He nodded. "Yeah. Me too. But he wants to leave. I

223

guess…he needs to. He has a career, and it's not here in Chicago."

"I know." Her voice wobbled. "I know that."

He wanted to say more, but held the words back. Maddie moved away from him and walked over to stare out the windows.

"We'll be okay, sweetheart."

Her head snapped around. "I know we will."

Despite their words, Aidan wasn't so sure. They needed to talk. But Zack came back with an armful of clothes and opened the doors to the small room where the washer and dryer were, and started stuffing them in.

He needed to go for a run. Running gave him the same kind of endorphin rush he got from giving up control to Zack, a place where he could let his head go quiet and peaceful. God, he needed that.

⟋⟋⟋⟋⟍

Zack knew he was acting like an asshole. He wanted to flee, just like last time, just like he'd ran from his mother, just like he always did when things got rough. But now he was stronger than that. More confident. In control. He wasn't going to run away. He was going to stay and say good bye like an adult. Maddie and Aidan deserved that from him.

He got that Maddie and Aidan weren't happy he was leaving. They weren't saying it, but the waves of negativity flowed off them. He didn't quite get why. Sure, they'd been having some hot sexytimes. But they'd known all along that was going to end. He'd always been open about the fact that he wasn't staying, that all he'd wanted was to get back to work. He'd had fun too while he'd been there.

Okay, maybe fun wasn't quite the right word. Well, it was. Yeah, he'd had fun. Lots of fun. But it hadn't been *just* fun. He'd healed. He'd grown. He'd given them something they needed, helped them learn about themselves and in return had gotten his need to dominate satisfied. It had felt great. It had felt…

Fuck. He didn't even want to go there. He had to shut down all those feelings. He was leaving and that was it. He had to do this. No fucking PTSD symptoms were going to stop him. He was healthier and stronger than he'd been six weeks ago. He was not afraid to get back in the saddle, or whatever the fuck the equivalent analogy was to what he did, and be out there documenting the heartbreaking crap that was happening in the world.

His gut cramped so hard he had to bend over. He set his hands on top of the vibrating washing machine, bent his head and closed his eyes. Fuck. *Toughen up, fluffy.*

He let out a breath and straightened. Okay. Walls up. Mask on. He'd get through this day. Laundry. Packing. Keeping it all light and pleasant.

Maddie and Aidan gave him his space. They apparently accepted that he was leaving. And why wouldn't they? Sure, they were all sad. They were friends. They'd gotten close. That was totally normal. But they weren't begging him to stay. Of course they weren't. Was he fucking nuts, thinking they'd do that?

He'd seen the way Aidan had pulled Maddie protectively against him, effectively showing him that they were a unit. A couple. They'd still be together when he left. He got the message, loud and clear.

He'd known his whole adult life that he was not going to have any kind of normal, lasting relationship. If he was going to be true to himself and his true nature, he needed to tie people up, boss them around, and fuck them — both men and women. That was definitely not conducive to any kind of relationship. And now Maddie and Aidan knew that about him too.

They drove him to the airport, although he'd tried again

to convince them they really didn't need to. Aidan parked the Lexus so they could go into the terminal with him. Zack didn't want to drag things out. He checked in, checked his two bags—he'd needed to purchase another one for the additional clothes and crap he'd acquired while in Chicago. He was taking his camera gear in the new carry-on sized bag he'd purchased onto the plane with him.

He headed to security. No point in lingering. They followed along behind him. He paused at the entrance. "Okay." He turned to them. "This is it. Thanks—" Fuck, his throat closed up. He coughed. "Thanks for everything. Can't tell you how much I appreciate you letting me stay with you."

As if he'd been a freaking casual house guest for a few days.

Maddie's eyes reddened, though she stretched her mouth into a smile. She had a hand at her throat. "You're welcome any time. Don't let another seven years go by before you come visit."

Right. He'd just drop in once a year, tie them up and fuck them both. Sure. That would work.

He was such an asshole.

"Yeah," Aidan agreed. "This time, keep in touch, asshole."

There. Aidan agreed with him.

"I will," he lied. "Of course."

Maddie sniffled, though she was still smiling. Was she about to cry? Or not?

Aidan's shoulders squared and his face remained impassive. "Take care, Zack. Take good pictures."

"I'll try." He smiled, but it felt stiff.

For a moment they all looked at each other, the air around them heavy and thick. Then Maddie moved and threw herself into his arms, much as she had the day he'd arrived. She hugged him tight, her face against his shoulder. He felt the tremors of her slender body and hugged her back, his chest burning.

Then she moved away and he turned to Aidan. They both hesitated. Zack's eyes smarted. And he reached for Aidan and pulled him in for a hug too. His body bigger and stronger, he felt different in Zack's embrace. Zack savored the feeling of holding this man, his bones big and strong, his muscles rock hard. He savored the feeling of Aidan's arms around him. He loved them both.

He clamped down on the stabbing pain that knifed through him and pushed it away as he stepped back from Aidan. They exchanged tight smiles and hearty back slaps. "Take care of each other." Zack turned and got in line.

He wasn't going to look back to know if they watched him until he was through, or if they'd gone home, but it was so fucking hard not to. His shoulders hunched up around his ears and his entire body felt stiff as he waited in the long line. He went through the routine that was so familiar to him after years of traveling, removing his laptop from the bag and setting it in its own plastic bin, taking his shoes and belt off, shoving everything along the conveyor belt, then walking through the scanner. On the other side, he kept his head down as he put his shoes back on, stuffed the laptop into its pouch and wheeled his bag down the concourse toward his gate.

His eyes burned and his gut was a huge empty crater as he slumped into a plastic seat. He leaned his head back and closed his eyes. There. He'd done it. This was what he'd wanted all along. So why did he feel so fucking shitty?

22

Maddie and Aidan drove home silently. She tried not to cry. It wouldn't do any good. She stared sightlessly out the window, remembering everything that had happened over the six weeks. Sadness swamped her, a hopeless heaviness that scared her. She'd just realized her feelings for Zack. She hadn't figured out what to do about it. She hadn't realized he was going to leave so quickly. She'd thought she had until next week some time before he actually left. Now it was too late.

How could she tell her boyfriend, the man she loved, that she was heartbroken over another man?

Aidan didn't seem too happy himself. Was it because of what had happened last night between him and Zack? Did he regret that? Or was he also sad because Zack had left? Did he want more of that?

God. Her chest and limbs felt tight and heavy with despair.

Aidan reached across for her hand with a sideways glance as he drove. His fingers were warm around her cold ones, despite the warm August day. She held onto him too. They still had each other. Hopefully that would be enough.

They walked into the condo. Aidan shut the door and dropped his keys onto the small table in the foyer. Maddie walked into the living room. She'd gotten used to Zack being there, and his presence left a gaping hole.

"Let's talk," Aidan said quietly.

"About what?" She bowed her head.

"About you and me. And Zack. I need to be honest with you."

She looked up at him, read the lines of grief on his face too. What was he going to tell her? "Oh, Aidan. I need to tell you something too." She sat on the couch and he joined her. He picked up one of her hands in his and curled his fingers around it. He looked down at their joined hands.

"Do you think less of me because of what we've done?" he asked quietly. "Because of how I am with Zack?"

"God no!" She gazed at him in horror. "You mean because you and Zack had sex?"

"Yeah, that. But also because I like it when he takes control." His fingers tightened on hers and she sensed his struggle. "Some people would think a real man wouldn't let another man order him around like that. A real man wouldn't do the things he told me to."

"Oh my god. You *are* a real man." She almost wanted to laugh at that, but he was so serious. "Aidan. Look at me." She touched his stubbled cheek and turned his face to her. "I love you, all of you, all the parts of you we're discovering now. I love you because you're smart and talented and you make me laugh. I love you because you look after me, in every way possible. You work so hard and do such amazing things, designing amazing buildings, running your business. I love how you feel responsible for your siblings even though they're adults now, how you looked after them when you were growing up. I love your stubbornness and how you push yourself. You are the best, strongest man I've ever known."

His mouth tipped up into a somber smile. "Thank you. I love you too, Maddie." He lifted her hand and kissed it. "You know that. I always have and I always will. I want to be the best man I can for you…but I know I wasn't giving you everything you need."

Her heart squeezed. How could she deny it?

"I thought maybe I could learn from Zack. While he was here." His gaze dropped back down to their hands. "But I don't know if I can ever do that for you, sweetheart."

The anguish in his voice made her throat burn. She gripped his hand tighter. "Is that why you're sad about Zack leaving?"

"Partly. Because I want you to have it all." He lifted his chin and met her eyes again. "But it's for selfish reasons too. I never knew…what it felt like to submit like that. How giving up control to someone else would be so freeing. I didn't have to think. Just feel. Like when I'm running, or lifting weights, and pushing my body hard…my mind goes quiet. I love it. When Zack took control like that, I'd've done anything he asked me to."

"Including let him fuck you."

"Yeah. But…" His mouth twisted into a wry smile. "I wanted that. I wanted it all."

"I know." She shifted closer and wrapped her other hand around theirs. "I know, honey. And *that* is something *I* couldn't give *you*. And I understand that you want me to have it all…because I want that for you too." She shook her head, took a deep breath and straightened her spine. "When I talked to Chelsea the other day, she couldn't understand why you weren't jealous watching me and Zack together."

He grimaced. "It's hard to explain."

"But we both get it. I never told her that I like watching you with Zack too. But I do. Here's the thing." Her voice wobbled. "I realized when I was talking to her that I have feelings for Zack. As in, I love him. And you. Both of you. I've been afraid to tell you that."

He stared at her, eyes burning. "Why?"

"I know you liked watching us have sex. Watching him flog me or whip me. But I didn't know if you'd be upset that I'd fallen in love with him. I thought...maybe you only did that stuff because you knew he was going to leave and eventually it would be just the two of us again."

Aidan's throat worked. "Yeah," he said slowly. "That's how it started. But then...oh Christ, Maddie." His eyes closed and his fingers convulsed on hers. "I love him too."

She blinked at him. Her head whirled. He loved Zack too? The way she did? He loved them both? She had to make sure she knew what was going on. "And me?" Her voice came out very small.

His eyes flew open. "Yes! Dammit, yes, Maddie, and you. I told you that. If *you* can love two people, I guess I can too."

"It's crazy," she whispered.

"I know." He rolled his eyes. "Believe me, I know. But that's just the way it is."

"We all need something. All three of us. And it only works when all three of us are together."

They stared into each other's eyes for long moments.

"What do we do now?" she choked out. "He's gone."

Aidan's eyebrows drew down. "I know. Usually I can fix anything. But this...I don't know. I wanted to beg him not to go, but how could we ask that of him?"

She didn't answer that.

"But Maddie...whatever happens...you and I will make it. We will."

She nodded, her lips trembling. "I know. I know we will." But inside she wondered how they would make it when there was always going to be this empty hole in their life, things they wanted and needed they could never have. "We can live without Zack." She paused. "But...I don't want to."

He nodded slowly. "Yeah. I know."

She sighed. "I guess I should make us some dinner."

"I'm not exactly hungry."

"I know, me either. I'll just make sandwiches or something."

She rose and listlessly wandered to the kitchen to find bread and tomatoes and cheese. She was assembling sandwiches on the counter when Aidan called her.

"Maddie? Sweetheart? Can you come here?"

She set down her knife and wiped her hands on a towel. "Where are you?" She started down the hall where his voice came from.

"In here. Zack's room."

She felt a tiny twist of a knife blade inside as she stepped into the room. All his things were gone, the bed was neatly made. Aidan stood in front of the closet.

"Look." He gestured at the closet.

She moved closer and saw stacks of picture frames on the floor, propped against the wall, all different sizes and shapes. The frames were all simple black. They both started moving them, bringing them out of the closet and leaning them against a wall.

"They're Zack's photographs." She studied them. "Why did he leave these?"

"Couldn't exactly take them with him."

"No." She paused. "He couldn't. So why did he get these done? Why would he print and frame a bunch of pictures when he has nowhere to put them?"

"Maybe," Aidan said slowly, "he wants somewhere to put them."

She tipped her head and gave him a curious look. "They're amazing."

There was no theme to the images but they all conveyed emotion...and mostly happy, positive emotion, or complicated emotion. A couple hugging and crying in front of a bombed out building. A beaming child holding a puppy in a barren street. A woman with a baby, love shining in her eyes. Landscapes that weren't desolate rubble, but rather depictions of the beauty in the world — a sunset over an ocean, a narrow cobblestone street, ancient temples in a desert glowing in rich sunlight. There were many more, and they pulled them all out and took in their beauty.

"He's so talented." Maddie ran her fingers over one frame. "I think he feels safe behind the lens of his camera. He can take these pictures, capture all those emotions without his own getting involved."

Aidan went still then sat heavily on the side of the bed. "Fuck."

Maddie pulled the last picture out. "Whoa." Her heart gave a bump at seeing it. "Look at this."

She carried the picture to the bed and sat beside Aidan, holding it in front of them. It was a picture of them, her and Aidan, taken seven years ago, probably one of the last pictures Zack had ever taken of them. She'd never seen this image, and wasn't even sure where it had been taken, but her chest constricted as she gazed upon her younger self smiling into Aidan's eyes. Their faces were close together, their gazes locked on each other, and the feelings they had for each other were blatant.

But that was long before they'd actually become a couple.

Her smile went crooked. "Guess my secret's out."

"What secret?"

She shot him a shy, sideways look. "I was in love with you for a long time before we actually started dating. Even back in college, I loved you." She nodded at the picture. "It shows, there."

"Kinda looks like I loved you too."

She nudged his shoulder with hers. "Men are just slower on the uptake about some things."

"A-fucking-men," he muttered. "How about seven years slow?"

She huffed out a sad little laugh. "I was so confused. I

had feelings for both you and Zack. I knew it was wrong and weird, especially when you guys just wanted to be friends with me. I remember thinking if I had to choose, which one of you would it be? And I knew I couldn't choose, and then I'd be all depressed because really...I couldn't have either of you."

"Oh, sweetheart." He turned and kissed her temple. "I didn't know you felt like that back then."

"I know. I wouldn't have told you. After Zack left...well, you were there and I still loved you. It was amazing and wonderful and thrilling that you loved me too." She sighed. Then she started thinking. "Zack took this. He must've seen it. How we felt about each other."

They both went rigid. They turned and looked at each other wide-eyed.

"I don't think he knew," Maddie whispered. "That I loved him too."

"Or that I did too," Aidan said. "I didn't even know it myself."

They sat and stared at the images.

"We should hang them." Maddie stood. She set the picture of her and Aidan on the dresser.

"Yeah."

They ate their sandwiches without much enthusiasm, watched a TV show, and went to bed.

Monday morning, Aidan and Maddie went to work as they always did. Neither of them had slept well, and though Maddie did a good job with her makeup, there was no hiding her puffy eyelids and the shadows hugging her lower lids.

But when Aidan got to his office, he didn't get to work. He asked his assistant to cancel all his meetings that day.

"But you're having lunch with the mayor," Julie said, bug-eyed.

"Doesn't matter. Tell him something came up and we'll reschedule."

Then he went online and booked a flight to Washington. There was one leaving at noon. He debated over the return flight, with numerous options, but ended up not booking one. He'd do it there, if he couldn't find Zack. He had a hard time thinking that far ahead. Then it took a bit of searching on Google and a few phone calls to find the hotel Zack was staying at. The Four Seasons. Jesus. And he'd worried about Zack having money.

That left barely enough time to pack up his laptop and cell phone and get to O'Hare.

He'd spent a good part of the night thinking about things. He might be crazy, but he found himself wondering if Zack really *had* wanted to leave. He found himself wondering the real reason Zack had left so abruptly seven years ago. And he knew he couldn't let him go without finding out.

A few hours later he was in a taxi and on his way to Georgetown from Dulles.

In the lobby of the Four Seasons, he called Zack's cell number. It went to voice mail. He swallowed an impatient sigh. "Zack. It's Aidan. It's Monday afternoon. Call me when you get this."

He looked around the elegant lobby. Though he figured Zack must be out somewhere, he used a house phone and asked to be put through to Zack's room. No answer there either, but he didn't bother to leave a voice mail.

He parked himself in a comfortable chair with a view of the street entrance, prepared to hang out there all day if need be. Zack had to pass by on his way to the elevators to get to his room. Assuming he came in the front entrance. Odds were on that.

Aidan pulled out his laptop and booted it up to check

email. Might as well be a little productive, after blowing off a whole day including lunch with the mayor, and with the mayor's schedule who knew when that was going to happen again. Some day he'd probably kick himself for that, but right then he didn't give a shit.

A couple of hours later he was bored and antsy. He debated going into the lounge for a drink, but with his luck Zack would walk by when his back was turned downing a scotch.

Another hour later he was fucking starving. His laptop told him it was nearly six.

And then finally something went right. He looked up as someone walked into the lobby, as he had all afternoon, hyper-alert and on edge. This time it was Zack.

Aidan stood. In his suit and shiny dress shoes, he didn't look out of place in the elegant lobby. Zack...well, Zack never looked out of place, but his worn jeans, Doc Martens, shaggy curls and scruff of beard stood out. Or maybe he stood out just because it was him.

Aidan grabbed his laptop case, squared his shoulders and started forward. Zack neared him, caught a glimpse of him out of the corner of his eye, then whipped his head around again in a double take.

"What the fuck?" His feet halted on the shiny stone floor.

Aidan gave him a grim smile. "Dude. You didn't return my call."

Zack's eyes shifted. "Uh. No. Christ, what are you doing here?"

"We need to talk."

Zack stared at him. "Can't believe this." He shook his head. "You came all the way here to talk?"

"Yep."

"Everything okay?" Zack frowned. "Maddie...?"

"Maddie's fine. Heartbroken, but fine."

"Heart...what?"

"Come on. Let's go to your room." Aidan jerked his head toward the elevators.

Zack muttered another curse, but started toward the elevator. They rode in silence to the fifth floor, then Aidan followed Zack into his room. A quick glance took in the small-ish room — paneled white walls, light-colored carpet, sleek dark wood bed, a night table and a dresser. Two dark leather chairs with beige upholstery flanked a round table in front of the window.

Zack tossed the key card onto the dresser and gestured at the chairs. "Have a seat."

"No. First I have to do this." He moved up to Zack, crowding into his space, grabbed his face in both hands and kissed him.

Zack's lips were rigid, his entire body stiff. He made a low noise in his throat and jerked back. "What the fuck?"

"Kiss me." It was Aidan's turn to take charge. He knew he had to do this. He tilted his head and crashed his mouth over Zack's again. Zack made another noise, half groan, half sob, and curled his hands around Aidan's wrists. But he didn't shove him way. He kissed him back.

Aidan opened his mouth on his and slid his tongue inside, tasting Zack, breathing in his scent. He shook off Zack's hands and slid one of his own around into Zack's silky curls, cupping his head. And Zack kissed him back.

Their bodies slammed together, hard chest to hard chest, both of them hot and vibrating. Zack's hands went to Aidan's waist, fingers digging in painfully as he pulled him closer still. Their pelvises bumped, Aidan's dick hardening almost painfully.

He licked inside Zack's mouth, then over his bottom lip, took it between his teeth and gave a sharp bite that made Zack hiss. Then he drew back. He stared into those neon blue eyes with steady intent.

"Why are you doing this?" Zack closed his eyes, his voice strangled.

"Because I fucking love you."

Zack's features tightened even more, his mouth becoming a thin, straight line, eyes squeezed up. "Fuck you."

"Yeah. I hope so."

Zack's eyes flew open and Aidan gave him a crooked smile. One corner of Zack's mouth lifted in reluctant response. Aidan shoved him away. "Sit," he said. "We still need to talk."

23

Zack tried to get his head around what was happening. And failed. He managed to take the three steps to the nearest chair and drop into it. Aidan sat in the other and leaned forward, elbows on his knees. The dark suit he wore was impossibly sexy, fitted to his broad shoulders, the silky gray shirt beneath stretched across what Zack knew was a wide, muscled chest. Narrow pants covered his long legs, hitched to reveal dark socks and shiny dark dress shoes.

Aidan loved him?

"Why'd you leave?" Aidan asked.

Zack shook his head. "I'm going back to work. You knew that."

"No. Why'd you leave seven years ago? You never said goodbye. You never came back. We never had that talk about why that was. We're having it right fucking now." Then he stiffened. "Wait. What time is it?"

Zack shook his head and glanced at the alarm clock beside the bed. "Six-thirty."

"Fuck. I gotta phone Maddie."

Zack watched in confusion as Aidan pulled out his iPhone and called Maddie. "I'm gonna be home late," he told her. "Go ahead and eat. How're you doing?" His tone softened. He listened, and nodded, eyes crinkling up. "Okay. Be there as soon as I can. Love you." He ended the call and dropped the phone to the table.

"She doesn't know you're here?"

"No." Aidan fixed a stern look on him. "I didn't want to get her hopes up, in case you're going to be a stupid asshole."

Zack swallowed. "Uh. Okay."

"So. Why'd you leave?"

Zack sighed. "I had a job. That was it."

"Bullshit."

Zack's mouth tightened.

"We saw the pictures you left in the closet."

Zack nodded slowly. "Yeah. That was a mistake. No idea what possessed me to get all those prints made and framed when I have nowhere to put them. Just toss 'em in the garbage if you want."

"As if." Aidan rolled his eyes. "They're amazing and you know it. Stop with the self-deprecating bullshit, okay?"

Zack drew back. Whoa. Aidan was kicking his ass here.

"We saw the picture you took of us." Aidan shook his head, forehead creased. "Neither of us remembers exactly where or when that was. But...it looked like we were about to rip each other's clothes off."

"Yeah." Zack bent his head. "That was what it looked like."

"Dude. Maddie never told me that before, but when we saw that picture, she admitted she was in love with me way back then."

Zack nodded, staring at the way the denim over his knees was lighter in color, ignoring the pain in his chest.

"But she was also in love with you."

Zack's shoulders stiffened and his head jerked. He looked up at Aidan cautiously. "What?"

"Apparently back in college she was confused. She

loved us both, but figured there was no way she could have us both. She was miserable about that."

Something fluttered in Zack's belly and heat spread through him. "I don't understand."

"I know." One corner of Aidan's mouth lifted. "As for me...in that picture it sure looks like I cared about her too. And I did. Maybe my feelings for her were more than friendship. Maybe I was in denial. I don't know. But there wasn't anything happening between us then." He paused. "Look at me."

Zack met his eyes, his entire body burning with the remembered pain and rejection.

"You know that, right?" Aidan said. "Nothing."

"I thought...something seemed to be happening between you two. I was leaving anyway, but I couldn't stick around and watch you two together."

Aidan's mouth softened and his eyes darkened. "Fuck." He bent his head. "Yeah, we ended up together, but it was years later. Maddie had a year of college after we graduated. It wasn't until after she'd finished school that things changed between us."

Zack stared at Aidan's bent head. "So you're saying I fucked off and tortured myself for years thinking about you two together for nothing?"

"Well, we did end up together. But back then...nothing." Aidan lifted his eyes to meet Zack's again. "If you'd stayed in touch you would have known that. Or if you'd stuck around long enough to find out the truth, you would have known that. But you ran."

Zack rubbed his forehead. "Sure. Call me a coward. I ran away. Because it fucking hurt, man! I loved you both, so fucking much."

He caught the relief that passed over Aidan's face, turning into...wonder.

"But yeah...like Maddie, I knew I couldn't have you both. When I thought you two were falling in love, that meant I was shut out. It fucking killed me." His voice broke and he paused, trying to get control. "Shit." He hated admitting his feelings, even if they had been seven years ago. It made him weak and pathetic. Rejected.

"I never knew that." Aidan pressed his lips together and turned away for a moment. Zack studied his profile, the straight nose, flat cheekbones and strong chin. "Not gonna lie. If you'd told me that back then, I don't know how I would've reacted. But I do know, when you left like that, it hurt. Like a motherfucker. I missed you so damn much."

"You had Maddie."

"Yeah, I did, thank fuck. And I love her. But she's not you."

Aidan had said he loved him. What did this mean?

Zack loved them both. Even seven years later, he loved them. But loving people only got you kicked in the teeth. Caring only got you hurt. He'd learned that all his life.

"Maddie loves you too, Zack," Aidan continued. "She always has. Somehow, you're the missing part of us. We need you."

Zack's heartbeat exploded into a galloping cadence. His hands shook and he set them on his knees. "What are you saying?"

"For fuck's sake! Do I have to spell it out?"

"Ah…yeah." All the little pieces were adding up, but he was fucking terrified that he was adding wrong.

And then Aidan was on his knees in front of him, grabbing his hands. "I know we have no right to ask you not to leave. It's your career. It's important to you. It's important to the world, what you do. But don't leave like this. We love you."

Zack stared at his friend. The man he loved. He took in the earnest expression, the sincerity…the love shining in his eyes. Wow. He had to admire the way Aidan put himself out there—especially since he himself was too chickenshit to do it. Aidan, who thought Zack had been brave and strong enough to survive captivity, had no idea how this was even more terrifying. He swallowed, sucked in a deep breath as if pulling courage from it. "Love you too," he finally said gruffly. "Both of you. Christ." His nose started to sting. Goddammit. He wasn't going to make this worse by crying. He hadn't cried since the day he'd been abused by that dickweasel drug dealer.

"Thank fuck." Aidan's hands gripped his even tighter.

This man, on his knees in front of him. Aidan, in his power suit, all polished and professional, was on his knees telling him he loved him. "Get up," Zack said gruffly. "Not that I don't like you on your knees, but this isn't the time."

Aidan's lips lifted. "I don't know." He glanced meaningfully at Zack's crotch. The air around them changed, going hot and electric. "But fine." He bent one leg and planted a foot into the carpet to stand. "So. Maddie and I want you to stay."

Zack wanted that. He wanted that more than anything in the world. And that fucking terrified him. To want something that much was only a set up for a huge disappointment.

To go home with Aidan...home to Maddie...the longing for it swelled up inside him so huge he felt like his skin might burst.

"We know we can't ask you to give up your career. But would you at least come and tell Maddie how you feel about her? Could we talk about a way to make this work?"

Zack had been thinking about his career a lot since he'd left them last night. He'd only slept a few hours in this quiet, elegant hotel room, his mind overrun with crazy recurring dreams, him chasing something, he didn't even know what, reaching for it but never able to grasp it. He'd woken numerous times, frustrated, heart pounding, sweaty. Lonely.

It wasn't the same as the nightmares he'd had after he'd

escaped. The fear he felt crawling inside him wasn't the same either. Before, he'd been afraid of dying. Now…he was afraid of living. He wasn't afraid to go to dangerous places and put his life on the line to take pictures and tell the world about the horrible things that were going on. He was afraid of being alone.

The last seven years, he'd worked long and hard, traveling the world. He loved his job. It was his career, his passion, what he'd always wanted to do. But now he could see his main goal had been to distract himself from his loneliness. And the idea of getting back out there held so little appeal, he'd been shocked.

He'd been turning over ideas in his head. The book proposal. The offer of a post in Chicago, starting with covering the G7 Summit. Professor Bridges' suggestion about teaching some classes at Northwestern.

He focused on Aidan who now sat on the edge of the bed watching him intently. A hot softness spread through his chest. Could this be for real?

"I don't know," he finally said, and the brightness in Aidan's eyes dimmed. "I mean, I want to. I want that so fucking much. You have no idea."

"Then what's the problem?"

"I just can't believe…this could be real. That the three of us can really love each other. Isn't that all kinds of fucked up?"

Aidan's lips twitched. "Yeah. Maybe so. But does it matter? If it's what makes us all happy, who cares?"

Zack stared in wonderment. Nerves still tingled. His stomach still felt knotted. "I need to see Maddie. I need to hear it from her too."

"Then come back with me." Aidan rose and moved to him, grabbing his hands and pulling him up out of the chair.

Face to face, their eyes met, mouths almost touching. He felt Aidan's body heat and his quickened breathing. He let out a slow breath. "Okay."

He sensed the relief that loosened Aidan's muscles. Aidan's eyes closed briefly. "Good." He leaned his forehead against Zack's. "Good."

Aidan moved off the other side of the bed and found his cell phone. He started tapping the screen.

"What are you doing?"

"Seeing what flight we can get on back to Chicago."

Despite their impatience, there were no seats on a flight to Chicago until morning. "Well, shit," Aidan said a while later. "Guess we're stuck here tonight. I'll have to let Maddie know what's going on." He picked up his phone. "Also I'm starving. Think we can find a steak in this dump?"

Zack laughed. "Yeah, probably."

"Hey, sweetheart." Aidan spoke into the phone. "How's it going?" He paused. "Yeah. Ah...I'm in Washington." He grimaced. "I'm with Zack...Yeah. Don't worry, sweetheart, it's all good." He closed his eyes and pulled in a breath through his nose.

This didn't appear to be going well.

"Yeah, sweetie. Look, everything's fine, except we can't get a flight home until tomorrow...I'm sorry. We'll be back first thing in the morning. Both of us."

Aidan lowered the phone and stared at it. "Well, shit."

"What?" Zack frowned.

"I think she's pissed. For Chrissakes, I was just trying to fix things."

"Maybe you should've told her what you were doing."

"Yeah." Aidan sighed and pinched the bridge of his nose. "I guess so. I was just trying to protect her in case things didn't go well. I thought she'd be happy."

"She's there alone and we're here, together. Can kinda see why she's not happy."

"Fuck. I'll call her back." He tried but she didn't pick up. "Now *I'm* pissed," he growled.

"Let me try." Zack jumped off the bed and found his

own phone, but she didn't answer his call either. Zack looked at Aidan, his hands curled into fists.

"Guess there's nothing we can do until we get back there."

"Yeah." Zack sighed too. "Come on. I'll buy you a steak."

"I just need to send a couple of business emails." Aidan groaned as he looked at his calendar. "Not good letting Julie know so late—she won't get this until morning when she gets to the office. She's gonna be pissed." Zack listened to him apologize profusely to his assistant and ask her to look after a couple of other things, saying he'd be there by noon for sure.

They didn't venture outside the hotel, heading into the restaurant on the premises where they found a wide selection of steak choices. They both ordered a Porterhouse, Zack a baked potato, Aidan mashed. They sipped bourbon while they waited for their food and Zack told Aidan about his meeting that day with some of the Reporters Without Borders folks.

Back in the room later, Aidan said, "I came with nothing. You gonna let me borrow your toothbrush?"

"I guess so. You had your tongue down my throat earlier, I guess we've shared any germs we have."

"I need antiperspirant too."

"Jesus. Want my shaver?"

Aidan rubbed his jaw. "I can go without shaving."

They faced each other in the small quiet room. Aidan moved closer and dipped his head to kiss him. Their mouths fused, hot and deep, tongues sliding against each other. Need rose in Zack, heat and longing and desire. He moved back, pulled his hands free of Aidan's and reached for the silk tie Aidan wore, twisting it around his hand. Aidan's pupils exploded and his lips parted. "This is how it is between us, right?" Zack murmured. "This is what you need."

"What you need too." Aidan lifted his chin.

"True enough."

"You knew from the start." Aidan's gaze dropped to Zack's mouth and lust kicked him in the balls. "How'd you know?"

Zack shrugged. He nipped Aidan's bottom lip. "Instinct. Experience. Some of the things Maddie said."

His hand went to Aidan's erection and rubbed him through his wool suit pants. Aidan groaned.

"I didn't know for sure until I started giving you orders." Zack brushed his mouth over Aidan's and gave a squeeze. Aidan twitched. "And you obeyed so beautifully. It made me so fucking hard."

"Fuck, me too." Aidan started to lift his hands then let them fall to his sides. "Tell me." He met Zack's eyes. "Tell me what to do."

Zack smiled. He tugged the knot of the tie until it was loose enough to come off over Aidan's head. "Take your clothes off."

He watched as Aidan did so, revealing that beautiful hard body as each piece of clothing came off. Aidan tossed his jacket onto a chair, unbuttoned his shirt slowly, eyes fixed on Zack's. Zack's dick was on fire, but he didn't touch himself, just let the strip of silk he held slide through his hands, over and over. Aidan's gaze flicked to the tie, then back up, and color washed into his face.

Aidan tugged the shirt out of his pants and finished unbuttoning it then shrugged it off. He tossed it to the chair as well. His fingers worked the buckle of his belt open, lowered his fly and he stepped out of the pants, one long leg at a time, leaving him in a pair of light-blue boxers. They sat on low on lean hip bones. Zack's gaze tracked over the defined pecs, abs and obliques, the trail of dark hair from chest to belly and then lower into the boxers.

He gave in to the impulse to touch, stepping forward to

rub Aidan's chest, then trail his fingers down over the ridges of muscle. One fingertip traced the arrow of dark hair. Aidan's cock was enormous behind the thin cotton, the head poking up out of the elastic. Zack let his fingertip brush over it too and Aidan sucked in a breath.

"Gorgeous," Zack murmured. "Your body is incredible. You make me so fucking hot, just looking at you. Turn around."

Aidan turned. Zack stroked his back, enjoying the small muscles, the firm ridge on either side of his spine, the dimples at the base. He palmed Aidan's ass through his shorts, one hand on each cheek, smiling as Aidan flexed and the big muscles became rock.

He kissed the back of Aidan's neck. With his hair cut short there, the nape of his neck had a boyish softness to it. Zack opened his mouth on it and sank his teeth into the skin, so slowly, so gently. Aidan hissed.

Zack soothed the spot with his tongue. "Don't worry," he murmured in Aidan's ear. "I won't mark you there. If I leave marks, it will be where no one can see them." Zack trembled. "Except Maddie. She'll see them. She'll know what we were doing."

"Marks," Aidan mumbled. "Not into pain…I mean, not like Maddie."

"Maybe you just need to experience it."

Aidan's body trembled.

"Trust me?"

"Yes." No hesitation.

"Good man." He pulled Aidan's arms behind his back and wrapped the silk tie around the wrists.

"Jesus."

Still he took his time, kissing and licking Aidan's shoulders, dragging his tongue down the groove of his spine. Standing behind him, he slid his arms around him to hug him from behind, caressing his chest, pausing at his nipples. He gave them each a sharp pinch that made

Aidan's body jerk hard. Zack kissed his shoulder again. "Like that?" He tweaked them again, then rubbed over Aidan's chest and abs and down into his shorts.

He curled his hand around Aidan's cock and Aidan groaned.

"Yeah," Zack whispered. "Your cock is gorgeous too. Love sucking on it...making you come in my mouth."

Aidan trembled and moaned again. "I liked it too," he admitted. "A lot."

Zack moved around him so they were face to face, and kissed him, long, hard, wet. Then he bent and found a nipple with his lips, sucking on it. The firm little nub fit perfectly to his tongue. Excitement pounded through him, pumping hot in his veins. The noises coming from Aidan's throat told him how much he liked that, so he played there for a while, sucking on each nipple until Aidan was a shaking so hard Zack was afraid he was going down.

"Okay," Zack said roughly. "On the bed, face down."

24

Aidan stumbled to the bed, hands tied behind his back, and fell face down. He pressed his hot cheek against the cool white cotton duvet cover, eyes squeezed closed. His dick was a throbbing spike and his balls ached. Christ, who knew there was a straight line from his nipples to his dick? He'd damn near lost it while Zack sucked on him like that. Now he was a trembling mass of lust and need.

He heard rustles as Zack undressed. The bed moved as Zack climbed on with him. Zack rubbed his ass through his boxers again, then tugged them down over his hips. Now bare, Zack's palm caressed him again and Aidan's body jolted when Zack's long middle finger slipped into the crevice between his ass cheeks.

There. There was where he wanted to be touched. To be fucked. Oh god. Longing for it blazed through him.

Zack wasn't gentle. Aidan didn't want gentle. Despite his protests about not being into pain, he relished every firm stroke, every hard grip. So different from a woman's touch. He loved Maddie and loved her touch, but this…it wasn't better, it was just different. Zack gave his balls a firm tug and squeeze, roughly stroked his cock, coarsely parted his ass cheeks. A moan climbed up Aidan's throat.

He felt liquid warmth and realized Aidan had drizzled saliva onto his anus. His thumb circled wetly there, then penetrated.

Aidan jolted. With Zack pinning his thighs to the bed and his hands fastened, he was helpless. A thrill raced through him. Fuck, *fuck*, he loved this. He let himself go, sink into it, let his head empty of thoughts. His mind had been busy since Zack had left, thoughts furious and fast, circling and tumbling and worrying. But now…it was quiet. He turned himself over to Zack's touch, Zack's thumb sliding in and out, his other hand squeezing his tortured balls.

Zack leaned over him. "Gonna fuck your ass."

"Yeah. Please."

"Gonna make you come. So hard."

Aidan groaned. Zack leaned in and took a rough kiss, pushing Aidan's head around to meet his mouth.

Aidan moved and Zack heard him open a condom package. "Please have lube," he muttered. "Please."

Zack gave a low laugh. "Yeah, man, I got lube, no worries. Your tender little ass will be safe. Sort of." He gave Aidan a smack on one cheek, a sweet sting.

Zack's slicked up fingers slid through his flesh, teasing then probing deep. Aidan's heart beat so hard he felt it in his throat, heard it in his ears. Fire burned beneath his skin. He sank his teeth into his bottom lip in anticipation of Zack's cock entering him. Fuck, that had burned last time, but with a heady, lovely fire, and his cock stroking over his gland had nearly blown the top of his head off. He wanted that again. Now.

But Zack had other plans, delaying that moment. He felt Zack's fingers roughly freeing his wrists. "This tie might be ruined." Zack paused.

"Who cares," Aidan mumbled. "Fuck it."

The silk fluttered to the floor.

Zack moved off him and flipped him over. He was

stronger now than he'd been when he arrived, but once Aidan realized what was happening, he helped. His hands were free but he didn't reach for Zack as he wanted to, lying on his back staring up at him.

"Wanna see your face," Zack growled. "When I fuck you for the first time, just you and me." He grabbed Aidan's jaw. "Wanna see your face when I'm inside you. Wanna see your face when you come."

Heat flared low in Aidan's belly at those words. He met Zack's gaze. For a moment he wanted to close his eyes. Yes, he loved Zack fucking him. Yes, he wanted it again. But looking into each other's eyes while doing it was…intimate.

He'd been brave enough earlier to tell Zack how he felt about him, taking the chance that Zack didn't feel that way and would freak the fuck out at the fact that he and Maddie both wanted him in their lives. It had taken every molecule of courage he could dredge up. The only thing that had spurred him on had been Maddie, knowing how hurt she was and wanting to make things better for her.

Now, he had to be brave enough to look his lover in the eye as they fucked. As they made love. So he held Zack's gaze. "Can I touch you?"

Zack's eyes lowered briefly, then opened. "Yeah."

Aidan reached for him, rubbing his chest, flicking his nipples. Zack pushed Aidan's legs up and back, and stroked his latex-covered prick up and down over his perineum, making Aidan's insides quiver and heat. Aidan's own prick twitched on his belly, thick and swollen. Then Zack was pushing inside him. There was that flare of fire, then heat spreading through his body. He cried out.

"Fuck." On his knees, Zack held Aidan's thighs and went deeper still. "Fuck, that feels good."

Aidan reached for his cock and began to pull, desperate and needy. Sensation whipped through him and over nerve endings.

"Yeah," Zack groaned. "That's it." His hips moved against Aidan's body. His skin wore a sheen of perspiration, highlighting the muscle he'd acquired.

"Damn," Aidan gasped. "You're pretty fucking gorgeous yourself. Look at you." His gaze tracked over Zack's body, the bulge of his biceps, the flex of his thighs, the ripple of his abs. "Fuck, that makes me hot. Watching you fuck me like that. Oh god."

"Shit." Zack's features contorted into a grimace. His dark curls fell over his eyes. "Not gonna last, dammit."

"It's okay." Aidan groaned, watching him through heavy eyes. "Just fuck me...like that. Christ." His hand moved faster, his dick pulsing and throbbing, begging for release. Pressure built deep in his balls. Jesus. Jesus Christ. Then ecstasy erupted in his balls and fire licked up his spine, burning out his brain cells. He cried out and hot semen jetted out of his dick onto his belly, his hand.

"Yeah." Zack released Aidan's legs and leaned over him, planting fists into the bed. "Oh fuck, yeah." He laid a hard, wet kiss on Aidan's mouth. Aidan's head spun and he kissed him back with all the hunger he felt. "Gonna come too, yeah...fuck, now..." He growled and trembled as he came, head going back, eyes squeezed shut, mouth open.

Fuck. Beautiful. Hot. Aidan slid a hand around the back of Zack's neck and brought his mouth to his again. "Love you."

"Yeah," Zack gasped. "Love you too. Damn."

They collapsed together in a tangle of sweaty muscled limbs, panting, chests heaving, hearts pounding. Aidan hooked his elbow around Zack's neck and once more pulled him in. Their mouths met in a long, fierce kiss. Undeniable. Now it was undeniable.

"Don't take this the wrong way," Aidan murmured, moments later. "But I wish Maddie was here."

Zack huffed out a laugh and stretched his limbs. "Know

what you mean. Wish she was too. Fuck. Never wanted to hurt her."

"I know." Aidan ruffled a hand through Zack's curls. "I think she'll forgive you." He winced, remembering the earlier phone call. Hopefully she'd forgive him too.

"Christ. I'm an asshole."

"Yeah."

Zack punched his shoulder, but it was a lethargic punch and when Aidan looked at him he was smiling. Then his smile faded. "Don't wanna be an asshole," he said quietly. "You both deserve better."

Aidan nodded slowly. "Then don't," he said simply. "Be the man you want to be. You don't need to be afraid anymore."

Zack's throat worked and his eyes went heavy-lidded. "Right." Zack rolled off the bed and disappeared into the bathroom. Moments later he slid into bed with him.

"You okay?" Aidan asked, rolling to him and pulling Zack against him.

"Yeah. You?"

"Yeah. Just thinking about Maddie."

"Yeah. Me too."

❦

After a crappy day at work where stupid little problems had irritated Maddie when something so devastating had happened in her life, she went home and waited for Aidan, still depressed and sad about Zack leaving. Then Aidan called to say he was going to be late. Fine. She made herself a bowl of soup, then poured a glass of wine and tried to read a book to distract herself. It didn't work.

She found herself wandering around the empty condo, staring out the windows at the evening view, then returning to Zack's room to sit on the bed and look at the framed pictures he'd left behind.

She still had so many questions and no answers. She missed him. She needed Aidan there with her. Heaviness settled in her, pulling her down as she returned to the living room to wait for Aidan. Darkness fell and the city lights sparkled, and he still wasn't home. Some of her sadness turned to annoyance. Why was he working so late on a night when she needed him so much? He'd been upset too about Zack leaving. Why wasn't he there with her, figuring out what they were going to do about this?

She reluctantly meandered into the bedroom, washed her face and changed into a nightie. In bed, she again tried to read. She was actually getting worried about Aidan and considering calling him to make sure he was okay when her cell phone rang again.

He wasn't going to be home at all. He was with Zack.

She reacted emotionally. She was hurt that he'd gone to Zack without her. She was hurt that he and Zack were together, so far away, and she was alone and miserable. She knew it was childish, but she turned her phone off and smacked it down on the bedside table. She turned off the lamp and hunched under the covers.

The bed was cold. Empty. Bad enough that Zack had left, now Aidan was gone too. God, she'd never felt so alone in her life. Sure, Aidan had gone on business trips where he'd been away a couple of days, and she'd slept alone, but this felt different.

What were they doing? Aidan had said it was all good, but how did she know that? What was going on? Why did he go without her?

She thought about her suspicions about Zack's feelings for Aidan. How she'd wondered if Zack had left all those years ago because he'd been in love with Aidan and thought Aidan would never feel that way about him. And Aidan loved Zack.

But he still loved *her*. She *knew* that. He loved both of them.

Her sleep was restless and uncomfortable. In the morning she felt almost physically ill, her body stiff and sore, her heart bruised. She showered and dressed and went to work where she had to pretend everything was fine. She took her cell phone with her but left it turned off in the bottom of her purse.

But she kept remembering Aidan saying that they were coming home. Both of them. Hope flickered inside her, a hope she was afraid to let grow in case she was disappointed again.

When she got back to her desk after a meeting, her voice mail was blinking on her desk phone. She checked it and it was a message from Aidan from about nine-thirty. "We just landed. I know you're probably at work but call me when you get this."

She deleted the message and hung up, her stomach in knots. Okay, they were back. That was good. Her phone rang as she sat there. The call display showed Aidan's cell phone number. She reached for the receiver and picked up.

"Hey." Relief colored Aidan's tone. "There you are."

"Yeah."

"I'm sorry, sweetheart. I never meant to make you mad."

"I know." She did know that.

"We're back. Zack's on his way home. I have to go to the office, but I'll try to get away as early as I can. After blowing everything off yesterday and this morning, I may have a few fires to put out."

"What's going on?"

"It's going to be okay. Shit. I'm at the office now. Gotta go. I love you, Maddie. I'll see you both at home."

"Okay. I love you too."

Now she was shaky and even more distracted, wishing she could just leave work and rush home to see Zack. She wanted to see them both, so badly. Her anger had dissipated. Mostly. Curiosity burned inside as to what had happened between them. Was Zack really back? What was going on?

Finally it was five o'clock and she could leave. Many days she didn't leave that early, but today nothing was stopping her from making a beeline to the elevator in the office tower where she worked and then running for the bus that would take her home.

She unlocked the condo door and stepped inside. Silence greeted her and she paused. Was he there? She swept the living room and den with her eyes, then started down the hall with brisk steps. Zack appeared in the door of his room. She halted, her heart skipping a beat, then bursting with a rush of joy.

Zack smiled.

Her chest hurt as she rushed at him and threw herself into his arms. He caught her against him and buried his face against her hair. His arms felt so good around her, his body so lean and hard, and she breathed in his singular scent. Tears burned behind her eyelids.

"Hey," he murmured. "It's okay, baby. It's all okay."

"Really?" She drew back and searched his face. Beard stubble darkened his jaw as usual, his dark curls tumbled over his forehead and around his ears in messy waves and his blue eyes glowed at her.

"Yeah. I think so. You and I need to talk."

"And Aidan. Where's Aidan? Not home yet?"

"Not yet. He'll be here. But I heard everything from him, last night. Crazy jerk, flying to Washington without telling anyone and stalking me."

She huffed out a laugh. "Yeah, I wasn't impressed with that either."

"Come on, let's sit down." He released her but kept her hand in his as he led her to the den. They sat on the couch, sideways, facing each other, legs crossed.

"I'm sorry, Maddie. Sorry for so much."

"I'm going to need you to be more specific."

He flashed a grin. "Yeah." His smile faded. "I'm sorry I hurt you. When I left on Sunday. And when I left seven years ago."

"Why? Why did you leave then?"

25

Zack told her what he'd told Aidan. This time it was easier. Maddie touched him and listened to him and asked questions and nodded. They held hands and he played with her slender fingers, caressing them and lifting them to his mouth to kiss. "I love you," he finally said. "I loved you then, and I love you now. I thought I could come home after all that time and see you two together and it would be fine. But it wasn't. It made me nuts."

"I'm sorry too." She curled her fingers around his. "We never meant to hurt you, Zack. I loved you too. Then and now. I didn't know how that could possibly ever happen, when I was so confused about my feelings for Aidan too. You two were everything to me. You saved me, you protected me, you gave me space to heal and get over what had happened. You were my best friends, but somehow I fell in love with both of you."

He listened to the words, hardly daring to believe they were true. Aidan had told him this, but hearing it from Maddie's lips made his chest constrict. "You're so loving, Maddie," he choked out. "So loving and good."

"Then you were gone." Her voice quivered. "I didn't understand why."

He explained that too. And the sadness that washed over her features made his gut ache.

"Oh, Zack. If only we'd known."

"Maybe it was for the best," he said slowly. "I've been thinking about what Aidan said. If I'd told him my feelings then, he probably would've freaked out. Maybe we all had to grow and mature enough to be able to accept this weirdness."

One corner of her mouth lifted. "It is weird. But yeah. Maybe you're right. I guess what matters is what's happening now. Dealing with it now. So…what *is* going to happen?"

"I'm thinking about staying," he admitted. "In Chicago." He told her about the options he had.

"Will you miss the traveling? The excitement? The fulfillment?"

"I don't think so." He looked past Maddie for a moment, considering it. "I wasn't really looking forward to getting back to it. In a way, I was dreading it."

"Oh no." She squeezed his hand and he turned his attention back to her face, the notch between her eyebrows. "Is it the PTSD? I thought you were doing okay with that."

"Yeah. It's not that. I think I was just denying that I didn't want to leave you. You and Aidan. I don't want to be alone any more. I thought that's the way I wanted my life, but now…" He paused. "After being held captive and knowing there was nobody who'd really care if I never made it out, it's made me question that. And now, after being here with you, being a part of something…I don't want to go." He met her eyes. "It's not that I'm afraid. Well, in a way I am, I guess. Afraid of losing you. Again."

"You don't have to lose us. We love you." Then she hesitated, panic flaring. "Um, Aidan told you that, right?"

Zack's jaw dropped. "What? He loves me?"

"Oh fuck. Oh fuck. Why isn't he here? Why am I doing this myself? Argh!"

He laughed. "I'm messin' with you. He told me."

"Oh. Oh well then, fuck you." And she gave him a punch in the shoulder. But she was smiling. He caught her hand, pulled her off balance and lifted her onto his lap.

"Kiss me first," he suggested. "Then you can fuck me."

She was laughing so much they could hardly kiss, but then they did, mouths opening to each other. Christ, she tasted good, like sweet woman and love and Maddie. He licked into her mouth, holding on so tight she made a little squeak. "Sorry, sorry. Love you. Love you so much."

They were lost in their kisses when Aidan's voice carried to them. "I see you're not missing me."

Zack's head turned and he blinked. Aidan leaned against the wall, wearing the same damn suit he'd worn yesterday, no tie, the gray shirt open at the collar, and he still looked smooth and authoritative. His eyes gleamed.

Maddie looked at him too, then back at Zack. They both remembered a time they'd jumped apart when Aidan had entered the room.

"I'm mad at you," Maddie informed Aidan.

He pushed away from the wall and sauntered toward them. "Get over it."

She smiled at him. "I am. Mostly."

He dropped to a crouch beside the couch where they were sitting. "Sorry, Maddie. I know you were upset last night."

She nodded, still hanging onto Zack. "Yeah. I was sad and lonely. Waiting for you to come home and then you phone and tell me you're in Washington with Zack and 'it's all good'. Well, I wasn't in Washington and I didn't know what the hell that meant. I was home all by myself, worried and depressed and crying."

"Sweetheart." He touched her cheek. "I'm so sorry. I just wanted to fix things. For you. For us. I didn't know how it was going to go. I wasn't sure I had the right to ask

Zack not to leave, to give up something he loves so much."
He paused. "You two have talked?"

"Yeah. Some. But I think all three of us better have a
conversation and make sure we're on the same page. I
almost had a heart attack when I thought I'd told Zack you
loved him before you had."

Aidan blinked.

"I was fucking around with her." Zack smiled.

"Okay." Aidan shook his head, lips quirked. "Let me go
change. I've been wearing this suit for two days." He
grimaced.

"Yeah, me too," Maddie said. "I mean, I haven't worn
this suit for two days, but I want to change."

"You look hot in that suit," Zack said. "And those
shoes. But go ahead, change into something more
comfortable. Like maybe a sexy little nightie. Or a corset
and garters belt and stockings."

She gaped at him, then laughed. "A corset and garter
belt does *not* sound comfortable. Also, I do not *own* a corset
and garter belt."

"We'll have to change that." He lifted her off his lap to
stand and patted her butt. "I'll get out my black leather
pants and gloves. And my whip." He waggled his
eyebrows.

Her eyes widened. "Black leather pants and gloves?
Really?"

"I used to have some," he admitted. "Don't any more.
Although I'm sure there's somewhere in town I can
pick up a few things. The outfit can really help set the
scene."

Her eyelashes fluttered and her lips parted. He smiled,
knowing he'd intrigued her.

"I'm picturing it." She touched his jaw. "Hot."

"I agree," Aidan said. "Definitely."

"For now, go put on your yoga pants," Zack said.
"Those are sexy too."

She laughed. "They are not. But that's what I'm going to wear."

"You're sexy no matter what you wear."

She smiled at him and it was like her smile filled his chest with light and warmth. He smiled back at her.

She and Aidan went to their room to change. Zack had taken his bag into the other room, but had hesitated. How was this all going to work? He had no fucking clue. Not only had he never really had a relationship with one other person, he sure as hell had never had a relationship with *two* people.

He went to the fridge for a beer. Aidan came back first, in faded jeans and an old T-shirt, barefoot. Zack reached into the fridge and then handed him a beer too. They eyed each other.

"Did you get her calmed down?" Aidan asked quietly. "Or was she okay when she got home?"

"She was okay." More warmth and light hit him remembering how she'd flown at him. "She's amazing."

"Yeah. I know. That's part of this deal, man. We look after her. No matter what."

"I know. I've got some time and some shit to make up for."

They poured Maddie a glass of wine and when she came out dressed in her yoga pants and a tank top, they all went out on the balcony and sat in the evening sun to talk.

"He's thinking of staying," Maddie told Aidan. "For good, right?" She looked at Zack.

"Not saying I'll never travel again. But yeah."

"And you'll stay here with us."

"If you'll have me."

"Want this to be your home," Aidan said quietly. "A place you can hang your pictures. Even if you travel, you'll come back here."

Zack nodded. He wanted that too.

"We need a bigger bed. King size." Aidan met Zack's eyes. "Unless you don't want to sleep with us."

Zack swallowed. "I do."

"When it comes to sex, you're in charge," Aidan said, as if he was negotiating a business deal. "But other than that, we're a team. All three of us are equal partners."

Zack nodded, his throat going tight again. He'd never felt good enough to be an equal partner for someone. In the bedroom or in the dungeon he was in charge. Outside...well, he liked the way that sounded. Partners. He'd do anything for them. "Not good at relationships," he admitted. "I'm too much of a selfish bastard. But I want to try."

"You're not a selfish bastard," Maddie protested. "Look at all the things you've done for the family of that missing journalist. For all the other families. The time you spent online, the fundraiser you want to have to help him. And look at how you are with us. Yes, you're in control, but you aren't just taking. You're giving. Giving us exactly what we need, always making sure we're okay, waiting to get your own satisfaction. That's not selfish."

"When you take control, it's not taking something away from me. You're *giving* me something," Aidan added.

Zack let their words sink in to his consciousness. Maybe they were right. Maybe he wasn't a complete asshole. Maybe he could have this.

Zack nodded. "I always thought if I wanted to be true to myself, to have the kind of sexual relationship I want—where I can be dominant and in charge, where I don't have to choose between male or female—I'd never have *any* relationship. So I pretty much fucked up any chance of that ever happening. But now...maybe I *can* be true to myself and at the same time meet someone else's needs. Maybe I can make you two happy."

"Zack." Maddie reached out and took his hand, then set her wine glass on the table and grasped Aidan's hand. "Let us make you happy too. We all need each other and none of us are going to be satisfied unless we're all together."

She was not wrong.

⚜

Maddie sat in the middle of the bed, Zack on one side of her, Aidan on the other. She closed her eyes and let her head drop back as they each sucked on a nipple. Pleasure streaked from her breasts to her pussy, converging in an unrelenting ache. With a hand on each of their backs, her fingers curled so her nails dug into their flesh.

They lifted their heads simultaneously and she opened her eyes to see their mouths joined in a long, hot kiss in front of her. She watched their lips move, their tongues sliding together as they kissed again and again, so close to her she could see every whisker, every eyelash, the slickness of their mouths.

So beautiful. She rubbed her hands up and down their backs.

They drew apart and looked at her and she smiled.

"We're all together," she whispered. "Really together."

Zack's lips lifted into a smile and he leaned in to kiss her. "Yeah. Really."

"Finally." Aidan kissed her too.

Yes, finally. It had taken a long time, but things happened for a reason. The people they'd become were open enough to admit what they all needed, brave enough to give it to each other...and strong enough to accept it.

She waited for Zack to direct things. Like Aidan had said, in the bedroom he was in charge. But to her surprise, Aidan spoke. "I want to fuck you."

He was looking at Zack.

Zack sucked in a sharp breath and his eyes met and held Aidan's. "Yeah?"

Aidan gave a short nod, his hand rubbing over Zack's shoulder. "You like that…don't you?"

Zack grabbed Aidan's face with both hands and gave him a fast, hard kiss. "I fucking love that." He nipped Aidan's bottom lip. "But I'm still in charge."

Aidan's eyes gleamed and Maddie smiled.

"Lie down, Maddie," Zack directed her. "On your back."

She slid down and reclined against the pillows, her body pulsing.

Zack shifted and grabbed the condom he'd set on the bedside table, next to the bottle of lube. He handed it to Aidan. "Put this on me."

Aidan bent his head as he did as ordered, his fingers steady as he rolled the latex down over Zack's straining cock. He fondled Zack's balls and trailed his fingers up Zack's chest. Their eyes met again. "You want me to wear one too?"

Zack's lips parted. She watched his chest lift and fall with his deep breath. "Your decision," he finally said. "I trust you. You and Maddie have been together a long time. You know your history. You don't know mine."

Maddie's eyes moved between them and she reached a hand out to set it on Zack's thigh. "We need to deal with this. Not now. Not tonight. Tonight we all use condoms. Tomorrow we talk."

Both guys nodded and Zack handed Aidan a condom. Aidan's lips tightened, but he suited up. Then, with a dirty smirk, Zack handed Aidan the bottle of lube.

Aidan's smile in reply was equally dirty.

Maddie's heart exploded into a rapid rhythm and heat swept from her hairline to her toes. Watching her two guys together like this, confident and accepting, brought her near to tears with joy.

Breaking eye contact with Aidan, Zack turned his attention to her. His smile gentled as he moved over her.

"Gonna fuck you, baby. While Aidan fucks me."

Her pussy squeezed hard. Her gaze moved from Zack's face to Aidan's behind him. Aidan gave another nod and a tender smile.

Zack kissed her, his mouth firm and hot, his tongue sliding against hers. "So sweet, baby. I love you."

"I love you too." Her breathing had gone short and choppy with excitement.

He kissed her cheek, her jaw, the side of her neck, then reached down between them for his cock.

She lifted her head to watch the head as he slicked it up and down through her wet folds where she was aching and burning for him.

"So wet." Zack probed at her entrance. "Love this tight, hot pussy."

His words inflamed her even more. She moaned as he eased inside her inch by inch, until he was fully seated. Flames licked over her body, heat spiraled through her and every nerve ending tingled.

He stretched out over her, sliding a hand down to pull her thigh higher against his hip, his mouth on hers, his other hand on the top of her head. Her hands framed his face, his stubble rough against her palms. Their eyes met in a shower of sparks, pausing in a moment of connection and beauty, then drifted closed as their mouths met in deep, reaching kisses.

"Okay, Aidan." Zack lifted his mouth but didn't look away from her. "Fuck me now."

Oh god.

Zack smiled into her eyes. "Felt your pussy squeeze me when I said that. It makes you hot, doesn't it?"

"Yes."

She heard Aidan snap open the bottle of lube, and felt the bed move as he knelt behind Zack. Zack drew in a sharp breath as Aidan touched him. Maddie swiped her tongue over her bottom lip and swallowed. Her gaze moved past Zack to Aidan, his expression tight and focused on where he was entering Zack.

Zack's cock swelled inside her and his head lifted. His jaw tight, he gritted out, "Oh yeah."

"Okay, Zack?" Aidan stroked his back.

"Yeah." He paused. "Been a while."

Aidan slowly worked his way inside. Zack's body shuddered against her and he buried his face in the side of her neck, one arm around the top of her head, the other on her jaw. She slid her hands into his thick curls and held his head.

"There," Aidan said in a low, hoarse tone. "There. You've given us so much. Want this for you. Want you to feel good."

"Fuck." Zack opened his mouth on the side of her neck. "You have no idea…"

They were all joined, so close, throbbing together in almost unbearable pleasure. She sensed they were both holding themselves motionless, fighting for control. Bliss flowed through her veins, hot and sweet.

"Do it," Zack groaned. "Fuck my ass."

He started to move inside her, rocking his hips into her, pushing back against Aidan. Aidan picked up the rhythm, one hand on Zack's back, the other holding his hip.

"It feels so good." Maddie stretched a hand out to find Aidan's strong thigh. "I feel you both. Oh my god…"

"Both…fucking…you." Aidan's hands ran up Zack's back and curled over his shoulders as his thrusts grew harder. "Love you, Maddie. Love you both."

Zack made a noise against her neck that almost sounded like a sob and she petted him, the nape of his neck, his hair, his shoulders.

Aidan pushing into Zack where he pressed against her clit had pressure building fast and hard inside her. The hot throbbing glow intensified, spreading through her body. She burned, sensation coiling inside her, twisting up into a tight, exquisite point of pleasure that burst into a million sparkling pieces. She cried out, her body trying to arch up but unable to beneath the weight of her two men.

"Sweet baby," Zack mumbled against her skin. He stroked her hair. "Gonna come too."

"And me." Aidan pumped faster. "Christ. Unbelievable..."

Zack's body went taut and still against her and she wrapped her arms around his shoulders and held on tight. His groans of pleasure filled her ears, her body still pulsing, and then she came again, shocking her. This orgasm was softer, ripples of pleasure, a second sweet tingling climax.

She dragged her eyes open to watch Aidan's face as he came, his mouth open, jaw clenched, eyes squeezed shut. The tendons in his neck stood out and he shouted, holding himself still against Zack's ass.

"I love you," she choked out. "I love you both. So much."

Her eyes met Aidan's above Zack. The open adoration that blazed there was for her. But also for Zack. And that was perfect and right.

Her heart swelled with love. This was how it should be, for them. Others might not comprehend. But they both knew. Zack was who they needed. He fit them together. And they fit him.

⁂

Zack stepped back and squinted at the framed picture on the wall. He reached out and adjusted one corner to make it perfectly straight. There.

That was the last one. All the pictures he'd had framed now hung on the walls in Aidan and Maddie's condo.

His condo. He lived there too, now.

His home.

He waited for the fear to rise up in his throat. It didn't.

He felt a blessed sense of peace and acceptance. The absence of fear in his life had made him realize what a huge dark presence it had been.

Not the fear of danger or being hurt or killed. Yeah, sure, he'd felt that kind of fright, many times. And when he'd been taken captive, he'd been fucking terrified.

The fear he was now missing was the one that had been with him most of his life. The fear of hoping for something, wanting something he could never have. The fear of being different and never fitting in anywhere. The fear of caring for someone and being betrayed or rejected.

Aidan had told him he didn't have to be afraid any more.

Those words had hit him like a punch. It had taken a while for them to fully sink in. It had also blown him away that Aidan had understood that about him.

Now he could be the kind of man he wanted to be without the fear. He could let himself feel, knowing he was safe. He could hope and dream. Loving someone didn't make you weak. It made you strong.

The fear hadn't disappeared overnight. In fact, when Maddie had suggested last week they should hang all those pictures, cold dread had squeezed his intestines. But he was getting past it.

The door opened and Maddie breezed in. "Hi honey, I'm home!"

He grinned. She dropped her purse and briefcase onto a chair and launched herself into his arms.

Something warm and sweet shifted in his chest as he wrapped his arms around her.

"You're so nice to come home to." She planted a kiss on his mouth. "Guess that's going to change, huh?"

"Yeah." He started teaching next week, and the G7 Summit was coming up which would definitely keep him busy. "No more coming home to dinner already made, with your slippers and newspaper waiting."

She choked on a laugh, squeezed his neck and released him. "Well, it was nice while it lasted. Oh hey, you got all the pictures up." She walked around the condo, studying them.

They'd decided on placement together, a grouping of images on one living room wall, more in the dining room and some lining the hall. The one he'd taken of Aidan and Maddie together all those years ago was in the bedroom, along with a new one.

Somehow Maddie'd convinced him to take a picture of the three of them. He'd set it all up, tested the lighting and flash, and then used the timer to get himself into the picture, him and Aidan flanking Maddie, arms around her but also each other, heads together.

That one also hung in their bedroom. It was private, not something they wanted to have to explain to the world. Not that the entire world visited their condo. And those who did were friends who would just have to accept their unusual relationship.

"Aidan should be home soon," Maddie said. "For our 'meeting'."

"Only Aidan would call a meeting for us." Zack shook his head.

"We have a lot of things to discuss."

"You mean argue about."

She frowned. "That's why we're having a meeting. So there won't be an argument."

"Like last week."

She nibbled her bottom lip. "Well, yeah."

Last week's argument had been about money. Zack wanted to contribute to their living expenses. It was only fair. He wasn't going to be a mooch. But the argument had really been about more than money. He had money, Aidan had money, Maddie made decent money.

No, the argument had really been about him being a part of their relationship. Did he really want to own one third of the condo? No. Did he give a shit that if something happened and this all imploded, he'd be out on the street? No. He just wanted to be on an equal footing with them.

But that discussion had opened their eyes to a whole lot of other things they were going to have to deal with.

Their other recent argument had been about leaving the toilet seat up. His lips twitched remembering Maddie's ire at nearly falling in the toilet in the middle of the night. He'd taken responsibility for that, had groveled and was now doing his damnedest to remember to lower the seat when he was done.

Who knew that was so hard to do?

Also, who knew that was so important to women? But compared to some of the issues they were going to face, that was miniscule.

"I'm going to change." Maddie kicked off her high heels and bent to pick them up, giving him a sweet view of her ass in a snug pink pencil skirt. "Be right back."

Zack headed to the kitchen where he had a pot of chili simmering. He wasn't much of a cook but found he kind of enjoyed it. Aidan and Maddie had suffered through a few unfortunate results of his efforts, but today's creation seemed to have turned out okay. He dipped a spoon in to taste the chili. Yeah, that was good. Then the heat kicked in. Whoa. That was…spicy.

He'd joked about being a 1950's housewife for them to come home to. He didn't mind doing things around the place, but he was eager to get back to work, excited about the new challenges he was facing in his career. He was ready.

Aidan blew in then, full of energy, slamming the door behind him. Today instead of his usual impeccably tailored suit, he wore dusty jeans, work boots and a plaid shirt over a crew-necked white T. Apparently he'd been at a construction site today. This look was possibly even sexier than his tailored suits.

"That smells fucking fantastic." Aidan strode to the kitchen and lifted the lid to peer into the pot. "Chili? You made this?"

"Yep."

"Awesome. I'm starving." Aidan dropped the lid, moved into Zack and pressed him against the counter. He too laid a kiss on his mouth, a long, hard kiss, one hand stroking over Zack's hair. "How was your day?"

Once again emotion swelled inside him at Aidan's touch. "Busy. I was at the university this morning, picked up some groceries, made chili, hung the pictures."

Aidan brushed his thumb over Zack's bottom lip. "You're really getting into this domestication, aren't you?"

Zack grinned and sank his teeth into Aidan's thumb. Aidan jerked it back but laughed.

Maddie appeared. "Oh good, you're home too."

Aidan stretched an arm out and pulled her in between him and Zack.

"Mmm. Manwich." She rubbed herself against them.

Zack choked. "Manwich?"

"Yeah. Me in the middle of my two men. Maddie Manwich. It's my favorite thing."

He shook his head, unable to stop from smiling.

What should be weird and fucked up felt fun and perfect and right with these two.

But he knew they were about to have a discussion about how to make the rest of the world see their relationship as perfect and right. There was a sobering thought.

"Let me go change." Aidan squeezed Maddie's hips then stepped away. "And I need a quick shower. I'm covered in dust."

A while later, they sat at the dining table with bowls of

steaming chili. Zack set a pitcher of ice water in the middle of the table. "You might need this," he said with a wince.

They all dug in.

"It's spicy," Maddie agreed. "But it's really good!"

"It's making me sweat." Aidan gulped some water.

"Sorry." Zack forked up more chili. "I might have overdone the spices. I remembered you like it hot and spicy." He winked at Maddie. "Actually, I kinda like it."

"I do too," Maddie insisted.

"I love you."

She laughed.

They all finished it, and it wasn't that bad.

"Okay." Aidan rose and walked over to his brief case. "Let me get the agenda for the meeting."

"You've got a fucking agenda?" Zack leaned back in his chair.

"Yeah. I printed it off at work."

Zack met Maddie's eyes and their eyebrows rose. "He ever done this before?"

She bit her lip. "Oh yeah."

"Oh my fucking god. Seriously?"

Aidan shrugged, taking a seat. He laid a piece of paper on the table in front of him. "Okay. We've argued about money, the toilet seat being left up, what movie to watch, toe nail clippings and whether vegetables should be crisp or cooked until they're a mushy mess fit for either a baby or a ninety year old with no teeth."

Zack couldn't stop the laugh that burst out of him. He and Maddie exchanged another amused look.

"Now shit's about to get real," Aidan continued. "We're talking…in-laws."

Zack reared back. "Fuck me." He stared at Aidan as if he'd produced an M24 sniper rifle and was aiming it at him.

"You met my parents," Aidan said. "When we were in college."

Zack shifted in his chair. "Uh, yeah. Couple times." He remembered going out for dinner with them once when they'd visited the campus. "Nice people."

Aidan snorted. "Sure. They're nice. They also don't give a shit about my life. So I don't anticipate much of an issue with them when we tell them what's going on with us."

"We're gonna tell them?" Zack's eyebrows shot up into his hairline. "What the hell are we gonna do that for?"

Aidan's lips twitched. "You think we can keep it a secret forever?"

"Sure." Panic flared inside him. Jesus, just when he'd thought things were going so well. "Why not?"

"Actually, with my parents, that could work. They're so self-involved, they may not even realize what's going on. Maddie's parents will be a different story, however."

"They are going to freak the fuck out," Maddie stated.

"Jesus." Zack moaned and slumped lower. "How often do you see them?"

"A few times a year, at least."

He knew they lived in Springfield, not that far away. Aidan's parents in Pittsburgh probably didn't visit often. "Christmas? Thanksgiving? Birthdays?"

"Um, yeah. Are you okay, Zack?" She reached out to squeeze his hand. "You look pale."

"I'm okay." He rubbed his face.

"I don't think my sisters and brother will be too much of a problem," Aidan added. "They're pretty open-minded."

"You're seriously going to tell them?" Zack gaped at him.

Aidan met his eyes. "Yeah. I am."

"You don't have to do that." What the fuck were they going to think about their straight-laced big brother in a relationship with another man? Jesus fuck. "Maybe I haven't thought this all through."

Aidan's eyes narrowed. "What the hell does that mean?"

"I mean...I don't want to mess up your perfect life." He switched his gaze to Maddie, then back to Aidan.

"Zack." Maddie reached out to squeeze his hand again, and this time her other hand reached for Aidan's, joining all three of them. "We've already figured out—our life *wasn't* perfect. Even though apparently our friends thought we had the perfect relationship, we didn't. We weren't being completely honest with each other."

Aidan nodded, his eyes on Maddie, the corners of his mouth lifted in a wry smile. He covered her hand with his other one and patted it. "She's right." He turned his gaze to Zack. "We needed you."

Zack swallowed and nodded.

"Look, we're either all in this or we're not." Aidan's eyebrows lowered. "Love is great and all that shit, but life is hard. We have to be together on this. There are going to be rough times. There are for every couple, never mind a threesome. Big decisions to make about money and careers and kids."

"Kids!" Now Zack did choke. Maddie patted his back as he bent over, coughing. He caught her smile, though.

"What our lives looked like on the surface may be some people's idea of perfect." Maddie rubbed his back. "But beneath the surface is where the important stuff is. We all need to be on the same page—do we want to adhere to what society thinks is perfect? Or do we want what *we* think is perfect?"

"Nicely said, sweetheart." Aidan nodded.

Well, that about summed it up. Terrifyingly.

"I'm sorry," Zack managed to say, straightening. "I guess I don't have my shit as together as I thought I did." He sucked in a big breath and squared his shoulders. "But when you put it that way...I don't give a damn what society thinks. I've lived my life by my own rules for a while now. I just...never had anyone else to be concerned about before." He met Aidan's eyes. "But I want what you want."

"I want a dog," Maddie said. "A puppy. Maybe a pug."

Yeah, Aidan had said it—love is great and all that shit, but life is hard. But they were in it together. Maybe with a dog.

Author Note

Thank you so much for reading **Loving Maddie from A to Z**! Make sure you're on my mailing list for news about my next releases. You can sign up at www.kellyjamieson.com.

If you enjoyed Loving Maddie, please consider leaving a review at the retailer of your choice or at Goodreads to help other readers find my books. You can also contact me at info@kellyjamieson.com to tell me what you thought of it or ask me any questions!

Other Books by Kelly Jamieson

Love Me
Friends With Benefits
Love Me More
2 Hot 2 Handle
Lost and Found
One Wicked Night
Sweet Deal
Hot Ride
Crazy Ever After
All I Want for Christmas
Sexpresso Night
Irish Sex Fairy
Conference Call
Rigger
You Really Got Me
How Sweet It Is

Power Series
Power Struggle
Taming Tara
Power Shift

Rule of Three Series
Rule of Three
Rhythm of Three
Reward of Three

San Amaro Singles
With Strings Attached
How to Love
Slammed

Windy City Kink
Sweet Obsession
All Messed Up
Playing Dirty

Three of Hearts

Heller Brothers Hockey
Breakaway
Faceoff
One Man Advantage
Hat Trick
Offside

About the Author

Kelly Jamieson is a best-selling author of over thirty-five romance novels and novellas. Her writing has been described as "emotionally complex", "sweet and satisfying" and "blisteringly sexy". She likes coffee (black), wine (mostly white), shoes (high heels) and hockey!

Subscribe to her newsletter for updates about her new books and what's coming up, follow her on Twitter @KellyJamieson or on Facebook, visit her website at www.kellyjamieson.com or contact her at info@kellyjamieson.com.